The Silence

The
Silence
Next Evolution

Kristi Buckel

NEF HOUSE PUBLISHING

The Silence: Next Evolution
Copyright © 2025 Kristi Buckel

ISBN 978-1-965393-07-9

As always, to my mom, who taught me how to read, and Josh, who taught me how to fly—bet you didn't see all these zombies in my future, right?

Dawn of the Undead

~ Sean ~

The taste of blood was like metal, pure iron dripping down my lips, so familiar yet so foreign. The walls were covered in gore. I looked at the doorway, at the dismembered leg hanging by viscera on the handle. My hands were covered in skin, the feeling startlingly similar to wearing winter gloves. The voice in the back of my mind screamed, but I couldn't make out the words. I rubbed at the skin, making it slide back and forth over the crater in the middle of my hand. I heard a rushing sound, and I realized it was my own heartbeat.

The person in front of me had no heartbeat.

My teeth were embedded in his skin, and I felt his muscles separating from his tendons. I heard him breathing, little stuttering steps coming quicker and quicker. I swallowed, and the entrails in my mouth slid down my throat. The movement stopped, but the screaming remained.

I sat up, hearing the echo of my screams in the living room, with Kiera asleep next to me on the couch. She woke to my voice, sitting up abruptly and rubbing her eyes. "Did you have another nightmare?" she asked.

I exhaled slowly, taking measured breaths to try to calm down. "Yeah. They're happening more frequently." She reached out to hold my hand, but I saw her hesitate. That'd been happening more frequently too. My nail beds weren't caked in red anymore, but she still saw the blood on my hands. In my mouth. On my body.

Life was supposed to go back to normal after the Cure was released. Instead, there were still places without power, though this wasn't one of them. There were still the bodies, stacked up by the side of the road, of those who hadn't made it far enough. And there was still murder in my mind, rolling around in the back of my head, saying that I'd never get myself clean from what I did.

I remembered everything.

I remembered what people tasted like in my mouth (like chicken) and what texture human skin had (silky, mostly). I remembered the feeling of ripping someone apart with my teeth and hands. No one should ever have to live with such knowledge. I couldn't tell Kiera, but I didn't deserve the Cure. I didn't deserve to be alive again. I didn't deserve to be with her after what I'd done.

I sat up, running my fingers through my hair. I didn't know how to tell Kiera the truth; I didn't know what to do about Zombie Sean versus Not-Zombie Sean. I could still see the marks on my body from what I'd broken. I was still healing, even after a few weeks. Walking into the kitchen, I wondered what the rest of my zombie crew was doing. It was too silent in my head.

In the kitchen, I started to make oatmeal for both of us. The TV stations still weren't on-hell, the power was still spotty, so I couldn't watch the news. I figured things wouldn't return to normal for weeks, if not months. People were still adjusting to nonzombie life. Some of the undead had dropped dead on the spot with their injuries. There was a massive plywood wall on the grounds of the campus covered in posted pictures of the dead, and messages and flowers and drawings from kids. It never failed to surprise me how resilient humanity was like that.

I stirred quickly; the oatmeal was close to burning. I heard Kiera getting up and ready for the day. We still had to use bottled water for showers and tooth brushing, but it was better than nothing. At least then, I could get the taste of blood out of my mouth.

It would haunt me forever.

After serving the oatmeal, I sat down at the table, slowly twirling the spoon between my fingers.

Kiera sat across from me, tucking her hair back behind her ears. "How did you sleep?"

I shook my head. "You were right. It was another nightmare." I kept it short; we hadn't had a chance to talk about what we'd been through after the Cure was spread. We'd returned to our old apartment despite no power or internet. I remembered Brett suddenly and I wondered what he'd be doing if he'd survived. Would he have been as drained, as weary as I was? Would the dreams follow him, too?

It seemed like my mind was haunted, and I could do nothing about it.

"What do you want to do today?" Kiera asked, stirring her oatmeal.

I hesitated. Part of me longed to find my previous crew, my zombie posse, to see what had become of them, but I didn't know if they'd dropped dead, moved on, or been killed. That last day was a blur of blood and gore, mixed with the shock of seeing Kiera again. I honestly never thought that I would. I had expected to be alone with my zombies forever.

I rubbed my hand over my stump. I'd been a pretty successful zombie with only one hand. At least I had that going for me.

"I guess inventory, and then the food supply? I know you went through a lot during . . . everything. There's no extreme couponing anymore, so we can't go to Costco."

She snorted, taking a bite. "It's gonna be a long time until I can go to Costco again." Sighing, she ran her fingers through her hair. "I think the food supply is a good idea."

We finished up breakfast and walked down the stairs. My mind flashed back to when Kiera left me here: I was turning, and there was nothing else I could do to keep her safe. I remembered the stairs were a challenge. I remembered finding my pack on the floors above.

The food pantry was at the college, the site of our last battle. The site of my Cure, my transformation. I'd never lost my memory, and it was catching up to me. We walked into the gymnasium and stood in line with other people in various states of unkempt. Not having modern conveniences shafted America. Maybe the world; I didn't know with no TV and no newspapers.

The line was long at the food pantry. I felt the bones knitting back together in my extremities—they itched on the inside, and I wasn't sure how to find relief. The CDC had doctors lined up after the Cure dropped, and I'd been bandaged and cleaned up, even though I didn't deserve Kiera had never left my side. Now she was still there, still holding on to my arm, letting me use her as a crutch as my support through the worst thing imaginable.

I didn't deserve her.

The line moved while I had an existential crisis, and we finally reached the counter. There was no chitchat in line, no sounds of community, and Kiera was silent as she wrote our names on the list. The worker slid a burlap sack over the counter, saying nothing, and I picked it up, putting it over the shoulder of my good arm. They gave the same kind of sacks every week, so it's not like I had to check it or anything.

We started to walk back toward the apartment, with Kiera's hand on the elbow of my bad arm; she had become very intent on keeping me close to her ever since the final battle. "So, what do you want to do tonight?"

She paused, looking up at the sky. "We can do a late-night walk with Gracey, if it doesn't rain."

I had never lived with a dog before. It took some getting used to. Of course, the dog slept in the bed with us, and her studded vest hung in the corner along with her booties. I was still in awe of how crafty Kiera had become during the zombie apocalypse.

"It'll be cooler then," I replied.

There was a sound. One I was familiar with. I heard it moving in the trees to our right, but I couldn't see it. I couldn't see anything now with my human eyes. Even after losing my colors, my night vision had been improved as a zombie. I wondered if opticians were even still a thing anymore.

I kept looking at the trees, straining to see what the noisemaker was, but nothing magically appeared in my purview. Before I realized it, we were back at our apartment, and I filed the sound away in my brain for later, hoping I could figure out what the hell it was before it drove me crazy.

Usually, those ideas came to me at three in the morning, after I woke up drenched in sweat from another nightmare.

But it was nothing. The end of the world had already happened, and now we were rebuilding it. Nothing else was out there. Nothing could be as bad as what had happened.

As we trudged up the stairs, I couldn't help but think we were being watched.

~

It was nice, really, that we kept the same apartment. Even though most of the kitchen didn't work, and there was no electricity in the living room(apparently, the people who ran electricity had not been Cured), we did have the radio. I'd bought it to go camping once, just to listen to music in the middle of nowhere; now it was our saving grace. The only thing we had to connect us to the outside world—now that phones didn't work and Brett was gone.

I tried not to think about Brett. Tried not to believe that it was my fault that he died, when I knew it probably was. He'd taken such good care of Kiera, and I owed him, at least, a proper burial, but his body was likely hauled away with the zombies that didn't come back. He was in a nameless burial site, a mass grave, or a burned pile. It didn't do him justice.

I was so angry.

Even as we unpacked our one bag of food (canned goods and MREs, mostly), I could feel tightening in my chest. The entire thing, the zombies, the end of the world—it made me *livid*. I had been a part of the destruction of mankind—at least for this corner of the world. And there was no way to fix it. I couldn't repair the electricity or make the factories and power plants start working again. Hell, I couldn't even pick up Kiera and carry her over broken glass, as having half my arm missing didn't do much for damsel-in-distress days.

"Fuck." I shoved the can of tuna into place in the dining room/pantry/Kiera's Costco Closet on the middle shelf. It didn't get offended or fight back, but I kind of wished it could.

Kiera's head shot up from the bottom shelves, where she was putting away some flour to make bread she could bake in the sun, theoretically. That's what the ladies at the food line said. Thank you, global warming.

"What fuck?" Kiera stared at me, eyes wide. It made

me realize that she was always a little on edge now, always treading water and waiting for the Next Worst Thing to happen. And it was all my fault.

"Sorry. I'm just . . ." I sighed. "I'm so fucking mad. I'm angry that I got Infected, I'm angry that you have to live in a house with no modern conveniences and shit in a bucket, I'm angry that I came back."

Did I just say the quiet part out loud? Fuck again.

Her hands stilled, holding a bag of sugar. I could see her fingers working, kneading at the bag, knowing that she was thinking—and that she was pissed. I definitely said the quiet part out loud.

"You're angry that you came back." It wasn't a question. Her voice was hollow.

I shifted uncomfortably on my feet, exhaling slowly to give myself time to think about the massive bombshell I'd just dropped on her. I gestured to the length of my body, the healing wounds, the bones that were still in splints from the CDC's health unit. "It's just that . . ."

"What, Sean? It's just that what, I spent every single day of your Infection feeling like it was the end of the fucking world? It's just that I fought an entire zombie army to get to you once I saw you. It's just that they finally, *finally* found a cure and brought you back to me, and now you're suddenly thinking it would've been better to end up dead for real?" Her eyes glittered in the low sunlight, and I could tell she was going to cry. Fuck.

"It's just that I did so much shit," I said in a rush. "I hurt so many people. So many people *got* hurt because of me, because of us, and so many families were broken apart. So many people weren't as lucky as we were to find each other. I can't count how many people I killed, but I remember the taste of every one of them, and that's fucking sick, Kiera." I leaned back against the shelves, closing my eyes so that I wouldn't have to see her hurt for even a second.

Grace had wandered into the room, pushing herself against Kiera's side and staying there. I always felt like Grace had some sort of vendetta against me, that she could tell that I was once the thing she went after and got treats for body-slamming into the ground. I had never spent much time around dogs, and I sure as hell didn't know what to do with one as smart as Grace.

She eyed me for a long time. Kiera stood still, holding on to the shelves for support. "So you feel guilty?" she said finally. "And you don't want to be here." Another statement.

I swallowed what felt like a metric shit ton of nervous spit. "It's not that I don't want to be here. I want to be here, with you, with Grace, even if she confuses me. I want to walk to the food pantry with you and listen to the birds because it's so damn quiet without the cars and planes. I want to help rebuild this world with you, to get back to normal. But, Kiera . . ." I hesitated.

"What?" she said shortly.

"I remember everything," I said again. "I remember what it felt like to lose control. To embrace the Infection. To have a master plan to Infect everyone. It's a hard thing to reconcile once the Infection is gone."

She sank to the floor with Grace, throwing her arm over her fur. "The nightmares?"

"The nightmares," I confirmed. "I keep having these dreams about all the things I did, and it's not getting any better. I'm still learning how to deal with things with only one good arm, and I'm still healing all the shit I broke while I was zombified. It's a fucking miracle that I'm standing here, and I don't feel like I deserve it."

"But I need you" came the quiet answer. She was staring at Grace, rubbing her fingers over the dog's soft ears, playing with the little tufts on top of them. "That whole time—all I needed was you. All I wanted was you. And now I have you, and you're having, what, a crisis of conscience?" Tears slowly fell from the corners of her eyes. Grace huffed a big sigh at me and leaned in further, pressing her head against Kiera's chest.

I sighed with her, sinking to the floor beside them both, canned goods momentarily forgotten. "I never stopped thinking about you," I confessed. "Not once. In one way or another, everything I did, I did because I wanted to get back to you. It's just . . . hard, knowing that I did such awful things. And with the amputation being my best-healing injury, I'm still a little off-kilter, you know?"

I paused. "Still not sure how something we did with power tools and duct tape ended up healing better than what the CDC did to me."

She cracked a smile. "They obviously hadn't watched as much *Grey's Anatomy* as I had," Kiera said softly.

"Totally." I put my good arm around her, and she snuggled against my chest, Grace lying across both our laps. "It's not that I don't want to be here. It's a dream come true. I never thought I'd see you again. But what I did . . ."

"You don't think that I did some awful shit? Yeah, they were zombies, but they were zombies we could have Cured. Grace and I and our little band of merry thieves killed a lot of actual *people,* and you think that I'm not haunted, too? Every one of us that survived is a fucking ghost house." She shook her head and buried her face in Grace's soft fur. "I killed people too."

We were at an impasse. We'd both done terrible things that we couldn't handle now that we knew those terrible things were done to people who could have been saved. How the hell were we going to get through this?

I held Kiera as she cried, rocking them both in my tattered arms. "We did," I said softly. "We both killed people. And that's never going to change. All that we can do is try to never get in a situation like that ever again."

She nodded slowly. "Well, it's not like the apocalypse happens twice, right?" she said, drying her face on her sleeves.

"Yeah," I echoed. "The apocalypse can't happen twice." Things could only go up from here.

~

As far as modern conveniences went, we could at least say that the natural gas hadn't died off. Apparently, it was easier to run than electricity with a skeleton crew. Either way, Kiera had rice on the stove-top, mixed with the little bit of fresh chicken they'd given us at the pantry, our weekly treat. I inhaled slowly, enjoying the scent, even though rice hadn't been my favorite food before all this had started.

I looked at my stump. Would we ever get back to the

place where people made prosthetics? Could I have some kind of awesome bionic arm in the future? I wondered if they came in cool colors. Fun aside, Kiera really had done a great job sewing me back together again, and the zombie virus had done the rest; it hadn't gotten infected, just Infected.

Kiera was spooning Grace's food into her bowl as I came up behind her. "It's time," I said.

She sighed, wiping her hands on her jeans, and turned off the burner. "Let me put this in bowls, and I'll be there."

True to her word, she came into the living room with two blue plastic bowls, offering one to me, and sat down in her favorite reading chair. She hadn't done much reading since the zombie war. I wondered if losing yourself in a world of unknowns was too triggering. I turned the radio on, grateful for the radio itself and the batteries the National Guard had given out when the dust had settled.

The broadcast went on every day, at six a.m. and six p.m. I didn't know where it was from, though I had to assume it was somewhere close unless radio waves worked differently than electricity. *"Attention, and welcome to the evening broadcast,"* it began.

We settled into our respective seats, and Grace wandered in, climbing onto the reading chair with Kiera. Seeing a dog sit in a chair like a person always made me smile.

. . . The electricians who survived the epidemic have worked tirelessly to restore civilization to its former glory. We urge you to continue using bottled water for cooking and hygiene. Water will be released every

Tuesday and Saturday at your local food pantry. Your refuse and personal waste . . ."

We listened closely. It was the same kind of message every day, but both of us thirsted for more information to know the state of the world. Had the Infection just been in America? Or just in the New England area? How widespread was this actually? We hadn't been in a state to ask when the CDC had distributed the Cure, as people were literally seeing zombies coming back from the undead. Water and toilets were not exactly on our priority lists at that moment.

The broadcast gave us the usual warnings about going outside, as the National Guard hadn't cleaned out all the bodies of the zombies who didn't make it and the humans who had died in the wake of warfare. We were supposed to go to a citywide meeting in the local high school auditorium two days from now, which was much closer to us than the college was. It wasn't a long broadcast, but the end of it made my hair stand on end.

And in notable news, the Cure that was given across the country has developed some side effects. It appears that those who were unInfected when the Cure was released have been exhibiting symptoms of a similar virus. This is an isolated incident at one location, but be aware that there is a possibility, no matter how small . . .

Kiera's eyes couldn't get any wider. "No," she whispered. "No, no, no—"

I found myself across the room before I knew I had moved. I scrunched myself into the over-sized chair with Kiera and Grace, holding them both, if a little awkwardly.

Grace didn't mind my stump, at least. She liked to lick it when she was nervous, and I was expecting a stump covered in goo by the end of this conversation.

"It's okay," I said softly. "He said that there's been, like, one case. So maybe that person just had some kind of co-morbid disease that reacted with the Cure. I'm sure it's just a once-in-a-million fluke. We don't need to worry."

She stared out at the dying sunlight, tears falling freely down her face for the second time that day. "It's happening again," she whispered. "It's happening again, and I can't do this, Sean, I can't lose you again, I can't lose Gracey, what if—"

I held her hand in mine and squeezed them both against my chest in a reassuring hug. "We won't," I said soothingly. "All we have to do is listen to the broadcasts and do what they tell us. They pulled us through the last war, and they can pull us through whatever weird shit is happening now." I was confident in my words and felt like I knew that it wouldn't get any worse.

It's funny how life happens that way.

Another Day
~ Kiera ~

They fucking came back. The zombies were back, and that meant that I was at risk. It meant that Sean might have to let me go like I'd sent him outside the apartment to his own fate. Oh my God, what were we supposed to do? I could feel panic rising in my throat, and I held on to Grace for dear life, burying my face in Sean's shirt.

"Shhh," he said. "We won't go outside unless we have to, so we won't run into anyone that hasn't been Infected but was Cured. We'll keep a close eye on you and the news and see what happens. This isn't a big deal, Kiera. You still have the space for Grace to use the bathroom inside, and we won't need dog food for another month. We just went to the food pantry for the week. They said it's like a one-off incident, Kiera. They did pretty well with the first outbreak; if this is a second one, I can't imagine it ending any other way."

He sounded so sure of himself. He sounded like he

knew what he was talking about, and I longed to listen to him, to feel safe in his arms, to know that we could take whatever was going to get thrown at us. Gracey's Doge suit still hung on the coat rack. My hatchet-mop had not been retired; it had merely migrated to the kitchen for some reason. We'd have to build a weapon for Sean. Some kind of containment for me. We'd . . .

Everything started spinning: the room, Grace, Sean. I felt like I was drowning. All I could think of was amputating his arm and hearing him scream. Finding him broken, zombified, at the college. Watching him "wake up" after the Cure had been deployed. It was all a blur. Something clenched hard in my chest, and I buried my fingers in Grace's fur, gasping. "I can't, Sean. I can't, I can't, I can't . . ."

"Hey," he said. "It won't come to that. Whatever it is, it won't come to that. I promise."

I closed my eyes against the swirling room. "You don't know that," I whispered.

He sighed. "No, I don't. I don't know that. But I got Infected before by another person. We aren't seeing other people. We don't go anywhere besides the food pantry and the roof for Grace to play. We can even make a place up there for her to potty so she doesn't have to do it inside. And I'm Cured, right? So I will always be here to take care of you."

"Yeah," I said. My voice was small. "I don't have PTSD at all, do I?"

He chuckled. "Well, if you don't have PTSD, I don't either."

I wondered if we'd ever be okay. The big kind of okay—where we got married at the courthouse, came home to our dog, and took her to the park. The okay where we'd have a family (or just a lot of books) and a future. Right now, it seemed like nothing would be okay ever again.

The broadcast was ending. I'd panicked through most of it. I could only hope that Sean had caught anything important while I was imploding. "Sean?"

"Yeah?" He was still holding me and Grace, who obviously knew that I was having a mental breakdown, as she wasn't budging from my lap.

"Is it . . . are we . . ." I hiccuped. "Will we be okay?"

He was quiet for a long time, rubbing my arm. "Yeah," he said after too long—long enough that the panic threatened to return. "Yeah, I think we'll be okay."

Sean took the bowl of somewhat warm rice and chicken, placed it in my hands, and grabbed his bowl to sit back on the couch again. "As long as I don't have to eat rice for the rest of my life, we'll be okay."

"Do you think it'll ever go back to normal? Like before it all happened?" I asked.

It took a few minutes for Sean to swallow and figure out how to talk again. "No," he said finally. "I don't think it'll be the same. But I think we'll be okay, even when it's different."

We sat silently and ate our dinner, Grace's tail wagging slowly against the chair. The *thump* sound was comforting, and I focused on that. I had Sean back. I had Grace. I had a home, food, and at least half of the supplies I'd hoarded from Costco back in the day, so we were doing pretty good on provisions.

Sean was right: I could hang up my hatchet-mop. We wouldn't see anyone besides the food pantry people, the National Guard, and maybe the CDC. It wasn't like we would go to the grocery store and get Infected. This one-off problem turned a regular person into some version of a zombie, details yet unknown.

Even though I knew Sean was okay, was sitting here in front of me, was Cured—my stomach rolled at the thought that I would be next, and I ran for the bucket in the bathroom. Rice didn't taste as good the second time around.

~

Somehow, sleeping in the living room felt safer, a habit I'd picked up before my merry band of adventurers had come into my life. Going into the bedroom, with the big bed, and the memories, and the smells . . . No. Couldn't do it. Absolutely not. Things were *not* the same, and if sleeping in the living room meant I could keep my sanity intact while the world was either ending or beginning around me, then I'd sleep in the living room in my comfy chair with my dog.

Sean was still asleep when I woke up. It was usually the other way around. Usually, his nightmares woke him up, and that woke *me* up. It was a little strange that he hadn't started screaming yet.

I watched him as he slept, looked at the bruises where bones had been broken, looked at the stump that I'd sewed with my meager home ec skills, the hollowness of his cheeks, and how skinny he was. I had covered the mirror in our bathroom a long time ago, unable to meet my gaze and accept the world as it was. I wondered if I looked similarly broken or if it was just him.

I brought Gracey to her potty spot as the sun rose beyond our windows. That was one good thing about the zombie apocalypse happening: I could realistically throw dog shit in the dumpster from the roof, and nobody would give a fuck. What we'd do when the dumpster got full was beyond my scope.

Grace was easy to please. She liked playing on the roof, showing off how she could get up and down the ladder easier than Sean could. She loved chasing balls, and we were careful to ration them in case she chewed them up and we couldn't get any more. She liked it when we returned from the food pantry because it meant new smells. She hadn't gotten a lot of outside time since Sean had come back; at least, not outside time on the ground. No sniff-walks for us. I didn't dare.

The CDC, the National Guard, and the radio said we were safe. I wasn't so sure about that.

I started the oatmeal—pretty much our staple for every morning; the only thing that changed was what I put in with it—and heard Sean getting up.

"You're up before I am?" he said groggily.

"I was confused, too." I rinsed out our bowls and spooned out our portions, leaving some for Grace. Oatmeal was her favorite. "No nightmares last night?"

He ran his hand through his hair as he wandered into the kitchen. "I always have nightmares," he said simply. "It's just a matter of how bad they are."

I didn't know what to say. I had nightmares too, nightmares that I didn't share with him. Nightmares of cutting his hand off. Of leaving him in that stairwell. Of being alone, with only Brett for company. Brett, who was dead now.

So many people were dead now.

We went back into the living room to eat after I added some blueberries to the oatmeal—a rarity from the food pantry fresh fruit was hard to come by. "So what are we going to do?"

He blinked. "With what?"

"The broadcast's coming on soon. What are we going to do if there's something else happening? Are we hiding? Fighting? What are we going to do?" I hesitated, my spoon halfway to my mouth. It felt too early to be making this kind of plan.

He swirled his spoon slowly, chasing after a blueberry. "What do you want to do?"

I shook my head, listening to Grace slurp down her oatmeal. "I don't know," I whispered. "I really want to be a part of this. This new world, you know? I want to contribute something. Make something better. But I don't know how."

We ate in silence; it was becoming a habit now. Finally, he looked up at me. "So we'll be part of this," he said. "Next time we go to the food pantry, we'll ask the National Guard. Or we'll listen to the radio broadcast, and they'll tell us what to do. We'll do something, Kiera. Together."

It was the "together" part that scared me. I'd dealt with a zombie apocalypse without Sean, without knowing if he was okay, and it had changed me. Who were we now? Were we still the same couple that had walked into this apartment for the first time together? Or were we something else, something new?

I clicked on the radio. It didn't play music anymore, just broadcasts. There was only one station. Even getting our news was different now. "Broadcast should start any minute."

I settled onto the couch beside Sean, resting my head on his shoulder. He'd cleaned up nicely after that first shower post-zombie apocalypse: a lot of injuries but nothing that couldn't be healed with time and effort. I traced my fingertips along the scar on his stump, remembering what it had taken to cut off his hand that day. I still wasn't sure if it had been the right answer; did it keep him from turning faster? No matter what I did, the Infection spread. I had only done what hundreds of hours of TV and books told me to.

He flinched a little but relaxed next to me. "It feels weird," he said.

"How weird?" I said, putting my hand back into my lap.

"I can still feel where the hand is supposed to be. I read in a book once that if you, like, put a mirror between your hands and look at the image reflected, it tricks your brain into thinking you still have two hands. I thought I should probably try it." He shrugged, laying his head back on the couch.

"That sounds cool. Complicated but cool. Oh, wait, here we go," I said. The radio clicked from static to sound.

It always began with the same spiel, telling us to be brave, help our communities, and basically be good little citizens. If this Cure that they spread over all of us was actually the next step in the apocalypse, I had no intention of being a good little citizen.

There have been five reported cases of the unInfected becoming ill in the wake of the Cure. Scientists are working hard to ensure that we understand why this is happening and how to stop it. The five patients have not turned into the exact type of creature that we'd seen in the war. They have evolved, with bodily fluids becoming acidic to the touch. If you see a newly turned individual, do not engage. I repeat, do not engage.

They are also faster. Faster than healthy humans. As we said, there have only been five cases so far that have been reported, but . . .

I couldn't listen any longer and buried my face in Sean's shoulder. "So it's the apocalypse times two but worse?"

He rested his chin on top of my head and sighed, listening to the radio a little more before answering me. "They still haven't said *how* someone is a second-time zombie. Like, transmission details. It stands to reason that if there are only five people with these . . . *enhancements?* . . . that it's just a small thing. Maybe they all have something in common, like . . . I don't know, lupus or something?"

I could tell he was grasping at straws to assuage my panic, but he didn't look as worried as I felt. "I guess," I said quietly.

. . . No other news to report. Please remain indoors as

*much as possible and contact your local food pantry if
you need assistance* . . .

I ate the rest of my oatmeal silently, staring at the
now-static radio. "Sean, what if—"

"Don't."

"Don't what?" I could feel my heart racing, and Grace
jumped up onto the couch next to us, resting her head on
my knee.

"Don't do this. Don't start panicking that it's happening again, don't start believing that you're next, don't start
living with anxiety every day from now until forever." He
turned a little, matching his gaze with mine. "I will do
anything to keep you safe, Kiera. I did it before, and I'll
do it again. It will be fine. Trust me."

The problem was that I did trust him. But I also trusted
what I knew from the previous war: zombies had a habit
of getting to you, no matter what your social circle looked
like. For all we knew, a rabid band of acid-spitting zombies would attack our apartment complex, and then Sean
would be alone—what if Gracey was Infected? Could this
new type of zombie-ism affect her too?

"Stop," he whispered, brushing his fingertips against
my lips. "We've got this, Kiera. I promise. All we have to
do is only leave the house for food pantry stuff. I replaced
the lock on the door after I came back, and we've got the
chain on the door now, too. Barely anyone still lives here,
so we don't have to worry about neighbors. I'm sure we
could find someone at the food pantry who wants to double up on security and walk home together as far as we
can."

Burying my head further in Sean's chest, I fluffed Gracey's fur with my fingers, making it stand on end. She gave a soft woof of encouragement, with just the tip of her tail waving back and forth. It was as if she knew what we were facing, and she was down to be in the thick of it with us, again.

"I'll have to get Grace goggles," I said finally. "If they're acid-spitting or whatever."

"You expect the dog to fight more zombies?" Sean said.

"Well, if we have to leave the house for any extended period of time, we can't just leave her alone like her previous owners did." I was already contemplating upgrades to her Doge suit, different ways to keep Grace safe. It never occurred to me that she *wouldn't* be with us to fight zombies. She had been such a driving force in my life during the first war that I couldn't imagine her not being with me for the second, even with Sean here this time.

"That makes a little sense, I guess," he replied. "We won't leave her to starve. But I don't plan on going on any zombie-killing expeditions either. It might not be a big threat, but it's still a threat, and we need to keep you safe until we learn more about what the hell's going on."

I gave my oatmeal bowl to Gracey, considering his words. Again, it hadn't occurred to me that we wouldn't be fighting zombies. There had to be a Plan, some great decision made by the powers that be to fix this, and of course, we'd fight our way to wherever they told us to go. But this war—if it even was a war—was different. We didn't *need* to go into town except to the food pantry once a week. And it was entirely possible that whatever triggered the fast, acid-spitting zombies was something I didn't have.

We would be okay.

Is It War?

~ Sean ~

It probably wouldn't be the last time I lied to Kiera, but it definitely felt like a stone in my gut. I didn't know if we would be okay. I didn't know anything other than what the broadcast had disclosed, and that wasn't much. I knew that I was fine, at least so far, since I'd already been a zombie, but what about Kiera?

I had to find more information, fast.

"Let's go to the roof," I said finally. "We can get Grace some exercise and come up with a game plan."

She quickly washed our oatmeal bowls in the sink, stacking them neatly on the strainer. Kiera said nothing, only whistling to Grace, and we went for the ladder. It always amused me to see a dog climbing as Grace did; I didn't know how the hell Kiera had trained her to do this, but she was definitely good at it and faster than I was getting up the thing.

Kiera had set up a small agility course on the roof,

and Grace knew exactly what to do. She began going through the weave poles, one after another, swiftly and without fail. Grace was a damned well-trained dog, and I had to give Kiera kudos for what she'd accomplished. She hardly had any experience with dogs, and yet she'd expertly taught Grace what she needed to know to survive.

I sat down on the lawn chair, a relic from the time before, when people used to come up here to drink coffee and watch the city. I didn't speak for a long time, not knowing how to make the problem better. As I squinted against the sunlight, I looked towards the city center, the streets that would lead us back to the university, where it all ended. There were no cars, traffic, or sounds, but I could see a single person staring into the sun until he turned to face me as if he knew I was there.

Something in my mind snapped. I could *feel* him. It wasn't the same as my Hex when I was Zombie Sean; it was something different. I hesitated before reaching out in my brain.

Killkillkillkillkill

Holy shit. He didn't have thoughts like my Hex zombie Links, nor were they like regular human thoughts (in my limited experience). It was all raw sensation, bloody red images, and I could barely translate what I felt into words.

"Kiera," I said after a moment.

"Yeah?" She sounded depressed. Grace was still playing in the obstacle course, going up and down a seesaw back and forth. I opened my arms toward her, and she snuggled into my lap, the lawn chair creaking slightly under our weight.

"There's a zombie down there."

I felt her stiffen. "You're kidding," she said.

"Look." I gestured toward the intruder on our peaceful roof time. "It's strange it's not like when I was a zombie, but it kind of feels like I know what he's thinking."

I let my mind drift back to where it belonged. Of course, I didn't know for sure that this was a zombie, but what else could he be? Someone I could commune with mentally almost *had* to be a zombie. But why was he here, and why could I overhear his thoughts? Was there something about the Cure?

Kiera paled, staring off from the expanse of the roof in the possible-zombie's general direction. As I looked closer, I noticed that he wasn't moving quite right. His actions were jerky but not from the various wounds or broken bones that I'd dealt with as a zombie. As he walked into the sunlight, I noticed how fast he moved, despite him being uncoordinated. This was definitely what they were reporting on the news.

"I thought you said there wasn't anyone to turn into a zombie in our neighborhood," she said accusingly.

"I said that we don't really have neighbors and don't really have to go outside," I replied. "That we have most of our apartment building to ourselves and the rest of the neighborhood only goes out when they need to. Obviously, something changed. I think we'll have to get out our raincoats and swimming goggles and try to figure out a way to get past him next time we go to the food pantry."

He looked relatively well-kept. There were no black, bleeding wounds, no broken bones, just some dude hanging out staring at the sun. A dude who could think of nothing else but to kill. "At least we know he can't sense us from up here," I said.

"Yeah . . ." Kiera trailed off as Grace came back panting and flopped down next to our lawn chair. She'd done the agility course at least three times, always stopping on her favorite tricks to do them again and again. "Okay. So there's a possible zombie down there. Why do you look like that?"

"Like what?" I had no idea what she was talking about.

"Like there's more to this conversation than what you're actually telling me." Kiera sat up straight, staring into my eyes. She wasn't going to back down.

"I mean, his thoughts are pretty much 'kill all the things' and nothing else," I said. "It doesn't feel the same, like what I felt from the others when I was Infected. It's just . . . like I can hear him thinking."

Grace laid her head on the edge of the lawn chair as if to contribute to the conversation somehow. I watched the zombie move so fast, toward the sunlight, away from the apartment buildings. "Well, at least we know there's something he's more interested in than us," I said thoughtfully.

"What?" Kiera had closed her eyes as if she didn't want to see what future might await her.

"He's, like, walking into the sun like a vampire with a death wish. I don't know what the endgame is, but he isn't sticking around here."

We watched the zombie damn near run away into the morning light until we couldn't see him anymore. I wondered what it meant, that I could feel what he was thinking. The news had said only people who hadn't been Cured of the Infection were zombifying, so it wasn't the start of a new Link or a Hex. I wouldn't turn. At least, not under current suspicions.

"Yeah," Kiera said, shielding her eyes from the sun. "Maybe that's all they want, to be in the sunlight."

After reaching out to him and hearing his *killkilllkill* urges, I agreed with her. Had to keep the peace. Couldn't let her know how worried I was about this new form of zombie. "Sure," I said, reaching down and petting Grace on the ears. "I'm sure the CDC has a plan, and this won't be such a big deal."

We carefully made our way back to our apartment living room, Grace leading the way as Kiera headed up the rear. As we sank into our respective comfy places—the places we slept now, anyway—I heard her sigh. I could tell that this was weighing heavily on her mind, but I had no comforting words, nothing to say that wouldn't be a lie at best. I *didn't* know if we would be okay. I *wasn't* sure that she wouldn't turn into whatever zombified-hell this was. At least for now, the zombies didn't seem too into harming people; they maybe had the idea, but they were far more interested in other things.

Then again, he'd been alone. With thoughts like that, I couldn't help but wonder what he would do when the sunlight faded to black.

~

I didn't "hear" from the zombie for the rest of the day. Kiera was oddly quiet, reorganizing our pantry and supplies. I was on the couch with Grace, who clearly did not know me and was somewhat concerned about it. It had only been a few weeks of me staying here and even less time healing from the various injuries I got as a zombie.

"Hey," I called. "The radio's about to go on."

She said nothing, simply walked into the living room and sank into her chair. I watched her, trying to figure out what was wrong. I'm not exactly the most observant person out there, but I could tell that the zombie from earlier had bothered her.

I rubbed my stump with my hand, watching Grace flump herself down on Kiera's lap. I couldn't figure out what to say. *Sorry, but you might end up a zombie* was not on my to-do list this year. I could reassure her that it would be okay, but would it? I was haunted by what I'd done. I couldn't imagine piling more on Kiera after what she'd gone through.

Welcome to the evening broadcast, came through our radio. *We want to caution you not to engage with anyone behaving unusually, such as moving mechanically. Please do not be alarmed if you have received the Cure; there is every bit of evidence that the citizens who are acting oddly are outliers. With that said, I would like to make a disclaimer.*

If you were one of the Infected and were Cured, you do not need to be alarmed. Citizens with prior undead experience need not worry. If you were not Infected and Cured but have been exposed to the vaccine or Cure, please monitor yourself for symptoms such as lethargy, difficulty seeing, a burning sensation in your mouth . . .

Grace had her paws on Kiera's shoulders, pressing her head underneath Kiera's chin. Looking up at her, I could only see her tears. She was sobbing quietly as if she didn't want to alarm me. As gracefully as ever, I fell off of the couch and army-crawled toward her, then rested my head on the seat of her chair.

"So, are you seeing weird? Or having mouth-burning goodness?" I said finally.

She sniffled, her eyes still closed. Grace was not moving one inch on her lap for me to hold Kiera, so this was the best she was going to get. "No," she said, almost too softly for me to hear it. "Not yet, anyway." She threaded her hand between herself and Grace towards me, and I took it.

"Well, it sounds like it's pretty rare. All we have to do is watch it and not go near anyone that acts funny. They didn't say to kill them on sight, or that they'll attack us, or any craziness like during the war. So what could go wrong, really?" I squeezed her hand.

Apparently, quite a bit could go wrong.

The radio was still squawking as I stood up. Something that sounded like thunder was pretty damn close. "It didn't look rainy today, did it?" I squinted to look through the blinds.

"N-no." Kiera sniffed. "What's wrong now?"

I tried to get a better angle out the window, but it just

wasn't happening. The sky was starry, with no trace of clouds or storms. The apartment building was still in one piece, far as I could see. Then something shifted and I heard a noise.

It was one of the very few neighbors who'd stayed in the apartment building, Ms. Barbie, out front of the building. She jerked her hands forward as she lurched toward the front, where the doors were. She wasn't growling, or groaning, or doing anything zombielike, except that her coordination was shit.

Maybe that was normal for her.

"Sean, what?" Kiera said, a little impatiently this time.

"It's Ms. Barbie," I said, trying to stay quiet. "Something's going on. Come look."

Kiera dried her eyes, petted Grace, and knelt beside me on the floor. "I don't think she normally walks like that," she said.

"I don't think so either." As we watched, the door of the apartment building opened, and another neighbor, one who remained nameless to us, started out the door. He wore business-appropriate clothes, which seemed weirder than Ms. Barbie awkwardly dancing in the alley. "Where the fuck does he think he's going, Starbucks?"

Kiera snorted a tiny laugh. "I don't think a shirt and tie are required at Starbucks."

"You never know." I was beginning to open the window for a better view when I heard it.

A deep, booming yell.

I couldn't see where it was coming from, but it didn't sound like Tie Man. Damn it, I wished I had a better view.

I could see Ms. Barbie but not Tie Man, as they had moved past my viewpoint.

"What the hell was that?" Kiera whispered.

I shook my head, waiting. Listening. And then I heard a sound: a sound I would never forget for the rest of my life. I didn't know what was happening to Tie Man, but he was screaming in his big, bass voice, sounding as if the world had fallen down upon him. I could only see Ms. Barbie's back, as she just stayed still. The screaming grew louder, and I could see Kiera next to me turning pale.

And then it stopped.

It stopped all at once. There were no noises, no movements, nothing. I could only see the back of Ms. Barbie's head, and that just faintly. No noises rose from the streets anymore, and I couldn't see a puddle of blood or anything.

I leaned back on my heels. "I think that's about the time we start saying 'fuck,' isn't it?" I said finally. "I don't know what that was. Someone clearly did something to Tie Man, and Ms. Barbie stood in the same place for most of whatever that was."

"Yeah," Kiera said quietly. "But who got him?"

Shaking my head, I sighed, leaning back against the coffee table. "So now we know that there *is* something going on." It was a sentence. A period. A full stop. Whatever this was, it had reached our little community of survivors, and it wasn't just some random guy staring into the sun.

Kiera crumpled into a ball on the ground, hugging her knees to her face. "Sean, I'm so fucking scared," she said.

My mind whirled, trying to find some spin on this that

was better than reality. It occurred to me that whatever happened to Ms. Barbie may have been the same thing that got Staring into the Sun Man. I would never be able to describe it, but I reached out mental "fingers" toward the front of the apartment, where I could barely see her.

!!!!!kill!!!!!

Well, that was quick. "So we aren't going downstairs for a while."

"Because?"

"Because I think our neighbor is a second-wave zombie, and I don't know what the fuck she did to that guy, but I don't want to see it happen to us."

"What if it happens to me? Sean, God, they said they were outliers, but if it's happening here, it's probably happening everywhere. We need to plan. We need . . ." I could tell she was lost in her own panicking thoughts.

I grabbed her hand. "Hey."

Her eyes slowly focused on mine, but I could see the fear still riding her.

"So we won't go outside," I said again. "Unless we have to. We don't *need* vegetables and bread. We don't *need* anything at the food pantry, and we won't for months. We can stay here, and we can watch, and we can wait."

"The last time I watched and waited, you became a zombie, and I had to leave you." Kiera was not happy with this train of thought.

Hesitating, I licked my dry lips. Damn, if that wasn't one thing I missed about the civilized world: ChapStick. "I know. I know what happened, and I know we're both freaking out about this, but we can't do anything about it.

Maybe we can break into some of the empty apartments and see if we get a better view of what happened."

She nodded slowly, and I retrieved my handy crowbar. We listened carefully at the door, unlocking the triple-safe locks with a click. I wasn't exactly expecting burglars to randomly show up, but it made Kiera feel better, anyway.

"Let's go." We made our way out the door and toward the front of the building. Most apartments had closed doors and very unpleasant smells emanating from them, but some of the doors were open. It made me think about just how different the zombie war was for all of us: some of us ran, some of us fought, some of us ate and Infected others. It was a still life that couldn't ever exist anymore; there was nowhere safe to run.

Once we had commandeered an empty apartment at the front of the building, I held my hand up for Kiera to wait. *She's been through enough,* I thought. As I opened the window, it creaked unhappily, and I winced. Would this new breed of zombie be sensitive to sound, like I had been?

I had a pretty good view of the front of the building from there. As the other supposedly-a-zombie had, Ms. Barbie stood there, looking at the sun. But Tie Man was different. Tie Man had collapsed on the front stoop.

Tie Man was melting.

"What the everloving fuck . . ." I couldn't help myself. "Kiera, come look."

"What is it?" She tried to fit beside me, between someone's couch and window. It was a tight fit, but she needed to see it herself. I gestured toward the front stoop, with no other words than *fuck* coming to mind.

He was bleeding. That was the first thing I noticed; it was a brilliant red against the concrete. He was splayed on the ground as if he'd fallen from a great height, which confused me. And then I saw it—Tie Man was being eaten alive by . . . something? His skin bubbled and burped as if on fire, and I could see his hands dissolving into bones. There was no other word for it: he was *melting*.

Kiera fell back the two inches we had to spare against the couch. I noticed it was extremely dated and ugly and wondered if zombie-ism had trained my brain to react to crises with a sarcastic tongue, expecting the worst. The skin on his head dripped down his face in little rivulets, blood following behind, and I could see his skull. One eye popped out of the socket—I swore I heard it, though maybe it was zombie memories—and dangled down the decaying skin.

"Do you . . . is he okay?" Kiera whispered, her breaths coming short.

"Uh, I would say he is very not okay, Kiera. He is having the most not-okay day in the world. He definitely isn't getting Starbucks any time soon." I looked at her, and it looked like she was in shock. Her face was pale, and sweat beaded on her forehead. Her hands were clammy when I went to hold one in mine.

She sat there with me for a long time, with the ooze outside just sitting there on the stoop, and I had no idea what to do. How could I take care of her when she was so broken, when *I* was so broken? Were we worse together or apart? My heart clenched; I didn't want to even think that way.

Kiera took a deep breath and squeezed out to sit on the couch. "So the zombies . . . liquefy people now?"

Again, not on my bingo card for this year. "I guess they weren't kidding when they said their bodily fluids or whatever are acidic." I struggled out from behind the ugly couch and gave my hand to Kiera. She took it, and I saw something I hadn't seen since the new zombies came to light: determination. She had a plan, and she would take hold of that plan and run as far as she could with it.

I couldn't help but smile a little, and she smacked me on the arm. "So what do we do about acidic zombies?" she said.

As we made our way back to our apartment, I considered the question carefully. "We monitor you, we don't go outside, we only use the roof for access. We listen to the radio. We prepare for the worst, even if it won't happen."

Kiera locked the door behind us. "What do you mean by 'prepare'?"

I didn't—couldn't—look her in the eye. "I mean, if something happens and you become an acid-shooting zombie, what should I do about it? What if I leave you here in the apartment, and you eventually get Cured like I did, and then we never see each other again?" My heart felt like a block of ice.

She leaned back against the closed door, shutting her eyes. "I don't know," she said. Her voice sounded hollow, haunted. "I guess lure me into an empty apartment and try not to get acid spit on you?"

Remembering Tie Man and his melting skin, I shuddered. It didn't seem like a pleasant way to go, melting from the outside in. "We'll figure it out, Kiera," I said. "I promise."

I didn't have the heart to tell her I was as lost as she was.

The New Normal

~ Kiera ~

I was up earlier than Sean, so I took Grace to the roof to blow off some steam. I knew Sean had figured out how freaked out I was. I'd thought about it briefly—what it might be like to be a zombie. Sean had told me about the urge to Infect, the desperate need to rip and tear into flesh . . . But this was different. This was new and absolutely fucking terrifying.

Grace wanted to play fetch, regardless of how bad a throw I was. "What are we gonna do, Gracey?" I whispered.

She was oblivious. I thought fondly of her Doge suit, the battle-ready outfit. Would it keep her safe from acid? How could we keep her safe if we had to abandon the apartment?

There were too many logistical problems to deal with in this new zombie world.

As we played, my mind wandered, and I soaked in the

meager morning sun. Vitamin D helped anything, right? It was actually a little relaxing until . . .

There's always an "until."

I heard what sounded like a car backfiring. There had been no traffic for weeks after the Cure was released. I gave Grace back her ball and went to the side of the building, holding on to the railing as I looked out. A car might mean someone knew what the fuck was going on. A car might mean we could get out of here.

Instead of a car, I saw a man sitting on his windowsill across the street. He was dressed head to toe in black. And he had a gun.

Holy fuck, he had a gun!

I knelt down quickly, peering between the rails, hoping he couldn't see me. Gun Man was quietly aiming at something down the street, and I heard that sound again. Silly me, thinking it was a car. Obviously, my privilege was showing.

I craned my neck to look as far as I could from my hiding spot, with Grace coming up behind me and panting on my neck. Someone had fallen on the ground, likely because of him. "What the hell is he doing?" I whispered to Grace. She licked my cheek and remained all up in my business.

The man sat quietly in his window for a while, looking down the street, and then lowered himself back into his (was it his? Did he steal it?) apartment.

What the hell?

I herded Grace back down to the apartment, then waited impatiently as she daintily stepped on every rung. After flinging the door open, letting Grace in, and slamming it behind me, I realized I was probably being a little dramatic about the whole thing.

"So, Sean?" I called.

He appeared from the nether regions of our apartment. "So what?"

"There's a dude with a gun picking people off on the street. He lives in the apartment across from us. Or he stole someone's apartment across from us, who knows."

Sean was rubbing his stump. The broken bones had healed fantastically, but the amputation still bothered him. "Like . . . picking off zombies or people?"

I shook my head. "I have no idea. I couldn't see far enough to tell. I'm going to try to assume zombies and not that we have a mass serial killer living across the street."

He exhaled slowly, coming into the living room fully. "So what do we do?"

"Well . . . if we're trying not to go outside, we can use that apartment with the window again and try to contact him? Maybe put up a giant note that he could read?" I shrugged.

"I mean, I appreciate that you want to make new friends, but what if he *is* a mass serial killer?"

"Well, then, he still won't know what apartment we're in, so by the time he gets here, we'll be ready." It made sense in my head, not so much when I said it out loud.

Sean snorted. "I guess that's true. Knocking door-to-door is probably not a serial killer's MO. All right, let's make a sign."

I grabbed my notebooks from school—God, how long had it been since I'd gone to school?—and started taping pieces of paper together to make one big poster. As I hunted for a Sharpie, I saw Sean looking out the window. "What's up?"

"I just . . . there's something about this that I don't like. Why does the Cure for being a zombie create more zombies? I know, I know, it sounds like a conspiracy theory. But what if there's something going on?" He rocked back on his heels.

It took me a long time to write in huge letters, "We Are Here—Who Are You?" The message was simple, but it got the point across. "Something going on like what? Like *X-Files* kind of stuff? The smoking man, aliens, what are we talking about here?"

Sean left the window and flopped down in his favorite seat on the couch. "I mean, kind of? The government just so happened to manufacture a Cure for the Infection; they didn't even have time to do clinical trials on mice, for fuck's sake. What if this is all a thing like the government driving us back into the Dark Ages, so we . . ." He struggled. "So we don't rebel against the shitty politics of our country and get the fuck out of it?"

I poured water from a jug into Grace's bowl and sat on my fluffy chair. "Seriously? We're talking government conspiracies now?"

"Well, wasn't that friend of yours, Callie or someone, working with the government?" He asked.

Frowning, I cracked my knuckles with a satisfying, if slightly painful, *pop*. "I mean, I guess. I'm not sure where she ended up after everything happened. My cell phone died, and I couldn't charge it or anything."

"And you don't find it slightly suspicious that within a year of the zombie apocalypse happening, there's a Cure for zombies? What if . . ."

I ran my fingers through my hair and sighed. "I think this is above our pay grade," I said simply. "Trying to figure out the whys and hows of this. All we can do is keep our heads down and try to get through this second wave."

Sean didn't say anything. He just sat there, watching Grace drink her water, and I wondered—not for the first time—if he was thinking with his normal brain or if it was a memory from Zombie-Sean. I knew it still haunted him, knew the nightmares were still bad, knew that he had regrets and sins of his own, just like I did.

"I don't think we should fully shelve this conversation," he said. "Let's put up our sign and see what happens."

Again, not for the first time, I wished Brett were here. It wasn't exactly *easier* with him, but he did seem to know what to do. Sean had his own ghosts, and I was too close to the issue to be partial. We had each made our own small community out of the disaster, and now neither of us would likely ever know what happened to our friends.

We marched back to the apartment facing the street and put up our sign. All we could do was hope that he wasn't a serial killer and that someone out there might actually be in the same spot we were in. Maybe he had a loved one he was protecting. Maybe he was a vigilante. Either way, it was worth the risk.

~

We spent another few days knowing nothing about what was happening in the real world. The broadcasts hadn't been very specific, only saying to "look out for acid-spitting zombies," but in fewer words. No reason was given for *why* people turned into zombies or what went wrong with the vaccine to make it happen. Of course not. Why would they admit fault?

It was time to go back to the food pantry. We left carefully, and I wondered if the man with the gun saw us—or cared that we were there.

My relationship with Sean was a little strained, and I didn't know what to do about it. We hadn't really talked since we "shelved" that little conversation, but we still woke up with each other and hung out with each other. I guessed it was about time for someone to make a move.

"Sean—"

"Kiera—"

We both laughed, and relief trickled down the skin at the back of my neck. "What are we going to do?" I said finally.

"We're going to get our weekly food pantry bag, go back to the apartment, and deal with whatever comes next together. Don't forget, we put in a request for batteries a few weeks ago for the radio, so let's make sure they don't stiff us," Sean said.

Standing in line, I felt like we'd be waiting forever. I didn't know how far away these people lived from the school, but apparently, we had neighbors we didn't realize we had. I didn't see anyone I knew; no one from the war, from Before, nothing. I wondered, not for the first time, what my little gang of zombie killers was doing.

If they were still doing anything. If they were even alive for the doing.

I sighed as we finally got to the front of the line. The clerk held his hand out for my requisition form and grabbed our food, as well as the batteries, and put them in a burlap sack. "Is there anything new on the requisition forms for next time?" I asked.

His answer was curt. "No," he said. "Move on."

Well, fine, then. We left Mr. Cheerful behind, making our way back toward the apartment. We made a pit stop at the front apartment we'd broken into, and Sean put down the sack as I walked over to the window.

There was a sign!

I am here—How many are you?

This was going to be a pretty slow-burning communication, that was for sure. I'd left the Sharpie and paper on the coffee table near the window and now got to work making a new sign as Sean peered through our pantry sack.

"Kiera," he said after a while.

"Yeah?"

"I think they're starting to run out of food. This bag isn't nearly as big as our last bag." He sat down on the couch, watching me draw.

An ice cube fell to the pit of my stomach. "But . . . they're the government. How can they run out of food?"

"Well, it's not like supermarkets are getting deliveries at this point, right? They're ransacking shelves from every store they can and passing out MREs. I think we're going to have to figure this one out on our own."

I started to color in my letters, black on white. I thought about how quickly the world had moved on after the Cure and yet how backward we still were. Infrastructure hadn't been repaired at all, and I didn't know when it would be. Did we even still have a government? Did this affect other countries or just the US?

Hanging my sign in the window, I sat down at the coffee table across from Sean and sighed. "So what do we do?"

"Well, last time you did inventory, we had enough stuff to keep us for at least two months. So if they are running out of food, we have two months to figure out what to do about it." He ran his fingers through his hair, and I looked at the scar on his hand from when he was a zombie. It would never fade.

None of this would ever fade.

"Let's go," I said abruptly, and stood up. Sean said nothing, only following after me with our sack, and we locked the door behind us. Something still wasn't right between us. It didn't feel like it did before, and it worried me. Sean was all I had left; I had no idea if my mother was okay, if Callie was okay, if any of my troupe was okay. I had no one else except for Sean.

I began to put the meager amount of food on the shelves in the pantry. As I checked out our storage, something clattered to the ground behind me.

It was my hatchet-mop; the tape on the mop handle was still stained a disgusting brown.

I wondered if I'd ever need it again. Sean and I could realistically stay here forever as long as the food pantry kept up. But if they were running out of food, we'd have to make a plan, and soon.

Grace came up behind me, and I grabbed a box of rice to make for her. We didn't have a ton of dog food, but we shared whatever protein we got with her when we could. I was planning on adding beef broth to it, a staple we'd quickly found was scarce.

My mind wandered as I lit the stove with my lighter and started the rice. If we couldn't stay here, where would we go? Could we take Grace with us? I would never leave her behind. If we went, she went, no matter what.

My thoughts spun around in circles as I cooked, and I set aside the rice to cool a little before I gave it to Grace.

"The broadcast's coming on," Sean called from the living room.

"Okay," I said back, cleaning my hands on a towel that I couldn't quite remember where we'd gotten it from. It was a nauseating green, and I wondered if it had been that color originally or if we'd done something to the poor rag.

"Welcome to the evening broadcast, the radio said. The new batteries sat beside the radio, ready to switch out as soon as we needed them. I was glad Grace wasn't the type of dog to eat everything in sight; what would we do without a vet if she swallowed some batteries?

We are experiencing a higher ratio of new Infected citizens than we were previously. The mutated Infection, the one that is affecting those who were not turned the last time, is spreading. There is no known cause or solution; we will update once we have more information.

Food pantries across the country are tightening their

belts," it said. *"Food grows scarce as we are now months into this pandemic. We highly recommend that you ration your food and consider growing crops in your backyards if you can to supplement the food given to you at the pantry. Please do not panic . . ."*

I snorted. "We're running out of food, but don't panic. People are turning even faster, but don't panic. Do they even know what the fuck they're doing?"

Sean lifted a brow. "Is my conspiracy theory growing on you?"

Shaking my head, I lay back in my chair, patting the spot next to me for Grace to jump up. She took her time, wiggling around the chair, before finally settling with her head on my lap. "I don't know, Sean. Something is going on. What are we going to do if we run out of food?"

The silent question was, *Or if I turned?*

"Well, we can play farmers on the roof if we can figure out how to get some dirt and seeds. Maybe the tractor supply store a few miles out of the center of town has stuff we can borrow."

He didn't answer the second question.

. . . Please remain in your homes. Do not engage with anyone who seems Infected. Remember, they have the ability to Infect you from a distance . . .

"So we're supposed to just be sitting ducks? Sitting here with no food?" I shook my head. "No. Fuck that. We have to be more prepared than this."

"What do you want to do, Kiera? It's not like we have a ton of options." Sean stretched, resting his head on the back of the couch.

I sighed. "Well, your idea to go to the tractor supply could be good. I'm sure we'd find something to make a little garden up there. And if anyone's kept feeding the baby chicks they usually have, we might be able to get some chickens for eggs for Grace."

"Then we'll go in the morning," he said. "It'll be fun. We can take a long walk with Grace; I'm sure she'd enjoy the scenery change. We've got this, Kiera."

Something in the back of my mind was screaming that no, in fact, we did not *have this*. Something was bound to go wrong. What if we never made it to—or back from—the tractor supply store? What if we ran out of food, and we had to watch each other starve to death? My mind was racing, and I closed my eyes against the room spinning.

"It'll be okay," Sean said, kneeling by my chair. He put his hand on Grace's head, scritching between her ears softly. "We'll figure this out. We found each other at the end of the war; the universe can't break us apart now."

I nodded. "Let's check our sign the first thing when we wake up. Then we'll go from there." It sounded like a plan, but it sure as hell didn't feel like one.

A Little Field Trip

~ Sean ~

It wasn't exactly bright and early, but it was definitely early enough that I should still be sleeping. A morning person I am not. Kiera walked with Grace, and I hauled a wagon behind us, a relic from trunk-or-treating that we'd done in the city before all of this had started. Back then, everyone sat outside their apartments and gave candy to kids who walked by in a little line.

I wasn't exactly sure why that was fun. At all.

We made it to the city center relatively quickly, as fast as Grace's nose would allow us to. I thought a little more about the gunman in the apartment across from us; we'd decided to check the signs after we returned (if we returned, I had to remind myself) and see if he'd left any response. The city center was deserted, shops boarded up, and streets quiet. I picked the fastest route to the store, and we began walking. Grace bounded happily in front of us.

"So, chickens?" Kiera said.

I sighed. "Yeah. Chickens. We're going to become chicken people. Who would have thought?"

"At least they can't really fly away. Worst-case scenario is they try and then fall off the top of the building." Kiera sighed.

It was sort of peaceful, the area outside of the city. There were big fluffy clouds, not obscured by buildings, with long tracts of grass. I even saw a horse dotting a field in the distance.

It made me wonder what would happen when the food ran out. Can a horse survive on just grass?

Or worse, the homeowner might eat the damn horse. I shuddered. "It's about two miles from here," I called to Kiera.

We walked down a mostly straight path, the paving leading off to gravel, which led to a dirt road. It took us nearly half an hour to traverse the path, even with Grace meandering across the road back and forth, trying to sniff out supper, I guessed.

"Here it is," I said. I pointed into the distance: a gray, nondescript building, low to the ground, with no cars parked in the lot and no signs of anyone alive.

It was just us.

I carefully tied Grace's leash to the open door, giving her plenty of room on her long lead to run around, go to the bathroom, catch birds, or whatever dogs did in the country. I had remembered to bring a crowbar in the wagon, just in case, and we pried the doors open cautiously, peering around in the darkness of the store. I had a somewhat dying flashlight and turned it on, and Kiera followed with the wagon as we carefully picked our way across a fallen shelving unit. "Hello?"

I heard nothing save some soft sounds of animals moving. At least, I hoped like hell that was what I'd heard. The windows provided some natural light, but I still would have trouble finding my own ass in the darkness. Kiera and I made our way into the store, and the first thing we saw: large bags of dog food.

"Oh, hell yes!" Kiera tried to stack some dog food in our wagon but almost fell over sideways.

"Let me get it," I laughed, pulling her up. I grabbed two huge bags, putting them securely in the wagon. Kiera started wandering the aisles, and I parked the wagon in the middle of the room with the flashlight shining onto the ceiling.

"I found some seeds!" I called over. As I looked through the aisle, I saw some little starter kits for growing plants: they each had a tray, a cover for condensation, and dirt. One was about as big as a loaf of bread, and I took two.

We walked around the store, calling out to each other and placing more things in the wagon, and it almost seemed like the good times. It felt normal, shopping with Kiera. Like we hadn't done horrible things to people in recent months, and it wasn't haunting us at all. Like the world hadn't ended, and we weren't actually scavenging and stealing.

Well, that did wonders for my conscience.

As I approached the back of the store, I smelled . . . something. I couldn't quite place it, but it was almost familiar, on the tip of my tongue. After peering around the counter, I finally walked over toward the corner of the store, where I saw it.

It was a body. Or what was left of a body.

Its face had run down its own bones like candle wax, pooling at the beginning of what used to be a neck. I could see scraps of overalls and a button-up shirt, as well as the ribs exposed beneath the fluttering fabric. His legs were relatively intact, but obviously, he wasn't able to outrun what had done this to him.

"Kiera," I said.

"Yeah?"

"Be careful. I think there might be a zombie around here somewhere," I replied, poking at the dead with my crowbar.

"Sure thing," she said, sounding a lot more at home than she had in months. Maybe that was it, the thing that would save us. Being out in the field, doing things together. Making new memories. It sounded like a good idea.

Right?

I hugged the wall and found a little pen full of half-grown chickens. I had absolutely no idea as to the gender of said chickens, so I grabbed five squawking birds, one at a time, and put them in the wagon. It was getting awfully packed. I noticed that they sold chicken wire—how ironic—and grabbed a roll, making a barrier around the edges of the wagon.

"I think we're done," I called. "There's no room in the wagon for anything else."

She came towards me with an armful of little things: de-wormer for Grace, tools for our new garden, and she was dragging a bag full of chicken feed. I pulled it over my shoulder and gestured to the wagon. "You pull the wagon, I'll carry the feed. It isn't far; I think we'll be okay."

"All right," she said, grabbing a plastic bag blowing in the wind from the open door and putting her finds inside it. "Let's go."

I had nearly forgotten about the zombie situation. It seemed so down-homey, so natural, as if the end of the world wasn't something to worry about but something to overcome. And we were a team, a true team; it didn't feel complete until we met Grace at the door.

It was us against the world.

It took a few tries to get the wagon to roll with all of its goodies. Kiera was panting with effort as she tried to pull it. "Let's switch," I said.

Then she dropped the wagon handle, staring behind me, her mouth open.

"What? What's wrong?"

She pointed behind me. "Sean, we have company." Her voice was high and thready.

I turned and grabbed the crowbar. It was apparently a multi-tool now. "We've got this," I reminded her. "Just keep Grace out of the way."

Grace was itching to move but Kiera put her arm around her neck as she hid behind the wagon, and I could see both of them watching me.

Turning around fully, I saw it. It *looked* like a person. Short hair, blue jeans, a button-up shirt. There were no broken bones, no vast amounts of blood, only a man standing in the field next to the store, staring at us.

The way it walked was definitely not person-like. As I waited, I hefted the crowbar in my hand like a baseball bat. He came closer, his movements jerky and uncoordinated—

My mouth was an inch deep in the chest cavity of someone who used to be a woman. I pushed apart her rib cage, using my zombie strength to get at her heart. It was the best part.

The best part . . .

I shook my head. I couldn't let the memories win; even though he acted like a zombie, he was something different, and I couldn't let my guard down.

"Should we just leave? We can walk faster than him," Kiera said.

"No," I said thoughtfully. "We can't risk leading him back to the apartment. No, I've got this." I carefully approached the zombie/not-zombie, who was hissing like a startled cat. He kept moving closer, one dogged step at a time, and I raised the crowbar. It would be just like baseball; I was sure of it.

I realized I'd never killed someone without being intimately introduced to their insides.

Could I really do this? On the other hand, could I afford not to do this? I had to protect Kiera and Grace, and he was coming faster and faster.

I circled around behind him, leaning down and throwing a rock the way he was going. He started to stumble towards the rock, and I raised the crowbar. With no further thought than keeping Kiera and Grace safe, I swung at that man's head like I was in Little League being scouted for the bigs.

He went down, his head falling to one side in a way no head should ever lie. Apparently, I'd broken his neck. I could see pink and gray flesh leaking out from behind his ears. Yep, definitely got him that time.

He was wearing a Star of David.

Oh, fuck, this was a real person. This was *a real person,* and I killed him. I killed him in cold blood, behind him, and even though he was an acid-spitting zombie, I—

My mind reeled. I couldn't think. Everything was bloody, including my shirt. I saw Kiera and Grace through tunnel vision; everything to the side of me was a static white-and-black, like the TV before we'd lost power but after the news had stopped. The crowbar dropped at my feet, and I only noticed because it hit my recently healed toe.

"Sean," Kiera said slowly. She put her hands on my shoulders. "What's wrong?"

"He was a person," I gasped. "He was Jewish. He probably had a family. Or he just liked the Star of David, who the fuck knows, but he was a *person,* Kiera, and I killed him!"

She pulled me down next to the sort-of-zombie's body, sitting on a large rock in the field. Grace was keeping watch, staring at the fallen form as if it would get back up again. It was somehow comforting to know someone would raise the alarm if something happened.

"This is why I don't sleep," she said quietly. "Because

after they were Cured, they could have lived. Everyone I ever killed could have lived, possibly, but they didn't get the chance because I ended things for them. It's not something I take lightly, Sean, and you shouldn't either—but I don't think you should beat yourself up about it either."

She gestured to the ground. Something was oozing out of his open mouth, and it didn't look like blood. It was a strange yellow, somewhere between urine and honey. It was thicker than any bodily fluid that I'd expected. As it trickled out, it hit the grass, and the grass sizzled, turning brown slowly.

"He was an acid-spitting possible zombie, Sean. We would've been sunk if you hadn't gone up behind him. I don't have any weapons on me, which was very fucking stupid of me, and will not happen again. He was clearly coming towards us. That's self-defense," she said.

I watched the grass dying. I thought about the worker inside, face melted into candle wax. I thought of the man Ms. Barbie had killed, left burning and dying on my front stoop.

This could have been Kiera, I realized. She could have had her skin running down her face in rivulets, liquefied by acid. It could've been Grace. I watched her chasing after a bird and grimaced. At least she'd get protein today.

"Okay," I said slowly. I tried to breathe. It's funny, isn't it, how you can forget how to do something so fucking simple that you do every day of your damn life? "Okay. So we don't have anyone following us now. Can we please go back home? I'll drag the wagon; let's tie Grace to the wagon handle, and you can carry the chicken feed."

Kiera nodded, laying a hand on my shoulder but saying nothing. I knew that she understood how I felt. I'd done many horrible things as a zombie, but Not-Zombie Sean was a hell of a lot more of a pacifist than Zombie Sean was.

She heaved the bag over her shoulder, unsteady on her feet for a moment, but she handled it. I realized she'd changed over the past months: fighting zombies had made her trimmer, for sure, but also more muscular. She definitely had some biceps that I hadn't noticed before. What were we becoming? I was all for women's health and all that, but why the fuck was all this happening that required us to become damned superheroes?

I pulled the wagon along behind me, slowly making my way back to civilization. At least we knew that the tractor supply store was relatively un-vandalized; it was in a backwater enough area that it hadn't been at the forefront of people's minds when the world went crazy. So we had that going for us, and could return whenever we wanted to.

Dirt turned to gravel turned to road. It ran like a black river toward the town center. We took a break on the broken-down fountain that still held water in it. Grace decided it was a good time to practice swimming.

"I don't know if I can do this," I said finally, not meeting Kiera's eyes.

She nodded. "I know. I couldn't do it either, but then I had to. And learning how to fight and prepare for the end of the world made me feel better. It made me stronger, and I knew how to take care of myself. We just have to do the same for you."

I looked at her out of the corner of my eye. "Do the same what for me?"

"We need to teach you how to fight. You were a zombie during the war, and you didn't really have combat experience. You just sort of ate people. So we get you a weapon—" I held up my crowbar as a question. "Maybe we can keep that for short-range, but we need to get you something that leaves you out of the range of the acid."

"You're going to teach me how to fight?" I said, a little skeptically.

"Don't look at me like that. Yes, I am going to teach you how to fight. We spent hours on the roof practicing and it kept me alive. We'll even practice with Grace, after I make a few modifications to her Doge suit."

We looked up at the windows of the apartment as we got there, but couldn't see our sign or the gunman's. It took more than a little effort to get everything up to the apartment, and I dreaded the thought of how much it would suck to carry it all onto the roof with those rickety-ass stairsteps.

I wasn't sexist. That wasn't the problem. It's just that the Kiera I knew had been . . . quiet. She liked books and studying. This Kiera was different: she was calm, much calmer than she had been earlier in the week. She was ready to fight, for sure. And I . . .

I wasn't.

~

As predicted, it took hours to get everything onto the roof. Grace was very interested in the chickens, so we used the wire to make a weird little enclosure from some spare pallets that people had used for sitting on. It wasn't ideal, but it was what we could do with what we had. Kiera was planting the seeds in their containers, and I wondered how long it would take for them to grow.

"So are we using the chickens for eggs, or meat?" I had to ask.

"Umm both, eventually? I think both. Meat for Grace, eggs for us. I think we've got one boy and four girls, so that should set us up fairly well."

I leaned over the front of the building, trying to see if the gunman had updated his sign. Surprisingly, there was a bigger mass of papers covering his window, and I saw his gun leaning up against the sill.

Just me—no one else. Join together?

It was a simple message, but it expanded our world exponentially. As I told Kiera about the sign, we went back to our apartment, where Grace was panting happily on my couch. Kiera opened one of the huge bags of dog food and shoveled a cup or two for Grace into her makeshift bowl, which had definitely been Tupperware in a previous lifetime.

"Do you think we should? I mean, he has a gun. What if he's crazy?" Kiera asked.

I shrugged, but felt a little cautious myself. "I think we just have to be careful. We've dealt with people that have had guns before, and came out okay."

"Okay," she said. She lay back down on her chair, upside-down, with her feet over the headrest. "I think we should. If the pantry's running out of food, we're going to have to go out more and more, and there's safety in numbers."

Watching Grace eat the dog food—pretty happily, I must admit—I considered the situation. There was a lone gunman across the street, and he wanted to join our little party of three. I was hesitant to open our ranks to anyone else: being in a group had gotten me to where I'd been as a zombie, ripping into people and killing indiscriminately.

But it had gotten Kiera safely to the college, to the Cure, and to me.

Groaning, I laid my stump across my eyes, blocking out the evening light. "I think if he comes bearing food and water, he's welcome. But I'm not particularly fucking happy that he has a giant rifle."

Kiera nodded, and I could feel her eyes on me. I remembered the night we'd amputated my arm, remembered the screaming, remembered how it felt to realize that the screaming was coming from me. I remembered the hope that it wasn't too late, and the crushing defeat when the Infection started to spread.

"I'll make a new sign," she said, pulling out the paper and the Sharpies. She shook the pens hard, trying to get the ink to spread, even though I'd never figured out if that actually worked for people or if it was just a habit, something comforting.

I looked at my watch—it hadn't needed a new battery yet, hadn't stopped yet—and frowned. I turned the radio on, listening carefully, and all I heard was static.

"Kiera," I said.

"Yeah?" She didn't look up from her paper.

"Isn't the broadcast supposed to be, like, now?" I scanned through a few channels, only to return to the one we'd been told to use. There was nothing. No one.

She stared at the radio. "Yes," she said slowly. "It's definitely supposed to be now."

I exhaled slowly. "What does this mean?"

"Maybe they're late. Or maybe their radios died. We don't know what kind of setup they have, though being government, they sure as hell should have better stuff than we did. Or . . . I don't know."

The "don't know" was the part that was getting to me. We *didn't* know. Didn't know if things were still okay, if the government was still out there. After a while, she said, "You're getting ahead of yourself. It's one late broadcast, it can't be that bad."

I nodded, but kept my eyes on the radio. I had put in the new batteries when we'd gotten home, so it should have been relatively set and ready to go. If there was a broadcast and we'd missed it, it wouldn't be our technology messing it up.

We listened to static for an hour. Every so often there was a hiccup of sound, and we rushed to pay attention, but it was always nothing. Cut-off words and noise. We waited for the entire time of the broadcast, but it wasn't coming on.

Kiera and I looked at each other as she turned the radio off. "Well, they weren't late," she said finally.

"Nope," I said finally. My mind was racing; those noises had sounded like words, a little bit. What if there was trouble? What if something was going on, and we didn't have a fucking clue here in our apartment?

She grabbed her sign and walked off toward the apartment at the front of the building. I wondered, not for the first or the last time, if we were in this together—and where that together would lead us. The world would never be the same, and we were just pawns in it.

Friendly Fire

~ Kiera ~

My sign said: *Two of us plus dog. How to meet?*

I sat down on the couch of the front apartment and sighed. There was something to Sean's words that bothered me. I couldn't figure out what it was, but I had an uneasy feeling that he was right, and the missing broadcast was something we needed to pay attention to. We had enough food stores to last for at least a month or two—well, less, if we took in Mystery Gunman, but we were relatively safe. So, what was it that haunted me?

Looking around the apartment, I had to wonder who had lived there. We hadn't gone to any of the neighborhood or apartment complex block parties or meetings, so we really didn't have many friends at the beginning of the war, much less now. I stood up and looked at the mantle, where there were pictures. A man and a woman, in an old-time photo, in their wedding accouterments. A child in various stages of growing up, until he graduated from college. New babies, two of them, and then the pictures stopped.

They would never see their grandparents again.

I would never see my mom again.

It hit me like a brick. This really was the end times, and I had been living through it, but I always imagined that somewhere, it would end up back to normal again. I always thought that cell phones, the Internet, and power would come back relatively quickly. That this zombie situation wasn't that big or bad.

Fuck.

It was that bad. If the government was missing broadcasts, that meant something; Sean was right. I didn't want to admit it, but something was going on, and it might mean our survival to find out. I left the apartment behind me, leaving the door open for the ghosts that haunted their former lives.

Walking back into our apartment and locking our door, I sighed. "So what do we do?" I said to Sean, who was sitting on the couch.

He stared at me for a long moment. "Did you walk in here mid-conversation or something?"

I shook my head. "No. But I think you're right, that something is going on. I think we keep listening for broadcasts, we start training you, and if we don't hear from anyone by next week when we're supposed to go to the food pantry, we . . ."

"We what?" Sean tilted his head curiously. Grace did much the same thing.

"I don't fucking know. We get together with the lone gunman and try to figure this shit out?" I leaned back against the door, groaning. "If we don't have the food pantry, we have two months, tops. Grace has more than that, but having kibble doesn't do her much good if we're both dead from starvation."

He hesitated. "Have you thought any more about . . ."

"About what?" I snapped.

"About what to do if you . . . you know. Turn." His eyes held mine, no matter how much I wanted to look away.

I slid to the floor, still leaning against the door, and Grace came over to sit with me. "I don't know," I said quietly. "We have to accept that it's becoming a possibility, I guess. Teaching you how to fight will keep you safe, even if you have to stay safe from me. I'll teach you how to work with Grace, she's really good in a pinch with her Doge suit. And if I turn . . ."

"If you turn?" he asked.

"Then leave me behind." There. I said it. I said the thing, the big elephant in the room, the unknowable future. "Leave me behind, go with the gun guy, and find somewhere that still has food and shelter. Use what we have in the apartment and lock me in the bedroom or something, I guess."

"What if they come up with a Cure for this new Infection?" Sean asked. "What do I do then?"

I shrugged. "I'll be locked in the bedroom and not a threat to anyone. You can figure out how to get me to it, or get the Cure from whoever distributes it." I paused. "Or . . . you know, not."

"Not? What do you mean, not?" He rose from the couch--still clenching his newly-healed toes tight against his feet.

"I mean . . . if it's too much, walk away."

"Kiera, you didn't fucking walk away. You had reasons to do what you did, and you found me in the end. I'd like to think you would have found me even if we hadn't run into each other at the last big battle. You didn't abandon me, and I'm not going to abandon you." His voice was firm, and there was no use arguing with him.

"I guess," I said quietly, playing with Grace's flag of a tail. "But it feels like I abandoned you in that stairwell."

"Well, you found me. We're together. And as much as I have my own doubts and my own terrible memories, we have to look to the future and make of it what we can. This isn't the end of the world if we can make a living somewhere." He shrugged. "Maybe we can find a farm out by the feedstore, one that still has livestock or sheep, and we could teach Grace to herd or something. She'd love that."

I managed a half-smile. "She would," I said, looking down at her. I closed my eyes. "Do you still think you don't deserve to be here?"

He paused. "Sometimes," he said haltingly. "I . . . did so many horrible things, Kiera. And I *wanted* to do the horrible things. They made sense to me, and it was comforting to kill and Infect. I can't get rid of the memories, no matter how hard I try, no matter how I scrub myself clean."

It took me a long time to find the words. "Thank you," I said simply. "For not giving up on me, either because you were a zombie or because I could become one." It wasn't a great speech, but it was how I felt.

"No problem." He shifted in front of me, gesturing with his stump. "So where are we at now? We have chickens. We have a wagon. We can bring the chickens in the wagon, theoretically, and throw them to zombies if we have to and use them for eggs if we don't."

"So you're suggesting a road trip?" I stood up slowly, and that thing that happens where you change position and your head swims happened. I held on to Grace, struggling to stay balanced, and sighed. "I think I need something to eat."

"Yeah, a road trip. We find out more about the gunman situation, we pack up our food and our chickens, and we take Grace and just fucking *go*. We don't have to stay here, Kiera. I know it's safe, but there's more out there than this apartment."

He led me over to the pantry, and I selected a cup of noodles. They didn't take much of our diminishing store of water and could be heated (somewhat) on the gas stove. Grace followed along behind us, always game for eating anything dropped on the floor.

"So we look for a farm and settle down like *Little House on the Prairie?* Like a homestead or some shit?" I asked, sitting down at the table while Sean prepared the noodles.

"I guess." He shrugged. "If we can find somebody that has cows or something, we could use them and the chickens to keep us fed. I know we have a boy chicken, so there's gonna be baby chickens, and baby chickens grow up into chicken nuggets."

I snorted. "That's horrible."

He came back with the noodles and a fork. "Yeah, but it's true. And maybe the gun guy knows some things that we don't. He has some type of fucking assault rifle and shoots zombies; he's gotta be at least a little knowledgeable about what's going on."

I ate silently, watching Sean meander past the pantry shelves. He was making a list of some kind, and I wondered where he'd learned to inventory. I figured at the outdoorsy store he used to work at. I frowned. "Wouldn't your outdoorsy store have some supplies for us if we're going rogue and finding our way in the country?"

"Possibly," he said. "It would require another field trip, and I don't know if other people had had the same idea, so who knows what's actually left at the store."

"Maybe Lone Gunman can come with us. He definitely seemed interested in getting together," I replied.

"I hate this sign-talking bullshit," he said, sitting down next to me. "Life was so much easier when we could just text people."

I snorted again. "You're not wrong," I said. "So I guess we'll wait for the broadcast tomorrow morning, and see what the gun guy says, and make a decision from there."

He nodded, reaching out to get a stray bit of noodle off my face. "Agreed," he said simply.

As if we were in this together, for real.

~

We spent the rest of the evening on the roof with my hatchet-mop and Sean's crow bar and cleaver-rod. After rummaging around in the leftovers from when Brett and I had armed our motley crew, I had given Sean a second weapon: not a hatchet-mop, but a big-ass meat cleaver on an old curtain rod. We worked on the patterns that Brett and I had taught to the crew so long ago. Was it really only several months since the end of the war? It felt like a lifetime.

Sean was better with the crowbar than he was with the cleaver-rod, so we focused on the latter. Grace was going through her obstacle course as we weaved between the makeshift chicken coop and the limited free space on the roof. We practiced footwork, getting out of the way of the zombies if they came at us. Sean swung the crowbar, and I heard a solid *thunk* as it hit the wooden targets Brett had put up for us.

"You're not bad at this," I mentioned, helping him pull the weapon out of the wood. "Do you have some hidden talents I don't know about?"

He snorted. "I took tae kwon do for, like, eight years as a kid. We didn't do weapon work, but I can still remember how to move."

"You learn something new every day." I watched him hack at the wooden stand, admiring his form. He looked good with a weapon in his hand, even if he had to balance it with his stump. The chickens were rustling around in their pen, making noises that obviously meant something to them, but not to me.

It was almost dark by the time we stopped training. Sean and I were both drenched in sweat, and we used one of the rain barrels we'd left on the roof to take an impromptu sponge bath, though we'd have to get back to the apartment to change out of our stinky clothes.

"You're really good with weapons," I mentioned as we locked the door behind us.

He shrugged, leaning his cleaver-rod against the wall next to the door. "Every little boy plays with lightsabers, I guess."

We went to the bedroom to change our clothes, and I was awfully glad that the pantry had given us little samples of deodorant; we definitely needed it. I watched as Sean dressed and wondered if anything would ever be the same again. When I saw Sean naked, my thoughts went immediately to the scars and bones not healed in perfect position; I saw the marks left by the zombie war. I wondered what he saw when he looked at me. Did he see my scars, too?

Would we ever see each other as true partners again?

I had to leave the room abruptly so Sean didn't see me cry.

I listened to him getting dressed and stuck my fist in my mouth to muffle my sobs. Everything was so different now. We didn't have the same relationship that we did before the war. What the hell were we supposed to do? How could we get back to where we were when everything was different?

Using a Handy-Wipe to clean the tears off my face, I sighed, flopping down on my usual chair. I was exhausted, still a little stinky, and my hair was wet. Nothing made sense anymore. As Sean came back into the room for bed, I turned away, feigning sleep. I didn't know what to say.

I didn't know if I'd ever really know what to say, ever again.

~

The next time that we went to the food pantry was the day we'd meet the lone gunman. We'd arranged that he'd watch for us to return, then meet us in our apartment lobby. I hated leaving Grace behind for these food drop-offs; it made me wonder if she thought we were going away forever, like the people I adopted her from. Border collies are supposed to be super smart, like an average three-year-old, and a three-year-old knows when their mom leaves.

It was a quiet walk to the food pantry that morning. No one was out and the sun was shining brightly, even though the weather was a little chilly. Fall was coming, and soon. I didn't have anything to say to Sean. What a surprise.

We walked along in silence, my hand and his hanging at our sides, sort of touching, but not really. It was a cop-out and I knew it. "So you really think we'll find a farm or something?" I said finally.

He glanced toward me as we walked. "Yeah, I do," he said. "There are tons of farms around the city. There's got to be one that still has animals. The Cure wasn't *that* long ago."

"And how exactly are we going to learn to run a farm?" I wasn't sure this was the greatest idea we'd ever had.

"If we stop at the outdoors store or the tractor supply again, they have magazines and books about homesteading. I think that's kind of like farming? Like, new-age hippie farming. Naming your cows and all that." He fell silent as we walked into the clearing where the food pantry usually was.

The table was still there, and an empty army truck. There was no food. No one there. The only hint that anyone had been there at all was a thick, oozing yellow substance on the ground. Sean walked up to the truck, looking around inside. "It looks like whoever left, did in a hurry," he said.

"How come?" I replied.

"Because there's still, like, bodyguard armor stuff, and bullets, and guns." He paused. "If I had any idea how to use a gun, I'd take one for us, but I don't."

I shook my head. "I don't like guns. I'm already having to deal with one lone gunman, I don't need two." I sighed, rubbing my face with my hands. "So there's no food pantry. That just cements the fact that we need to get the fuck out of here."

He turned back to me and shrugged. "I guess so." It took him a minute, but he held out his hand for mine.

I took it, and we walked back to the apartment, slow and steady. We didn't see anyone—or anything—on the way home, so we sat on the stoop to the apartment building after we got there, waiting for the lone gunman to appear.

We sat for about an hour, chatting about farms and plans, and I felt better about us than I had in some time. Maybe we *could* still connect. Maybe there was hope. "So—"

I didn't have a chance to finish my thought. The door of the apartments across the street opened, and

I saw a man with brown hair, body armor, and a rather impressive-looking rifle at the entrance/exit. He nodded once and walked over to us, his eyes sweeping the streets.

"I take it you're the note leavers?" he said curtly.

"Yes. I'm Sean, and this is Kiera," Sean replied.

"My name is Owen. How long have you been here?" His eyes never stopped moving.

"Since the end of the war. We lived here before that, we just came home together after Sean got Cured."

His gaze sharpened. "He got Cured? You were a zombie?"

Sean hesitated. "Yeah," he said simply. "I was. And now I'm not."

"Good," he said. "That's at least one of us who we don't have to worry about. Do you have a plan, or . . ."

Sean stood up from the stoop, shielding his eyes from the sun with his hand. "We planned on hitting the outdoors supply store where I worked and then going out to find a farm or something. We've got some chickens and a dog upstairs, and we were going to bring them with us."

Owen thought about it for a minute or two. "That's not a bad plan," he said at last. "Do you mind if I join you? My wife . . . she turned." He shrugged. "She was exposed to the Cure the same as I was, but she . . . just turned."

So the lone gunman—Owen—had been just like us, a little family against the zombie apocalypse. But he'd lived through the worst of both Infections. I wondered if he would be able to take care of Sean if I turned.

It was never far from my mind.

I stood up. "Okay. So let's all pack our shit—we have a

wagon, we'll load it up with the chickens and other stuff we might need—and we'll bring our dog down, say, after the evening broadcast?" *If there is an evening broadcast.*

"Sure. I have a portable radio and I'll scrounge something up to use as a transport for some canned food and MREs. I've got a lot of ammo that can come with us too," Owen said.

"Sounds good," Sean said, reaching out to shake the man's hand.

Owen hesitated, and Sean closed his fist. They touched fists in a weird show of masculinity, and I wondered if it was human contact or germs that bothered him. "We'll meet here."

We watched Owen going back to his apartment, walking carefully across the street as if a rogue zombie would jump out at any time. *He was definitely a little nervy, maybe a little traumatized,* I thought. I wondered how great of an idea this was.

Sean, holding my hand once more, led me up the apartment and to Grace. We had a lot to do, and not a lot of time to do it in. It would be a bitch to bring the chickens down from the apartment.

The Yellow Brick Road

~ Sean ~

We spent the rest of the day packing and repacking. We didn't have a huge wagon, but it was a good enough size that we could fit a few chickens on top and shove some food and supplies beneath. It was a weird little wagon, with two tiers, and I was damn glad we had it.

Grace was extraordinarily interested in the chickens. I used a little bit of chicken wire around the sides of the wagon to block them off. I didn't know if she wanted to eat them or herd them, but I wasn't going to find out until we were safe.

Kiera and I sat next to the radio, with Grace between us, the chickens cackling softly behind us. I thought longingly of elevators, and wondered how Kiera and I would manage bringing all of this plus the dog down to the street level. We turned the radio on and waited.

It wasn't precisely on time, but we did hear something

other than static this time: *If you hear . . . then we . . . fallen. There is . . . longer any . . . food pantries or National . . . Do not leave . . . Stay where you are . . . The army is . . . and deploying . . . safety. Do not . . . be alarmed.*

It was hard to follow, having to make sense of the blank space between the words. It sounded as if whoever was speaking was hushed in a room somewhere, with bad reception. I wondered if they were hiding out from acid-spitting zombies, or if something worse had happened to the government. They'd said something about the National Guard, I thought; whoever decided that we should not be alarmed deserved to get fired.

"So there we are," I exhaled as the radio went back to static. "Somebody, somewhere fucked up, and we're on our own."

Kiera pet Grace absentmindedly. "They said something about 'army' and 'deploying,'" she said after a while. "So I think that someone is still out there, but I doubt they're going to be coming somewhere like here. We got lucky with the Cure, but I don't think we can count on being that lucky again. We were only saved the first time because of Callie's interference, and I don't know where the fuck she is now."

I stretched slowly, looking at our overburdened wagon. "Well, we've taken what we could take, we've made a plan, and Owen has his own radio, presumably with batteries. Speaking of Owen, what did you think, by the way?"

She frowned. "He's definitely not friendly," she hedged

carefully. "But it feels like he knows what he's doing. Ex-military, ex-cop, maybe?" I could see the wheels turning in her head. "But he said his wife turned, so . . . does that mean he shot her?"

"Yeah," I replied heavily. "I think he did. And he's had to deal with that every day since the beginning of this second round of bullshit. So I think we can cut him some slack for being a little weird."

Kiera nodded. "Yeah," she said eventually. We watched the radio in silence, listening to the static until the sun began to set, and then we put on our newish travel backpacks—I'd had them in the closet from the outdoorsy store in case we ever, you know, went anywhere—and Kiera gave a signal to Grace.

She was smart enough to know that this meant to walk herself, and to follow us. I didn't know how Kiera had trained a dog during the zombie apocalypse; then again, what else was she going to do with her time?

We rolled out of the apartment, pausing at the threshold. "So this is goodbye," I said.

She leaned her head against my shoulder. "It is," she said quietly. "I loved living here with you."

I nodded, leaning down to brush a kiss against her forehead. "I did too. But now we get to love living together in a real house, one Grace will love, with our chickens and miscellaneous farm animals in the middle of nowhere, and we can adopt every single stray cat we see."

"Promise?"

I smiled. "I promise," I said.

We rolled down the hallway to the stairs, and it was

a circus trying to get the damn wagon down. We would slide a few steps, skid to a halt when it was too much, and then go again. I was at the bottom, walking backwards, and Kiera was at the top, steering. We each had our makeshift weapons strapped to our backs.

"We packed a lot of shit," she gasped as we paused. "Canned goods are no joke."

"The MREs are lighter, but I'm sure they don't help, either," I panted back. We were finally making progress, Grace walking herself behind Kiera, and when I looked at my watch, I estimated that it'd taken us over an hour to get the wagon down the stairs.

Owen was standing on our stoop waiting for us. He came over to help with the wagon, for the last few feet to the street. "I wish we'd thought to call you earlier," I said.

"Call me how, with magic?" He snorted. "I would've helped, though."

We took a breather, with Grace dancing beside Kiera in her Doge suit. Kiera had added some extra protection; an old raincoat covered most of Grace's face and neck, with two eyeholes and a nosehole cut out. She was wearing makeshift goggles from the swimming gear I'd had in our bathroom for years for no real reason, seeing as how we never went swimming.

I looked at Owen after I caught my breath, and realized that he had a wagon as well. Wait; no, that wasn't a wagon, it was . . . a baby carriage. Two tiers, like our wagon, but definitely for a baby. My eyes met Owen's and he said nothing, did nothing, but I knew he didn't want me to ask. He had food, ammo, first aid supplies and more, but I couldn't shake the idea; what had happened to the baby that this carriage belonged to?

It was like mystery piled on top of mystery, and it frustrated the fuck out of me.

"Let's head to the store," I said abruptly. "It's about five miles outside city center, and once we're done there, we can keep going on the same road to look for some farms."

Owen nodded. "Ten-four," he said. "Anything specific you're looking for at the store?"

"Homesteading stuff?" I gestured around. "I don't know. Instruction manuals on how to be a farmer? Tools?"

"We could definitely use some tools. Maybe a shovel, a pick. I see you have some seeds, that'll be good. And the chickens will be a big help, too." Owen peered through our goodies, and then to our weapons. His expression changed from serious to surprised.

"You, uh . . . you have some weapons, there," he said finally.

"They don't look like much, but they work," I said, my tone a little short. "Kiera's hatchet-mop got her through the zombie war just fine, and my cleaver-rod and crowbar work pretty good for getting zombies the fuck away from us."

His gaze slid to Grace. "And . . . what exactly is that?"

"That is Grace, she is in a Doge suit, and she knows how to attack zombies," Kiera said firmly. "I've made some modifications for the acid-spitting situation, and I'll keep her back until we know if it's only the saliva that is acidic or if it's *all* body fluids. But she can hold her own in a fight, and we're not leaving her behind." Her voice was confident. It surprised me; she'd gone from crying, to speculative, to sobbing, to determined in a very short amount of time.

Maybe she was dealing with this a hell of a lot more healthily than I was: all I had was anger. Anger that the world was doing this to us *again*. Angry that Kiera was at risk. Angry that we had to leave our world and our apartment to make a new life somewhere else. Just fucking angry.

"Let's go" was all I said.

We started walking, heading north towards the city center, and I looked at all the damage from the previous war. There was blood coating several doorways, bones scattered in the street. Not much, but enough evidence that something had happened, and it had been big. I wondered if I'd contributed to any of the blood or the bones.

. . . I tore at a tendon, relishing the snap when it finally broke free. My face burrowed in his chest, I grabbed his aorta between my teeth and bit down hard; a splatter of blood accompanied a moaning grunt, and then silence. The blood slid down my throat easily, tasting like metal, and it was a taste I would do anything for . . .

I shook my head. That was then. This was now. This was something to work towards, a future for Kiera and I. What I did before didn't matter.

~

We made it to the city center and kept going south. The streets were peaceful, quiet. I wondered how many of these houses had people in them, what the community was like after the war. I had no idea how affected places had been by the Infection; was there even a community left? Had they all received the Cure, or had they remained zombies out in the wilderness? Were they human now, and at risk like Kiera was?

I really didn't want to finish that thought.

It took us about two hours to get to the store trailing our zoo behind us. I gave Owen my crowbar—it seemed like this required two hands—and he pried the wood off of the doors. We pushed the doors out of the way, and Owen held up the flashlight that he'd stored in his baby carriage.

I really, really wanted to ask about the baby carriage.

"The books are near the registers," I said. "Camping is in the back-left corner. I think Kiera and I should look for books, and Owen, do you mind seeing if there's anything that would be helpful back there?"

He grunted. "Ten-four," he said. It seemed to be his catchphrase. He wandered off toward the back of the store, and Grace sat quietly in the vestibule with the chickens. For some reason, she didn't want to pass those doors.

We meandered around the checkout. Kiera found several magazines about homesteading, and I had a few books pulled out of the stand, flipping through them slowly, trying to see what would be helpful.

Kiera tucked the magazines into her backpack. I stored a few books in my own backpack and wandered over to the impulse buy sections. There were a few solar-powered flashlights, and I took one for each of us. Keychain fire starters, threw some of those in the backpack. Seeds for fruit trees, check.

And strangely, there was . . . a woman's peeing device? I stared at it for a long moment. It was a female urinal, with a tube that you could aim at the ground or out of the way. I had absolutely no idea how it worked, but it looked helpful, so I grabbed one for Kiera. I shook my head; such weird shit we've cooked up in this world.

I wandered back toward the front of the store and sat with Grace. Kiera came back a few minutes later, and I offered her the San-e-fresh Toileting Device. She stared at me like I was insane, and laughed.

It was good to hear her laugh.

I heard some glass breaking, and what sounded, again, like a car backfiring. Once, twice. I stiffened, staring at the depths of the store, and Kiera looked startled next to me.

Owen came back, his backpack fuller than when he'd left. I had gotten a better look of it on our way to the store; he was definitely ex-military. "I found some camping gear and more ammo. I had to break the glass at the ammo counter, but I got quite a lot from it. Are you two ready?"

As ready as we'd ever be, I supposed.

"What was the gunshot?" I asked quietly.

"There was still someone in the store," he said simply. "I didn't particularly feel like melting today."

That might have been a coworker of mine. Or a coworker's family. I sighed, closing my eyes briefly for the dead. What the hell was this world coming to?

We began our long trek southeast. The chickens were not particularly happy to be quarantined to a wagon-with-chicken-wire, but they rode along as well as could be expected. Grace was dancing in her Doge suit, the spikes glittering in the sunlight. My cleaver-rod was strapped to my back, and my crowbar was looped through the left strap of my backpack.

There was very little to look at as we walked down the road. The highway was in surprisingly good repair; there weren't too many potholes, and the zombie apocalypse had happened gradually enough that there weren't a ton of stalled cars, either. I adjusted my backpack, bowed beneath the weight, and exhaled sharply.

"You okay?" Kiera was walking beside me. Her face was a little red, and I could tell it was a workout for her too.

"As good as can be expected, pulling a wagon and having a huge backpack on me," I muttered. "I don't mind, but I wish I'd have eaten my Wheaties."

She snorted and we walked on. A gas station rose in the distance, and we made for it. My watch said we'd walked for three hours by the time we got there, and Owen peered in the glass doors, searching.

"I don't see any zombies," he said finally. I offered him my crowbar and he broke the windowed door and climbed through. "I'm going to see if they have any water; it's a long walk and we need some hydration."

"We'll be here," I said. I was so fucking glad that Grace could walk herself; she sat next to Kiera, wagging her tail (which was now covered in raincoat) and just generally being a really great dog. We'd gotten so damn lucky with her.

Grace stirred slightly, her wag slowing down. Her expression changed from one of patient love to something else. I watched her carefully, and saw her body tense, could hear the low, thin growl that escaped her lips. "Uh . . . Kiera?"

She had been messing with the chickens and the wagon, but she stopped as soon as she saw Grace next to her, and listened to her growl. "Something's wrong," she said.

That was all the warning we had. A zombie—the new kind, of course—staggered out from behind the building, where the bathroom was. I unclipped my cleaver-rod, and Kiera got out her hatchet-mop. Grace steadied herself in front of us, bowing down instinctually, ready to strike.

"Here we go," I said through my teeth, and I got out of range of Kiera, swinging my cleaver-rod in the zombie's general direction. That did nothing except for piss the zombie off, and she was spitting, I could see the acid trickling down her chin. If she had more force than that, we'd be sunk; as the acid touched the gray hoodie she wore, the material started to melt away.

"Fuck," Kiera said. I thoroughly agreed. We stood on opposite sides of the zombie and tried to brace ourselves as far away as we could. The zombie's mouth pursed, as if ready to spit, and I swung with all my might.

My cleaver-rod stuck straight in her ribcage. Kiera came up from behind, using her hatchet-mop to go for the throat, but the zombie staggered from the weight of my weapon, and she missed. Swearing again, she held her hatchet-mop securely, waiting for the next opportunity to strike.

I swung again, this time at the zombie's body. An arm

clattered to the ground, oozing thick, black blood. So it was related to the zombie war and the Infection; that was the same blood I remembered having when I was a zombie. Fuck.

Her blood was spurting out of the wound and I wondered what else had changed about the damned zombies. Kiera aimed her hatchet-mop and swung, catching the zombie in the back of the neck.

Grace bared her teeth and circled behind Kiera, ready to charge at the word of her mistress. Kiera shoved with all of her might, forcing the hatchet through the zombie's neck, and as the zombie tried to turn, she put her weight into it and it snapped the neck, the zombie falling to the ground.

Acid seeped into the ground from the zombie's open mouth, the grass sizzling and dying. I knew the zombie hadn't gotten close to either of us, but I couldn't help but check over Kiera with my eyes; if something happened to her . . .

I didn't want to think about it. "So that was fun," I said lightly.

She raised a brow. "Tell me how you really feel."

Sighing, I pushed the body further away with my foot. "It sucks. It all fucking sucks. We don't know what these new zombies are capable of, we don't know if there's a Cure around the corner for them, and we just have to . . . deal with it as we go."

"I know," she replied. "That's what I had to do, too. You get used to it," she said, but I could see the haunted look in her eyes.

Owen stepped back out from the door and eyed the zombie on the ground. "You guys had fun without me," he commented. "Where did she come from?"

I gestured toward the building. "Back toward the bathrooms. Find anything good?"

He grunted, hefting his backpack and going over to his baby carriage. "Some water, and travel packs of ibuprofen. I figured we might need some before this was all over."

All I could say was a-fuckin'-men.

To the Homestead

~ Kiera ~

It was nice, in a way. A sort of vacation/road trip, but walking and dragging heavy stuff behind us. My backpack was digging into my shoulders, and I was glad Grace was walking herself, rather than giving me one more thing to hold on to.

The chickens, still small, were squawking in the wagon, and Owen and Sean were deep in conversation about . . . God only knows. I didn't feel left out, though; I was enjoying seeing the country right outside of my city. There were flowers next to the road, little purple ones, and I thought about how something so beautiful could grow in the middle of nowhere.

It took us another hour to get to farm country. We picked the farm by rock-paper-scissors, figuring if it was occupied, we'd just try again with one of the others. It was a stately house, white with a big wraparound porch, and a big, red barn in the back. I could hear horses somewhere, and scattered across about an acre around the building were a handful of cows.

Sean stopped at the threshold of the fence. "Should we, like . . . knock?"

Owen snorted. "I don't think they'll assume we're zombies if we knock."

Rolling his eyes, Sean walked up to the porch and up the two stairs that led to the house. He knocked hard, bang-bang-bang, and I swore it echoed. We all stood there waiting, chickens rambling and dog stretching, to see if someone would come out.

After a second knock and a good five-minute wait, we left our wagons at the front and tried to open the door. It was locked, but Sean's crowbar made quick work of that. "Hello?" I called.

I sneezed. There was definitely dust in the air. Grace was hugging my side as I walked, as if she were nervous about this new place. Sean and Owen began to explore, and I walked into the living room, with the now-defunct TV, and the family album sitting on the mantle.

I put Grace in a sit-stay and pulled down the book to look at the pictures. There were two farmers and three children. I wasn't sure if the farmers were brothers or husbands, but they looked like a happy family. I wondered where they'd gone during the first war. Were they Cured, like Sean? Or at risk, like me?

"Clear," Owen shouted from somewhere upstairs. He sneezed, too.

"So obviously we've got some work to do," I said as he

came back downstairs. "Let's get the chickens situated, unpack our shit, and get to it."

There was a rabbit hutch next to the house, big enough that it would do for the chickens, especially at their size now. We carefully pushed them into the "yard" of the hutch, and I put some of the bird food I'd brought in the wagon in the grass. There was a barrel collecting rainwater just to the left of the hutch, and I found a bowl in the "yard." I filled it for the chickens and walked back into the house with Grace to find Sean and Owen.

Sean offered me a can of Pledge and some rags. "You dust, we sweep," he said.

"This is not how I pictured my second zombie apocalypse going," I replied, taking the can. I tied one of the rags around my face to protect me from the dust and went to work, Grace lying on a dusty couch that needed beating.

Sean wasn't particularly *good* at sweeping with one hand, but he managed to at least make piles for Owen to scoop up. There was dog hair everywhere, and I wondered what had happened to the dog that lived here. Was it still around somewhere? Did it get eaten in the first war? There were so many questions about this house that I knew I'd never get answers to.

We spent the rest of the sunlight we had cleaning the house, and by the time of the broadcast, we were exhausted. I sat on the dusty couch with Grace and Sean, Owen on the chair across from us. He pulled out his portable radio and set it on the newly Pledged coffee table. There was nothing but static.

We waited.

And we waited.

There were no voices tonight. No words, however strung-together. No person on the other end to tell us what to do or where to go. It cemented the idea that we'd done something good by coming out here, finding a homestead of our own. We waited the full hour of the broadcast that wasn't, and finally Owen clicked it off with a sigh.

"We're on our own, aren't we?" I said.

Owen nodded. "Let's unpack our backpacks and call it a night. We can unload the wagons tomorrow." I noticed that he called his baby carriage a wagon. I did not think that that was a mistake; it seemed very intentional.

I started up the creaky stairs with Grace and Sean trailing along behind me, slightly off-balance with how heavy my backpack was. I hadn't chosen the master bedroom for Sean and I; there was one farther down the hallway, with a queen-sized bed, and we decided to make camp there. It had posters on the walls of various boys and men that I couldn't name; obviously I wasn't a cool kid anymore. There was a wide dresser with a single jewelry box on top, and I opened it. There was nothing inside except a small agate rock, and the jewelry box sang its sad, slow song until I closed the lid gently.

Sean and I looked at the bed. It would be the first time we'd slept in the same bed together since the war. I'd done that deliberately; I needed the reassurance that we were still in this together. I could only hope that it was okay with Sean.

"Let's unpack," he said suddenly, so we did. I put all

my toiletries in the bathroom across the hall, seeing Owen taking the master bedroom as I walked between the two rooms. More power to him, I didn't want to think of taking the farmers' bed—I assumed at this point that they were a couple, with children—but Owen clearly had no reservations.

"Sleep wherever you can," he said to me in passing. I could only nod.

Grace hopped up onto the bed. It had a handmade quilt covering it, and I pulled it back. We would have to investigate water for baths tomorrow, but for now, we had to deal with each other as we were. I slid into the bed silently, watching Sean across the hall brushing his teeth with a little bottle of water that Owen had found.

He came back into the room and hesitated. It was only for a minute, but I saw it. I wondered what he'd been thinking, what was going on for him at that moment. I knew I had some level of anxiety, but I couldn't read him, even after all this time.

Sean slipped into bed next to me, fluffing the pillow behind him several times. We'd already beaten the dust out of them earlier. "So," he said.

"So," I said.

He turned to face me. "Are you okay?"

I turned as well. "As okay as I can be, I guess," I said slowly. "I wasn't particularly fond of killing that lady, even if she was an acid-spitting zombie."

Sean nodded, and tentatively reached out a hand to touch my shoulder. "It was her or us," he said softly.

I watched him, and thought I could recognize

something familiar in his expression. I raised my hand to touch his cheek, wondering what this meant, until—

There was an explosion.

There was no other way to describe it. It was louder than gunfire, louder than anything I'd heard before. It almost reminded me of fireworks, but that couldn't be it. Who the hell would be shooting fireworks in the middle of nowhere?

Sean hopped out of bed and looked out the window. The bedroom we were in faced the back and side of the house, so he couldn't see much. We both got up, and Owen was waiting for us as we entered the master.

"What the fuck is going on?" Sean said.

Owen lifted the blinds. "There's some kind of . . . party? Gathering? Something?" he said after a second.

I looked out the window next to him, and saw not just one person, and not just two people, but several people dancing around a trash can fire across the way. As I stood there another firework went off, with brilliant red flashes across the sky, and I heard howling. It didn't sound like wolves; it sounded like . . . well, people.

Sean was next to me, and we all watched as a naked man approached what looked like a cauldron. "What the fuck is that?" I said.

"It's, um . . ." Owen shook his head. "I have no idea."

The man looked peaceful as the rest of the mob screamed and danced around him. I noticed that there was a fire beneath the . . . pot? . . . Surely, he wasn't going to . . .

"Oh, fuck," Sean whispered. The man was pushed into

the pot headfirst, into what I could only assume was boiling water. The water was spitting angrily as he struggled and shouted, flailing in the hot liquid. "What in the hell is going on here?"

"I think we're watching a human sacrifice," I said, after a long minute of watching the man struggle.

"So there's zombies and . . . whatever the fuck this is?" Sean shook his head. "Maybe we should rethink this plan."

Owen turned to Sean. "I think staying here is a good idea," he said. "We have water, there's a creek at the back of the house and they've been catching rainwater in barrels. We've got animals. That house is closer than I'd like it to be, sure, but it's still far back from the road. Hopefully we won't cross paths with them at all."

Sean's mouth worked but no words came out. "Okay," he said finally. "But if they come to the door like Jehovah's Witnesses, I am *out* of here."

We stood at the window for a long time that night, watching the . . . whoever they were dance and throw their arms at the sky. The pot/cauldron thing was bubbling, and they were throwing in what looked like dirt. I realized suddenly it could be spices. They could be boiling this man alive to eat him.

Oh, no. Nononono. What did we just walk into?

~

It wasn't until, like, two in the morning that the crazies went back into the house. Well, houses—there were a bunch of little buildings on the huge plot of land. I had no idea who the hell they were or what they were doing, but

I was definitely not going to mess with them if I had anything to say about it.

We cautiously went outside, the three of us, early the next morning. The chickens were fine in their bunny hatch. The cows were lined up next to the barn, and I wondered what kind of routine the family that lived here had had.

"Do you know how to milk a cow?" Owen said to us.

"Not a clue," I said. "Do you?"

He shrugged. "It's not rocket science. I've milked goats before. Should I milk the cows while you guys start planting?"

I remembered the vast array of seeds we'd found at the tractor supply store and nodded. It was kind of nice, being a farm family. I could hear the cows mooing softly across the way, the chickens clucking loudly behind me, and Sean and I started playing with the cool dirt. There were already crops sprouting in the field behind the house, but I couldn't tell what kind yet.

"This isn't so bad," I said.

Sean was digging holes for the plants and seeds that we had, and I was coming up behind him to put them in and cover them up. "I'm a little worried about our neighbors, but I think farm life might be a good idea," he said.

It was relaxing, to plant the seeds. Moving the earth, sifting it through my fingers, patting it down tightly became a routine, a familiar one, and my mind wandered. I thought about the neighbors; who the hell were they? Were they dangerous? Should we move on?

I knew that Owen felt that we should stay, but . . . "Sean?"

"Yeah?" He was stamping down some loose soil.

"Do you think we should stay here? With the, um, partiers and stuff?"

He shrugged. "They didn't shoot any fireworks at the house, so that's a plus. If they keep their creepy party away from us, I don't see why we can't stay. This house has everything we need. If they want to boil people alive, Owen's got a pretty nice rifle, but I don't think they're a danger to us."

We finished up planting and went back inside to wash up with the rainwater. Owen came in with a few buckets of fresh milk, and I looked through the kitchen to find jars or bottles. This house really *did* have everything we needed. Creepy neighbors aside, this had been our best idea in a while.

Grace was napping on the tile floor as we worked in the kitchen. It was . . . nice. Normal. It seemed as if we could live like this forever, farming and taking care of each other. Aside from the creepy party, this could be home.

We were putting the milk into mason jars when I heard a sharp rat-a-tat sound at the door. I froze. "You've got to be fucking kidding me," I whispered.

"Unless they're door-to-door missionaries, I think we're safe," Sean said.

"Are you going to answer it?"

Owen clipped the lid of a mason jar shut. "I'll do it," he said abruptly. He disappeared from the kitchen, walking toward the front of the house, and I could hear the door opening—not a lot, just enough.

"I think I saw a basement off of the pantry," Sean remarked. "We can store the milk down there to keep it cool."

I tried to ignore the rising voices and concentrated on what we were doing. There was a not-insignificant amount of milk jars and bottles; it would last us for a little while, at least. I decided to start going through the cupboards to toss anything expired and inventory what we had. There was flour in abundance, and lots more baking supplies besides that. The oven was an antique, one where you started a fire underneath and opened the little door to cook or bake. It would do nicely; there was an entire drawer full of lighters and matches next to the stove.

The door slammed shut, and I heard the locks clicking into place. Owen came storming back to the kitchen, and I could tell that something had happened.

"What's wrong?" I asked.

He snorted. "Fuckin' crazies is what's wrong."

"I'm gonna need a little more info than that," I said.

"It's a cult. They want us to join them for their next bonfire. They were particularly interested in you, Kiera. They saw us yesterday unpacking everything. So if you go outside, make sure one of us is with you. Just in case." He grunted as he leaned down to light the stove.

"Interested how?" I started putting up the still-good baking supplies, leaving out a few things to make us some bread. I had seen some fruit trees off beside the barn and figured the homesteading books and magazines could teach me how to make jam, and then we could have PB&Js. I was no baking connoisseur, but even I could read the recipe off the page.

Owen cracked his knuckles, one at a time. It made me wince; that noise grated on my nerves. "They just had a lot of questions. Who are we, why are we here, do we plan to stay, who's the female—and just for the record, when men start referring to women as females, something's up—and what side we were on."

I frowned. "What side? There are sides?"

He shrugged. "Us versus them, I guess. I didn't ask too many questions, their crazy was showing without me interrogating them."

I had found a large mixing bowl and started making the dough, looking at the recipe after every ingredient. I wasn't a baker, but I wasn't stupid. "Do we need to move on?"

"We just got here," Sean sighed. "And unpacked. And made room for chickens." He paused, then looked at me. "But I agree, don't go outside alone. If they're willing to boil a dude alive, they're certainly capable of doing something to one of us."

As I kneaded the dough, I watched the cows out the window. They were so peaceful, grazing out there next to a small pond. I wondered if the pond had fish; we could probably cook fish on the stove too. I wished life was as simple for us as it was for the cows.

Something flashed in the corner of my eye. I frowned, trying to see what it was, and suddenly it was in full view—

There was a bear.

There was a bear and it was coming toward the farm.

"Owen," I called, almost dropping the dough on the floor. "Owen, there's a bear. Like a big fucking bear."

"On it," he said, swinging his ever-present rifle around to his front. I wondered if he slept with the damn thing. I followed Owen and Sean outside as he said, "If he comes towards you, make yourself big and shout a lot."

Sean and I came forward with our backs to the cows. We needed these cows: for milk, for meat, for everything, if we were going to stay here for the long run. The bear walked on its hind legs, then fell to all fours. Something about the bear wasn't right.

Owen leveled his rifle. The bear roared, running at him. I clutched Sean's hand. "I really fucking hope that we don't have to act big and yell," I whispered.

A loud *bang* echoed across the farm. The bear staggered, but didn't fall down. Owen frowned, and took more careful aim. The bear was about twenty feet away from him.

And it was spitting acid.

"Oh holy shit," I said.

"Is that—" Sean started.

"That's a zombie bear," I replied numbly. In the zombie war, I hadn't seen any Infected animals. Now I had to worry about zombie cows and bears and foxes and whatever the fuck else lived in the woods behind the fields. "That's a fucking zombie bear. Owen, be careful!" I called.

The bear lurched forward as Owen shot again; this time, I saw the splatter of an eyeball and brain matter leaking out of the bear's head. It fell to the ground heavily, and things got really quiet. I could hear the cows mooing unhappily behind me.

"What are we supposed to do with a dead zombie bear?" Sean asked.

Owen shook his head. "Don't know," he replied, seeming a lot more calm than I felt. "Maybe burn it? To keep the acid from eating into the fields?"

It made a modicum of sense, I supposed, but I wasn't sure we knew how to torch a zombie bear. "I'm going into the barn for a second, I saw a gas can in there," Owen called over his shoulder.

It didn't take him long to get there and back. The cows were still freaked out, all huddling in a pile next to the barn, except for the bull; he was staring at the bear, and he looked pissed. I guessed scaring his women wasn't in his plans.

Owen doused the bear in gas; it was pungent, burning the hairs in my nostrils, or so it felt. "You're a pretty good shot," I said.

He grunted. "Put in a lot of practice back in the day" was all he said. He reached into his pocket and pulled out a matchbox.

"To a zombie bear funeral!" he cried, then lit the monster on fire.

"To a zombie bear funeral," Sean and I echoed.

I was definitely keeping Grace inside or with me at all times. If a bear could become Infected, who knows what else could happen?

I was *not* going to let this Infection take Grace, Sean, or Owen away from me. There was no way.

At least, that's what I thought as we watched the bear burn, hearing the crackling as the fire hit the acid, and the smell of rotten, burned meat permeated the air.

A fucking zombie bear.

Lions and Tigers and Bears

~ Sean ~

S
o that was an adventure.

We'd puttered around the house and watered seeds and plants in the afternoon, checking back on the bear periodically to see how it was going. It stank; it stank like death, necrotic all-encompassing viscous liquid permeating the air. By the time evening rolled around, the bear was as gone as he was going to get, and Owen put the fire out with some rainwater.

We were all getting ready for bed by lantern light when we heard it: more fireworks. They just wouldn't shut up. Kiera and I slept fitfully, tossing and turning to the sounds of a cult in full swing. We didn't stay up to see if they sacrificed—cooked—someone this time.

The next morning it rained. Owen went around to all the barrels and made sure they were open; we needed the water, especially if we wanted to stay here. Kiera and I were playing a game of cards on the kitchen table while Owen cleaned his rifle.

Grace was under the table, whining a little as a thunderclap echoed through the sky. Kiera reached out and put her foot over her, hugging her a bit. It made me smile; they were definitely bonded after all they'd been through.

. . . lightning shattered the sky, illuminating the room. I could feel that someone was here; feel their heartbeat, feel their fear. I hunted, searching for the source of the red that I craved. Turning over tables in the apartment, I finally found her hiding under the bed.

I grabbed her by the throat and she screamed. I squeezed harder, thinking maybe if I squeeze hard enough her eyes will pop, and I can have them, too. I threw her to the ground and pounced as thunderclaps resounded outside. I clawed my way past her clothes and nuzzled her neck, feeling the heartbeat against my lips.

She screamed again as I bit down, hard, tearing my mouth away to let the red flow freely. I watched her struggle and swallowed the bit of skin and muscle I'd taken. Her eyes didn't pop out—so I dug my thumbs into the hollow, forcing my way behind the spherical meat. They made a satisfying sound when I finally worked them free.

The screaming was fading as she bled. The red was so beautiful. Everything was so beautiful . . .

I hadn't realized I'd fallen asleep until I jerked awake, panting. Grace lay at our feet, wagging just the tip of her tail as she saw me sit up. "It's okay," I whispered to her, reaching out a hand to tap her on the nose the way she liked.

I was clammy, and the shirt I was wearing didn't seem like enough. Would I ever get free of these memories? Would there ever be a time where I wasn't haunted?

Kiera was next to me. "Sean?" she murmured.

"It's fine," I replied. "I just fell asleep for a second." I wanted to be alone with my nightmares.

I slid out of my chair, Grace following not far behind, and went into the living room. I sat in the rocking chair and Grace laid her head on my knee. We rocked back and forth for a while, as I watched the bonfire still burning outside. I wondered if there was another person in the cauldron.

You didn't even have the courtesy to cook your meat before you ate it, the voice in the back of my head said. You know the voice—the one that tells you you're being dumb as shit, or that this is the right moment to propose. The little-god in your head that oversees all of your decisions. And right now, my little-god was tormenting me even as I sat awake.

I could feel the skin making its way down my esophagus. I remembered the taste of it, and how pleasant it was to Infect someone who had been wearing perfume. I remembered the Hex, and the Links, and wondered not for the first time what my newly unzombied friends were doing.

I heard Owen pacing in the kitchen, talking to Kiera. I didn't know if that man ever slept, much less relaxed. We had left embers on the stove to heat up the house against the slight chill, and I could feel it behind me as I sat in the rocking chair.

"I don't know what to do," I told Grace. She tilted her head in that way. "I keep having these nightmares . . ."

She said nothing, but I didn't need her to. I just needed to talk. I heard a pause, a small silence, and then Owen coming into the room.

He sat across from me on the couch, avoiding my eyes. "You having nightmares too?" he said.

I nodded. "I didn't mean to fall asleep like that. I guess all the walking did me in."

"At least the yahoos finally finished their party last night," he replied. "God only knows what they do after they dance around the fire like lunatics."

I wasn't sure I was in the mood to talk, so I simply nodded. We were quiet for a long time. "You really need to be careful with Kiera," he said, surprising me.

I looked up. "What? Why?"

He sighed. "Because they're a fucking cult," he said. "And they want to recruit us. They were extremely interested in Kiera. How old is she, has she been exposed, was she Cured, was she Infected. I don't know what exactly they're doing over there, but I don't want to fucking find out because we have to do a rescue mission."

Nodding, I absently petted Grace's head. She was a good dog. If all dogs were like her, I could get behind this dog thing. "So we protect Kiera," I said finally.

"Yeah," he said. He paused. "So nightmares?"

I blinked a little. "Yeah. A lot of them. You?"

"A lot of them. Of the war overseas, the zombie war,

every place I've been deployed or served has night-mares attached to them." Owen shrugged. "I'm a haunted house."

"I am too," I admitted. "I remember everything. I remember being a zombie, eating people, Infecting them. I remember killing people. And now . . ."

"Now you just can't shake it," he finished for me. "That's unusual. Folks that I've met that had been Cured don't remember much of it."

"They're the lucky ones," I muttered. "I remember every damn day."

We sat in silence, listening to the sounds of the outdoors. Grace was starting to fall asleep on my knee. I sighed. "How do you do it?"

"Do what?" Owen, for once, was not fiddling with his rifle.

"Compartmentalize. Accept that you've killed humans and there's nothing you can do about it. Think about them like a target. They were an objective, nothing more," I said. I listened to Kiera in the kitchen.

"I don't think I can," I added. "It wasn't objective at all. It was up close, personal, and right in my face. It was intimate. I never killed someone cold-blooded; I always felt their last heartbeat in my hand or my mouth. I just . . ."

He nodded slowly, leaning back on the couch. He was quiet for a long time. "Done that, too," he said finally. "If it's not an objective, it's harder. You have to separate yourself from humanity, a little bit."

"Doesn't that come back to bite you in the ass?" I asked.

He shrugged. "Of course. But being a little bit separate lets you do horrible things in the name of better things, like freedom. Not the yahoo-fireworks-screaming freedom like the freaks across the way, but true freedom, like being exactly who you were meant to be."

That was awfully profound for Owen. I felt a lump in the back of my throat. "Be who I was meant to be?"

Our eyes met briefly before I looked down. "Sean, you didn't want to turn into a zombie. You didn't cause this. You dealt with it as best as you could at the time and now you're feeling bad about it. But you can't let those feelings overrule your common sense.

"We have a purpose here: to survive. Whatever we all did before coming to this farm doesn't matter. We're in this together, and we'll take on whatever horrifying zombie animals come to the farm and the crazies across the road. We'll figure it out." He spoke firmly, as if he knew absolute truths.

I let my brain struggle through that, winding my thoughts around the ideas. Was it really that simple? Put it behind you, it's done and that's it? I could feel the skin skimming down my throat. I remembered what it felt like to put a hand inside a chest and grab a heart. I remembered Infecting people that would do the exact same damn thing. I created more of the problem, not less.

I could only hope that somehow, here, I could set the record straight. Be who I was meant to be, according to Owen. I was not a killer; zombies were zombies and people were people.

At least, that's what I kept telling myself, until the sun rose.

~

We spent most of the morning taking care of the animals, who most definitely did not appreciate a good rainstorm. Grace hated to get her feet wet, and the cows were mooing loudly in displeasure as we trailed muck behind us.

The bear had melted into a congealed goo, and I could see some kind of animal poking through it. I decided it was better not to know. Kiera was feeding the chickens, and I was milking the cows. It wasn't hard, really. Owen showed me. It was just messy if the cow decided it hated you and kicked.

Luckily, I encountered a very small number of cows who wished death upon me.

It was peaceful, rhythmic work. The sun was shining, the birds were singing, and there was no zombie bear threatening to attack our cows. Or us. I grabbed the big pail we'd been using for milk and started to haul it to the kitchen. Kiera went towards the chicken coop.

Out of the corner of my eye, I saw something toward the front of the house. *It must be Owen,* I thought to myself. He had meandered off to do his own thing after a quick breakfast of—surprise—oatmeal. It was easy to make and even I couldn't fuck it up.

I tried to balance the pail in my one hand, leaving my stump to wave beside me in a desperate quest to not fall in the mud and the "presents" from all the animals who lived here. I dropped off the milk, cracking my back as I went back outside. It had taken several hours to milk the cows, and I went to find Kiera.

Who wasn't there.

Let me restate: Kiera was not there.

I figured she must have gone back inside, so I searched the house. It wasn't a very big house, so it didn't take long, and there was no sign of her. Owen came in at about the same time as I'd finished searching, and he took one look at my face and sighed.

"We're going to have to make a field trip, aren't we?"

Owen slung his rifle over his shoulder and I brought my crowbar. We marched across the street to the biggest house on the lot and knocked hard enough to shake the windows. Nothing. No sound, no movement, nothing.

I was starting to get worried. We split up, checking each building on the acreage, and no one was home.

I pounded on the main door again, and used my crowbar to pry it open. I kicked the door in and Owen and I went in guns a-blazin', so to speak. We searched the house room by room until we finally found a note in the kitchen.

The Messiah has come
We Are Rebuilding the future
She is in better Hands now
Well fuck.

"So they've got Kiera," I said, trying to sound normal. My heart was racing. They *boiled people alive* and they got Kiera. I didn't fucking know what to do with this knowledge. It felt like the entire world dropped out from beneath me.

Owen came over to me, putting a hand on my shoulder.

"We'll go after them," he said solemnly. "Get her back, and burn these buildings down so the fuckers have no reason to be here ever again."

"How?" I could feel my brain struggling to compute. The world faded to white, just a little, around the edges. "I don't think arson is the best solution. What else do you have?"

"In the service, I did a lot of recon work. Tracking, finding people, finding hiding places. It's not rocket science; we just have to come up behind them and get them before they get us." He shrugged, letting his hand fall back to his side. "It's doable."

I didn't think I was breathing. I thumped my chest until I coughed, exhaling finally, and gasped. "Okay," I said as my head swam. "Okay, so we go after her."

"Let's go pack our backpacks," he offered. "Then we can start to follow them."

I didn't quite hyperventilate, but it was close. I had wanted to be back with Kiera so much when I was a zombie; and now that we finally were together, it was a wall separating us. A wall with a bloody handprint. And now . . .

Yeah. That train of thought did not go anywhere fast. I started packing the essentials as fast as a one-handed man could, rifling through the things we'd unpacked, ready to start our new lives at the farmhouse. The animals had free rein to walk around, eat grass or birds or whatever, and drink rainwater, so they would be fine. One loose end fluttered at the back of my head.

Grace.

"We have to take Grace," I called out to Owen. "We can't leave her behind."

Owen came in with his backpack stuffed to the gills and his rifle around his neck. "So we have a zombie-fighting dog," he mused. "All right. I'm in."

I gathered up some stuff for her and shoved it in my backpack, and I decided not to bring the leash; I didn't have the same bond with her as Kiera did, and was nervous walking her without a safety net, but I trusted in the training that Kiera had done with her. My heart lurched as I realized how hard Kiera had worked to train these little things into her. Kiera . . . What was she doing right now? Where was she? Was she scared?

I had no idea, and it haunted me.

Witchcraft

~ Kiera ~

I struggled to wake up. Something was wrong, and I couldn't open my eyes. Everything felt so heavy, and I couldn't move. I took a deep breath only to realize that there was something covering my face. I panicked, but it did no good.

I heard people. My hands were bound, as were my feet, so I couldn't run very far if I tried. I exhaled slowly, trying to think in my muddled mind. What the hell had happened?

. . . had finished feeding the chickens . . . heard a sound . . . turned and saw . . . Something pressed up against my nose . . . falling . . . being carried . . .

Okay. That was as clear as mud, but I figured out a few things: I was caught, likely by the freaks across the street. I was *not* with Owen and Sean. I was drugged and brought to some unknown location and blindfolded. Kidnapped.

Holy fuck, I was kidnapped!

I struggled against what felt like duct tape on my feet and hands, but couldn't move an inch. I bit at the blindfold, trying to move it, and it finally fell past my eyes. I was seated on my behind, which was wet from leaves.

I could hear indistinct conversation. There were six men around the fire, and three women. The women looked about as good as I felt; they were serving the men dinner, in old-fashioned dresses, and they seemed absolutely miserable.

Great. So I'd been kidnapped by misogynist males that wanted me to be a good little woman.

I watched as they ate from tin cans, trying to listen to the conversation. There was something moving behind the group of men, and I strained my eyes trying to see it. There were three more people, one woman and two men, chained to the ground. More kidnappees?

One of the men threw a tin can at the chained people, and I heard a low growl. It didn't sound human. It didn't sound like anything I'd heard before. Wait; *were they zombies? And they were naked?*

One of them spit acid in the general direction of the man, and they all laughed as it hit the ground, the grass sizzling beneath. My mind whirled as I tried to figure out what the fuck was going on. I was kidnapped, they were keeping naked zombies on leashes, there were several men and women, and we were going somewhere unknown. At least, it seemed like we weren't at our final destination. Nobody bothered to unpack.

The only thing I could think to do was lower my hands to the ground and use my fingers to write *Sean* as best as

I could; maybe he'd see it and know that this was the way we were going.

It didn't take long for them to realize that I was awake. A burly, lumberjack-looking man stumbled over to me, with alcohol on his breath. "Our guest has awakened!" he crowed.

The men around the campfire cheered, and the Lumberjack grabbed me by my hair and pulled me towards the fire. It fucking hurt. I yelled, struggling as best as I could, only to be cuffed in the back of the head by his fist.

"Aren't you much happier with us?" he said, unceremoniously plunking me down next to the zombies. "You have purpose here."

I looked at the women standing back away from the fire. They wouldn't meet my eyes. I struggled against the duct tape, trying to find the littlest rip in it, but it was no use. "More beer!" my captor called.

A petite brunette walked off toward the tents behind the zombies, and quickly came back with an armload of beer. Where the hell were they getting their supplies from? She faded into the background, but not before looking at me.

I watched her, desperately trying to send a message through my eyes. She only shook her head and bit her lip. *Don't do it,* she seemed to be saying.

"Do you like our friends?" A skinny, black-haired fellow was speaking to me now. "We've found the Messiah. One of those three is our savior, and we only need to listen to their teachings to find enlightenment."

I stared at him. The messiah? A zombie? What in the hell had I gotten into? From behind the blindfold that was now around my mouth, I tried to speak. "Let me go!"

The Lumberjack cuffed me again and I saw stars. My head was throbbing after his blows and I wanted nothing more than to curl up with Sean and go to sleep. Where was Sean? Was he looking for me? What about Owen? There were so many questions and so few answers.

"Aw, look, she's a good little girl," Lumberjack laughed. "Knows when to keep her mouth shut."

If looks could kill, he'd be in that fire. I tried to make a plan: something, anything to get me out of this situation. Some way of signaling to Sean and Owen where we were going. Owen was in the military, did he have some skill in finding people? Jesus, I hoped so.

The sun was down completely. The only light I had was the fire in front of me, and I had no way out. I missed Sean. I missed our stupid cows. I missed everything. Tears were springing to my eyes and I blinked hard; I *would not* cry in front of these men.

The big pot from the front yard was sitting on a wagon behind Lumberjack Man. Another kidnapper, this one ginger and portly, pulled the wagon toward the fire. It took him, the Lumberjack, and the skinny guy to get the pot onto the massive fire.

They were talking, but it didn't make any damn sense to me. I kept hearing "messiah," and "Infect" and "the end times," but that didn't tell me more than I already knew. I could only sit and wait, trying to wiggle my hands free of the duct tape as best as I could, a little at a time. The zombies were pressing against their chains, trying to get free, and spitting acid.

There was water sloshing around in the pot. It wasn't full, but they'd been carrying the damn thing with them with water inside. I guessed they were committed to whatever the fuck they were doing.

Another man, this one tall and gangly, unchained one of the male zombies. He grabbed it by the scruff of the neck and dragged it over to the pot as the men cheered. The zombie spit furiously, but the tall man was strong, and as he held the zombie near the pot, the rest of them started chanting.

Messiah! Welcome! We await your direction. Messiah! We look for your coming. Messiah! We atone for our sins and offer you this sacrifice.

He grabbed the zombie and shoved it headfirst into the pot. The zombie didn't quite fit in there, and was howling, squirming, trying to get out. I wondered if it could feel the water boiling around it. What senses did zombies still have? Were they similar to Sean's zombies?

Tall and Gangly grabbed a pitchfork and pressed the zombie down deeper. Water sloshed over the sides as it struggled, and he stabbed it a few times, causing even more splashes. Finally, after way too long, the zombie stopped trying to get out.

Was it dead? Did boiling water kill zombies? Or had he hacked it to pieces with the pitchfork? Jesus, I did *not* want to be in this situation.

Two of the women, a tall blonde and a plus-sized brunette, started carrying things to the pot. I could see potatoes, carrots, all the makings of a hearty soup. Only . . .

The zombie was the meat.

I shuddered and continued to work on my taped hands. It didn't take long until I smelled it.

It smelled like pork. I gagged, leaning over as best as I could, and threw up on the ground, coughing. The fucking zombie smelled like pork, they were cooking it, and they had kidnapped me. The Lumberjack's eyes met mine as I vomited, and he smiled. "You'll get your share," he said. "Don't worry. We feed our women."

As opposed to not feeding their women? And *their* women. I didn't want to be one of their women, for sure. I had to find a way out of this, and soon.

Where was Sean? Where were Grace and Owen? Would they come for me? Did they know? I sat there beside the fire, duct-taped up, silent, and fighting my tears. They had to come for me.

They had to.

~

It took a while for the zombie—gag me—to be cooked with the vegetables. I swore to any god paying attention that I would never eat pork again. Hell, I'd be a vegetarian if it meant I could escape what was happening. The tall man was stirring the pot with the pitchfork, presumably breaking up the zombie's flesh.

I had hoped they were sated with their tin can meals, but evidently, that was just the appetizer. The fifth man, Asian with a long ponytail, produced bowls that looked like a kindergartener had made them in art class. The group around the fire were cheering, jeering, making noise and stomping their feet. It was chaos; I couldn't figure out what they were doing, aside from the inevitable.

"Are you ready?" Lumberjack Man prodded me with a finger, and I mentally prodded him back with both middle fingers. Fucker. "You'll do just fine, I promise."

The portly man waddled over to the pot and dunked in a huge ladle. He came up with soup. It smelled and looked like *real soup*. I gagged again, throwing up around the second blindfold that had slipped to my chin by that point. Lumberjack Man only smiled.

The zombie soup was passed around to every man around the fire. "To the Messiah!" the black-haired man cheered.

"To the Messiah!" they crowed.

I wondered what eating a zombie would do to a person. They were obviously acidic; wouldn't it hurt them? Or did the boiling neutralize the acid? This was so not in my wheelhouse. As they ate, the women stood near the tents, staring at the ground. "They fed women" my ass, half those girls looked skinnier than I'd ever been before. I tried to get the petite brunette's attention, but she wouldn't meet my gaze.

The lumberjack came toward me with a fork and a piece of meat. I shut my mouth as hard as I possibly could. He grabbed it with his strong fingers, prying my mouth open even as I fought against it. "Nononono!" I screamed.

Screaming just gave him what he wanted: my mouth was open and ready. He shoved the meat in my mouth and used his big hand to make my jaw chew. I was gagging again, and the stars above were spinning fast. It tasted just like a pork roast. I choked on the meat, unable to breathe, until the lumberjack hit me on my back, hard.

The zombie meat went down my esophagus.

I had fucking eaten a *person*. Not by choice, unwillingly, but nevertheless, there was human muscle and skin in my stomach, or at least heading towards it. Tears sprung to my eyes, and this time, I let them fall as the men laughed.

"Tastes good, doesn't it?" The lumberjack cuffed me on the head again, and I groaned. "I told you we feed our women."

He did the same thing to the three women by the tents: offered them a large bite of zombie meat, pushing it into their mouths with his fingers and using his hands to make them chew and swallow. Their eyes were dead. Whoever they had been before this cult had gotten a hold of them, they weren't at home in their heads anymore.

I did something I didn't do very often: I prayed. *God, the universe, or anything . . . please, let me get out of this. I don't know what you want in return, but I need your help. Please . . .*

The men were eating out of their little misshapen bowls and talking. I tried to focus on what they were saying while my head swam from the blows of Lumberjack's fist.

". . . move to the next farmhouse, a few miles away," the skinny, black-haired man said. "We can regroup there and look for more Infected."

So we were going to another farm. Great. I watched the

women clean up the bowls, and they started to empty out the cauldron/pot into big bowls with lids. I started working at the duct tape a little more, trying to get my thumb out from beneath it.

". . . set up camp," the ginger said. I wiggled my thumb as hard as I could. "And we can continue our search for the Messiah if these two"—he gestured toward the leashed zombies—"do not end up being the Messiah."

What fucking messiah were they thinking about? As far as I know, you only joked that Jesus was a zombie; it wasn't real. A zombie as the savior of mankind? And what did that have to do with boiling them alive? Or boiling them undead, depending on your view of the Infection.

A thumb was free! Oh, hell yes. I started working on the rest of the duct tape on my wrists.

One of the women, the tall blonde, was looking at me. She shook her head again, and I tried to figure out what she was trying to tell me. I held out my duct-taped wrists in her direction, and she did the same movement. She gestured toward the fire with her eyes and put a finger to her lips.

The third girl, with an average build and locs in her hair, was taking the rest of the bowls back into the bigger tent. I kept wiggling slowly and carefully, trying not to attract attention. The men were cheering now, howling around the fire, and I shrank back as much as I could.

This was too fucked up.

As I continued to work through the duct tape, I felt another *thunk* against the back of my head, and I went down.

~

As I woke up, I realized I was in a wagon or a wheelbarrow. Stuffed into it unceremoniously like some garbage. I groaned and tried to rub my head on my bound hands; so far, this was not going my way.

Then I remembered: my thumb! I started working at the duct tape again, only to realize I'd been retaped. Son of a bitch.

It was bright outside. The wagon was being pulled by the Asian man with a ponytail. He grunted as he pulled me uphill, and I saw a rickety house at the end of a long drive. This was definitely not as great of a setup as Owen, Sean, and I had had; this looked like nobody had been in this house for decades.

I looked around, trying to find the women. They were behind me, with large backpacks, trudging up the driveway of this old house. None of them would look at me or even acknowledge that I existed. Clearly, I wasn't going to find an ally there.

We finally made it up the drive, and I was unceremoniously picked up and thrown over the shoulder of the lumberjack, then plopped down on a dusty couch. With blindfolds no longer around my face or throat, I coughed, my eyes watering.

I wanted to scream, but it wouldn't do me any good. I had woken up too late; now we were in the house, and I was trapped. But like a good little soldier, I worked at the duct tape again, relieved to feel that they hadn't just *added* more duct tape; they had actually taken off the tape and rewrapped my hands. Fantastic.

"What the fuck is this?" I was spitting fire.

The ginger man approached me and grabbed my chin in his hand. "That's not how you speak to your superiors, missy."

Oh gag me. "I am not your *inferior,* I am someone you fucking kidnapped. Now let me go!"

He shoved me back onto the couch by my chin and gave me a nice, firm slap across the mouth. "I warned you once. Don't talk back again."

My face stung. I refused to let the tears fall. The average person could walk twenty miles a day, and it wasI turned my head as far as it would go. It was late afternoon. So, theoretically, we'd gone about thirty miles from the original house. I had to believe Sean was coming for me. Had to believe they weren't leaving me behind.

But it still niggled at my heart, just a little bit. We hadn't been on firm ground that night. I knew that our relationship was having trouble adjusting to what we had done. Sean still had nightmares, and I still couldn't splash water on my face, because it felt like blood spurting onto me. What if he didn't come? What would happen to me? To Grace?

I made myself small against the couch and closed my eyes, listening to the men working around me. I didn't bother to try and find the other women. There was no reason to. No one was going to help me.

I was going to have to help myself.

Reconnaissance

~ Sean ~

We had packed our backpacks full of food, dog food and toiletries: everything we might need on the road. Owen and I followed the wheelbarrow tracks in the dirt road, hoping we'd catch up to them eventually.

"It looks like we're following the trail," Owen said.

I felt horrible. "I'm glad," I said, looking down at Grace. Grace was a godforsaken mess. She kept looking ahead for Kiera, behind, sideways, any way she could. I was a very distant second; it was clear. "It's my fault. I thought she was safe feeding the chickens."

He shook his head. "Doesn't matter. We just have to find them now. And be aware of zombie bears," he added as an afterthought.

"Fucking zombie bears," I exhaled.

It was not a particularly interesting walk: we saw farmhouses, cows, horses, and grass. Lots and lots of grass.

The most interesting parts of the walk were when Grace took a detour for a potty break, and we got to stretch our legs and arms a little, cracking our backs. The trail wasn't particularly difficult to follow; we just had to catch up with the bastards.

We walked all day, stopping only for water and bathroom breaks. I felt like we weren't getting any closer, that we were going to be too late, and it shattered me. I left Kiera alone. She was somewhere, in god knows what situation, alone.

At least, I hoped she was alone. Jesus, the things that men could do with a woman were exponential. There was definitely a block of ice in my stomach. I was grateful that I'd healed all the bones and bruises I'd gotten while I was a zombie, or else this would have been torture.

We didn't talk much. We were just two dudes on a field trip with a dog. We had left the gate for the chickens open so they could eat bugs to their hearts' content, and the cows were set for a while. I wondered if we'd ever go back to that farmhouse. I wondered if I'd ever see Kiera again.

The trail veered off into the fields, and Owen tracked it. "They stopped here," he said. "Looks like they're dragging an entire camp all over creation. There was a fire here"—he gestured at the blackened wood—"and something heavy on it, likely that zombie cannibal pot."

"I have no idea what I'm going to do if Kiera is a zombie, a cannibal, or worse, when I find her," I admitted. "Obviously, none of this is her fault, but the nightmares she's going to have will be insane. I really didn't believe that they'd take her. It was my stupid fucking mistake."

Owen grunted and hefted his backpack, adjusting it a little on his back. "Well, it's done now. No use in crying over it."

We started following the tracks again, this time through the fields, through cornstalks and beans and peas, and something tomato-like. I felt bad trampling over the plants, but at least we knew there was a little food hanging around if we were in this for the long run.

Grace was chasing after a rabbit in the field. At least one of us was having fun. Or having lunch, I realized. "Hey, we should stop to eat soon."

We slowed to a stop, and I put out some dog food for Grace, who happily left the bunny alone and came back to us. "How far ahead of us do you think they are?"

He shook his head. "Not far," he said. "They don't have much time on us. Couple hours, really. I'd say once they make camp for the day, we'll catch up to them no problem."

"And then what?" God, I hoped he had a plan. Because I certainly didn't.

Owen smiled grimly. "And then we get Kiera back."

We ate in silence, and I wondered what exactly that entailed, getting Kiera out of there. Were we fighting people? Would we sneak up and set her free? Owen wasn't forthcoming with information at any fucking point, and I was panicking. I somehow needed and didn't want to hear the answer at the same time.

We finished our meals and packed back up, Grace wagging alongside us. "We can walk at a pretty fast clip," Owen said, "and we should make up some time.

Hopefully, they've stopped for the night, and we can figure out what to do when we get there."

It was a long walk. A long, boring, stress-filled walk through fields. And more fields. I didn't know why there were so many damned fields or who would tend them. Maybe their farmers were caught in the war and now they were growing out of control and were ready to eat me like *Little Shop of Horrors*.

Owen wasn't much of a talker. I kept looking at his gun as if it were going to go off by itself, though I felt much safer with my cleaver-rod and crowbar, both strapped to me. I didn't want to initiate the conversation, but it felt so fucking awkward.

The sun was setting, and we still hadn't found them. Owen was certain that they'd be camping somewhere in the next clearing between the fields. As we made our way around the wheat, I saw firelight and heard sounds.

"Owen," I whispered.

"I see them," he whispered back. "Let's sit and watch for a bit, not jump in rashly."

I definitely wanted to jump in rashly. Like, now. I couldn't find Kiera in the circle around the fire, but seeing through wheat wasn't great either. I inched as close as I dared, wanting to stay hidden as best as I could.

They were eating something from the pot. Oh, fuck, they were *eating something from the pot*. They put zombies in the pot. I gagged, turning around to find a space to throw up.

Owen said nothing, he stayed watching the group. There were six men and three women. If I strained, I thought I could see two zombies as well. And then . . . *there.*

Kiera.

I sighed in relief. She looked okay, if a little pissed off. She wasn't hurt or anything, but she definitely wasn't happy to be there. "She's okay," I whispered to Owen, just in case he hadn't seen her.

He nodded. "I see her. I also see the zombies tied up behind her, and I can hear someone coming from the far side of the campfire. We need to be careful what we do to keep the risk low. We don't want Kiera getting hurt."

From the look on her face, we were a little late to the party for that. I sighed, watching her as she sat there bound in what looked like duct tape. What the fuck?

They were scooping meat out of the pot and giving it to the six men around the fire. A skinny, black-haired man jeered at Kiera, and I tensed. Owen put a hand on my back, willing me to calm the fuck down before I ruined the whole thing.

A red-haired, kind of fat guy disappeared into the fields only to reemerge with two acid-spitting zombies in tow. I hadn't noticed it earlier, but the zombies had some kind of muzzle on them. Something to block the spit, I guessed. They sat the zombies down by the fire and started laughing as they . . .

. . . just a zombie, Sean . . . You'll never be anything else . . . you're too broken . . . think of the Link, the Hex, and how much you enjoyed what you did . . .

I really needed to find a therapist.

I sat back on my heels, drumming my fingers against the dirt. "So what do we do?"

Owen was thin-lipped. "We sit here until the idiots go to bed, and we watch where they put Kiera. Then, we break in."

I nodded. It seemed like a good enough plan.

~

It took a long time for them to go to bed. There was beer, there was zombie taunting, and there were horribly sexist jokes to tell. The woman standing behind Kiera led her to the smallest tent closest to the fire, and all four of them went inside. There was no light in there, and the woman who'd gone in first zipped up the front.

The men meandered their way over to the tents; they had three, two men each. I wondered what they expected to do with the women if there were more of them in their tiny tent. I could only imagine they'd be stacked like logs.

"Let's sneak around back," Owen said finally. It felt like it took forever for him to speak. I put Grace in a stay.

"Okay," I whispered back. We crouch-walked through the wheat slowly so we weren't seen by anyone coming out for a last-minute bathroom break. It was about half an hour later when we finally made it through all of the crops and to the little tent off to the side of the fire.

"What now?" I asked.

Owen reached into his pocket and pulled out a knife. Because of course he had a knife. Why wouldn't he have a knife. He carefully made an archway in the back of the tent, cutting the fabric easily, and there stood five women huddled in a little tent. Kiera was in the middle, hands bound behind her back.

"What the fuck do you think you're doing?" a petite brunette hissed at me. "They're going to see a giant fucking hole in the tent!"

"So sew it up," Owen said. "We're here for her." He gestured to Kiera.

Kiera fought off the hands on her shoulders, headbutting the tall blonde, and came rushing out of the tent into my arms. I exhaled slowly in relief as Owen started to cut the duct tape off.

"What the hell happened?" I said.

"They're going to notice she's gone," said one wearing locs. "I don't know what you expect to get out of this night raid."

Owen smiled. It wasn't a nice smile. "Let them find out. Stay out of it. You have no quarrel with us."

The other woman sighed. "That's not going to work for me," she said. And then she screamed.

Fuck.

Fuck fuck fuck. I panicked and grabbed my crowbar; Owen grabbed his gun. The men poured into the small tent, pushing the women out, and saw the hole that we'd made, saw Kiera next to me, saw Owen and I ready for them. So they charged.

And we responded. Owen climbed up on a nearby boulder in the field to get some height and distance for shooting, and I put Kiera behind me. I could see Grace's eyes from across the campground and gave her the hand signal to continue staying, even as she twitched with excitement.

"You fuckers! You're taking our women! We won't stand for this!"

"Yeah, they're *ours,* and we got them fair and square!"

We met in the middle. I started swinging my crowbar against the mostly unarmed men, who were surprisingly strong. I could feel Kiera behind me as I whacked a guy's face in; his skin turned in on itself, opening up a huge wound in his cheek that showed his teeth. He stood there, dazed, and I grimaced. This wasn't like killing zombies, or being a zombie and killing a human. It was beating up another person, and I felt guilty.

Where were the other women during this? I saw Kiera, but I couldn't find the three women that had kept her captive. "Kiera, where are the girls?" I called.

"I don't know. I'll find them," she said.

It was a melee. It was chaos. It was crowbar thwacking against bone, fist meeting my face, bruising ribs, and breaking bones (theirs, not mine). I heard Owen shooting, and the remaining four men fell in quick succession. They were still alive; he had shot them each in the leg or the side. They were incapacitated for the moment but alive.

I didn't know the prognosis of the guy whose face I busted in, though. He was lying on the ground, bleeding with the others.

Kiera and Grace herded the women toward the scene. Grace was baring her teeth, looking as menacing in her Doge suit as she possibly could. Kiera was clearly in charge. The women knelt down by their fallen men and started to tend to them.

"Do we agree that Kiera's going to come with us?" Owen called pleasantly.

Moans and groans were heard across the field. Owen hopped back down from his boulder and nodded at Kiera. "I think we're good." He cleared his throat. "Ladies, would any of you want to leave this hellhole and go somewhere else?"

The petite brunette stood up and walked toward us. "Hi," she said simply. "I don't want to do this anymore."

Kiera held out a hand and they shook. "My name's Laura," she said. "These guys are fucking nuts, and I'm over it."

I looked at the ground, at the groaning and bleeding men and the two women catering to them. I felt some remorse, as I was pretty sure the guy I'd whacked with my crowbar was dying. I had done that. Me. And it was a person, not a zombie.

Just more food for nightmares, I guessed.

. . . he blood dripping down my face. I buried my head in her body cavity, eating the dark, sweet meat of her. Her hands twitched with every bite, but she wasn't in any condition to resist anymore . . .

Fuck!

Kiera, Owen, and Laura looked at me like I was a little crazy. I shook my head. "Let's head back to the farmhouse. You,"—I pointed at the group on the ground—"don't follow us. This was only a preview of what we'll do if you follow us."

The women were pissed, but they had enough to do without getting involved with our shit. We started the long journey back, Grace at the front of the group in her Doge suit, Kiera and Laura in the middle. At least we'd be safe at the farmhouse. Unless another cult came to live across the street, I guessed.

Out of the Frying Pan

~ Kiera ~

I t took a while to get back to the farmhouse. Owen played with his radio as we walked, and I listened to the static while watching Grace lead the merry band of travelers. She was prancing through the fields, chasing after mice or birds, leaving a wide swath of wheat for us to push through. It made me smile.

I had fucking eaten a zombie.

I thought I was going to throw up. Laura noticed I was a little green around the gills, and she looked over at me. "It won't kill you, you know."

"What?" I spit the overload of saliva onto the ground, that unfortunate warning before you puke.

"The zombie flesh. It's disgusting, but it won't kill you or turn you into a zombie. At least it hasn't for as long as I've been with those guys," she said.

I bent over the side of the path and hurled. Sean came

up behind me, holding my hair back, and Grace stopped in her tracks. "What is it?" Sean asked.

"They made me eat zombie," I groaned, leaning against my knees. I wiped my mouth with the back of my hand and straightened. "I don't know how to process this." Laura was standing next to me, awkwardly showing her support.

Sean's face was a fixed mask, and I couldn't tell what he was thinking. Was he remembering his time as a zombie, eating human flesh? Or was he thinking of me differently after knowing what I'd done? Well, been forced to do. It definitely wasn't my idea.

He adjusted his cleaver-rod on his back and offered to hold my hand. "I don't know what to tell you," he said finally. "But hopefully, it's just a bad memory."

"Yeah," I said quietly, and we started to walk.

I had missed most of the walk to the clearing in the middle of the fields; I had been unconscious. Walking back was taking a significantly longer time than I'd thought. The sun was lowering in the sky by the time we started seeing houses again.

Right after sunset, we arrived at the dark farmhouse. Owen went to check on the cows and the chickens, and I went to feed Gracey. Sean was left starting lanterns and the stove for heat and light. Laura went into the kitchen to investigate food for dinner. When I was done, I rejoined Sean and watched him finish.

"Did they hurt you?" he said finally.

I shook my head. "Not really. But they kept talking

about the messiah and zombies, and I'm a little freaked out, truth be told."

"So it's a zombie-worshipping cult. Great. Okay," he said, adjusting the light of the lantern. We sat down on the slightly dusty couch, releasing a soft puff of air from the cushions.

"I don't know how you did it," I blurted out. "Ate people, I mean. It was horrible. It tasted like—"

"Pork," he supplied, his face expressionless. "I remember." We sat in awkward silence for some time, and he finally sighed and turned to me. "The nightmares haven't stopped. It's still happening in my head. I don't know how I'm ever going to be free of what I did."

I rested my hand on his shoulder, moving closer to him on the couch. "You weren't you," I said softly. "It wasn't like you had a choice."

He sighed. "I know," he said reluctantly. "But I can still taste it. I can still feel it. And I don't know how to stop being haunted by what I did."

I leaned my head against his shoulder and said nothing for a long while. I had no advice. I certainly didn't know what to do with the thought of eating zombie flesh; eating people's flesh must be ten times worse.

Owen came back in, holding his lantern up to see. "The animals are fine," he reported.

Laura came back out into the living room. "I think I can make us some rice and beans," she reported. I wondered what her role was in the zombie cult; was she the caretaker of the crazies?

"That sounds good," I said simply as Owen sat down

in the armchair next to the couch. "Laura, are you okay?"

She stiffened, the lantern in her hand glistening in the dark. "I'm just . . . glad to not be there anymore," she hedged.

"Did they hurt you?" Owen asked quietly.

Laura stood there silently for a long time before nodding. "They hurt all three of us," she said slowly. "In various ways." It was clear that she didn't want to elaborate on exactly what that meant.

"Do you want help making dinner?" I offered. It was random, I knew that, but it was the only thing I could offer.

She shrugged. "Sure." I rose and walked with her into the kitchen.

Laura found a pot in the cupboards and settled it on the stove-top. I started pouring in rainwater that we'd collected, and we set it to boil. "How did you get tangled up in this anyway?" I asked her after a long moment of silence.

Shrugging, she cracked her knuckles, one at a time. "I lived next door to one of the men. He said he'd heard from the government that they were going to start bombing cities to keep the zombie problem under control and asked if I wanted to come with him. I didn't have any better ideas, so I did."

I paused. "Wait, is that true?"

She looked at me for a moment. "I don't know," she said finally, stirring the water a little bit as it began to boil. "Do you guys have a radio or anything?"

"Yeah. Owen!" I called.

He appeared at the doorway as Laura poured the rice and beans into the pot. "Yes?"

"Have you heard anything through your radio in the last few days?" I asked.

He shrugged. "A lot of static and random shit," he said. "Why?"

"Laura thinks that they might be starting to bomb the cities to deal with the zombie problem," I explained. "At least, that's what she was told when she joined their group."

Owen frowned. ". . . It wouldn't surprise me," he said. "But I haven't heard anything. Last thing I heard was stay indoors and keep away from strangely acting people."

"Well, let's listen to the radio tonight and see if anyone comes on."

"It's a two-way radio, so if someone is broadcasting, we can theoretically talk back," he explained. "Theoretically, because I don't know if anyone can hear us way out here."

I nodded. Laura stirred the meal slowly as the rice absorbed the water and the beans began to cook. "I guess we'll have to see what happens," I said after a while. "They wouldn't bomb such a rural area as this, right?"

Owen shrugged again. "They might if they thought there were enough people and animals that were turning into zombies. Hell, we might have an entire forest of zombie deer for all we know."

"Zombie deer?" I blinked, trying to imagine a deer coming at me with its blunt teeth. "That . . . is not something I had thought of before."

"I've seen a few zombie bears and a zombie cougar," Laura noted. "They skinned the cougar and made a coat for Jason, the leader of the group. The zombie bears—they let their pet zombies go against them in a fight. The zombie bears won. There were originally seventeen people in that group, we lost eight from sheer stupidity."

I shook my head. "I'm glad we got out of there," I said sincerely. "So you're out here alone? No family?"

She took the pot off the stove and started bowling up the rice and beans. "No family. My fiancé died in the zombie war, and I haven't made any friends since."

I carried my and Sean's bowls to the living room, Owen and Laura trailing behind with their own. "Sean was a zombie in the war."

Laura blinked. "Really?"

Sean waved his stump at her. "We tried to avoid it, but yes, I became a zombie."

She stared at his arm for a long time. "Are you telling me you . . . you . . . *amputated* your arm? Like, by yourselves?"

"Yep. Well, I didn't have much to do with it besides screaming the house down," Sean admitted. "Kiera did all the work. It didn't take, though; the Infection was too strong."

She whistled through her teeth as we began to eat. "What was it like?"

I couldn't answer that for Sean, no matter how badly I wanted to. "It was equal parts exhilarating and absolutely devastating," he said after a minute of thinking. "I still retained a lot of thought, unlike a lot of zombies I met. I still remember what it felt like to have the zombies in my mind."

"That's incredible," she gushed. "I was always interested to know what it was like after the government announced the Cure."

Sean nodded. "It was like having a family in your head all the time and the voice of your conscience in the back of your mind. I could always feel them, sometimes hear them, and I knew where they were without looking. We communicated mostly in pictures and feelings."

Owen raised a brow. "I'm guessing you were at the college when the Cure was produced?"

"Yeah," I said. "Sean was attempting to start a zombie coup, and I was attempting to get to the National Guard in one piece with my group."

"What group?" Laura stiffened as Grace came up behind her. "And what the hell is that dog wearing?"

"Sean's friend Brett looked out for me after Sean got turned. We gathered together a group of zombie hunters with makeshift weapons. It worked pretty well until we got to the college," I said thoughtfully. "That's when all hell broke loose." I paused, holding out my hand for Grace to come across the room and lick it.

"She's wearing a Doge suit," Sean explained. "Do you remember that meme of the dog with the coyote vest so it wouldn't be taken in the dark? It's kind of like that, except with a lot of metal and goggles and raincoats."

I eased the goggles off of Grace's face and set them down on the end table. She wagged happily, and I knew she was just glad to have me back. I looked down at my watch, somewhat surprised that it was still keeping time. "Hey, turn on your radio, Owen," I suggested.

He nodded and grabbed it out of his huge backpack that he'd leaned against the wall. We heard an awful lot of static at first as he changed channels. There were voices periodically, sure, but nothing that sounded official or even well-put-together.

Then we heard it.

. . . bombed the city, the voice gasped. *They're coming for everyone. Everyone who was exposed to the Cure that wasn't a zombie at the time . . . they're coming.*

Owen's gaze sharpened. "Who's coming?" he said over the radio.

The voice sobbed in relief. *Thank God! I thought I was alone. They're coming; the government, with helicopters and bombs. I barely made it out of the city alive.*

"Where are you right now?" Sean leaned forward, trying to hear better.

I'm in a feedstore about six miles out of the town, she said, her voice shaking. *Where are you?*

I replied, "We went southeast from the city center and ended up in a farmhouse." I touched Sean's elbow and whispered, "We can't leave her there."

"Which feedstore did you find?" Owen said.

It's the one on Route 33. There's still food here, and I didn't know what else to do except run. The voice was shaking, and I could almost hear her tears.

Owen nodded. "That's the feedstore we went to on our way to the farms," he said. "We can come get you. Are you safe right now?"

She exhaled slowly. *I think so,* she said after a while. *There's nobody else here and there are granola bars for days.*

I leaned in. "Well, we have a farm with chickens and cows, and you're more than welcome to share the house with us," I said firmly. "Let us come get you."

Really? Her voice was high and shaky. *You'll come get me? How many of you are there?*

"Four," Sean and I answered in unison. We chuckled a little bit, then Sean began again. "We have an ex-military guy named Owen, myself as a former zombie named Sean, Kiera as the one who kicked zombie ass, and Laura, someone we saved just recently from a zombie cult." He paused. "Oh, and we have a dog. She knows how to fight zombies. It's kind of awesome."

It took a few moments to get a response. *You . . . you have a dog?* she squeaked. *That's . . . that's great. That sounds normal. Oh, god, I need it to be normal.*

"We'll start out in the morning," Owen said firmly. "It shouldn't take more than a few hours to get there if we don't stop. Just stay at the feedstore, don't let anyone in, and stay hidden. Have you heard any broadcasts from the government?"

I could almost hear her shaking her head. *Not since I heard about the bombs, and I don't think I was supposed to hear about that,* she answered. *I just got on the wrong frequency and got lucky, I guess. They're supposed to bomb the city tomorrow at noon.*

I swallowed hard. That was home; it would always and never be home again. I didn't know how to feel about another piece of my life splintering off and rolling into the abyss. "We'll leave at first light," I said. "We should be there well before noon, and you won't have to worry about it."

She sniffled a little. *Thank you,* she said in a rush. *Thank you. Seriously. I had no idea what to do except leave the city.*

"We'll figure it out together," I said softly. "What's your name?"

Aspyn, she said, spelling it out. *My parents didn't know how to spell. Or were drunk, I guess. Either way.*

I nodded, even though she couldn't see me. "We'll be there. Get some rest, and wait."

I will, she said, her voice slightly more determined.

Owen flipped the radio through a few more channels, hearing nothing but static. We ate dinner together in silence: Laura, Owen, Sean, and I (and Grace had her own dinner in the kitchen). It was beginning to feel a little like a troupe, like the group I'd been with during the zombie war. It was somewhat familiar and comforting to adopt people like that.

"I'll show her to the bedroom down the hall," Owen said abruptly, standing up, his gun still stowed on his back. Laura trailed along behind him with a small wave, and Sean and I were alone.

"So we're really doing this," he said after a few moments.

"Really doing what?" I asked.

"Creating a little mob here on the farm. A farm family. A farmily, if you will." He chuckled. "I swear, the two of us seem to collect people without trying. Me with my Hex and Links, you with your merry band of zombie hunters."

"And Grace," I reminded him as she came to sit next to me, signaling that it was time for bed. She was very insistent on bedtime.

"And Grace," he said back, offering her a few fingers to lick. "Let's go to bed. We have a rescue mission in the morning."

Grace led the way toward the bedroom, and Sean followed. I went into the bathroom to brush my teeth and wondered if Sean was going to fall asleep before I finished. I still didn't know what to say to him after being kidnapped; there was this weird disconnect between us that I really didn't like.

I climbed into bed next to him, and he stirred, not quite asleep yet. "Are you doing okay?" he whispered.

I threaded my fingers in with his. "A little banged up, maybe, but they didn't hurt me or anything. I was more pissed off than scared."

"I'm glad we found you so fast," he said quietly. "I was afraid . . . well, you know what I was afraid of."

I snorted. "The usual array of male-dominated society problems, like rape and battery, and then the added surprise of potentially turning into a zombie or zombie bait? Yeah. I'm pretty glad you found me quick too."

It took me a few seconds to adjust, but I leaned my head against his shoulder, and he slid his arm underneath me. "I missed you," he said simply. "I don't want to be without you ever again."

I rested my hand on his chest, feeling the reassuring beat of his heart. "Me either," I said back, and it was a long time until we said anything else.

~

We left early the next morning, Grace in her Doge suit, Laura in some clothes that were left by the farmers. We'd given Laura an old kitchen knife Owen had brought for emergencies. We traveled light, opting for speed over comfort. It was a windy day, one where the trees bowed and played in the crisp air. The wind seemed to push us along as we walked back to the store.

"Do you think the cult people will come back?" I asked Laura.

She shrugged. "It's hard to say. They'll be pretty pissed that you broke in and took both of us. They're lazy and good for nothing, but they're also vindictive and think that they're righteous."

"What's with the zombie worshipping?" Sean asked.

"I don't know what started it," she began as we walked. "The guy I was originally with—David—wasn't like that at first. The skinny Asian guy with the black hair, Mark, he's the one that started in on that crap. He told us that zombies were the next step to evolution and that Jesus was a zombie. Told us that if we ate the flesh of zombies, we would transcend like Jesus, rather than rot like a zombie."

"Some people really have too much time on their hands," I muttered.

She chuckled. "No, I agree with that. He got the rest into it—Paul, Lincoln, Shen, and Jason. I don't know where he picked up the other girls—Cara and Blue. They were there before David and I came. Once Mark starts talking, though, people tend to listen, and it wasn't long before David got swept up into the movement."

"So what's Mark's role in all of this?" Owen asked.

"He's like the leader? Like a prophet," Laura explained. "He communes with zombies and transcends them to enlightenment. And then the rest of the group eats zombie soup."

"That is the biggest pile of bullshit I've ever heard in my life," Sean said simply.

We all started to laugh.

"No, you're right," Laura said. "I absolutely hated it. I tried to leave several times, but David wasn't having it, and Mark made sure that the girls' tent was always behind the men's tents. We hadn't really had a stable place until we got to that old farmhouse."

"And then Mark saw Kiera?" Owen asked.

Laura nodded, confirming his theory. "Mark saw Kiera and said that we needed another female in the group to balance out the energies. We hadn't seen anyone in a long time, you guys were the first group we've come up on since we started walking out here. So he took it as a sign from the gods and said that we needed to release her from her bonds and have her join the holy party."

I snorted. "I'm sorry I wasn't ready to be 'enlightened.'" Shaking my head, I adjusted my small backpack and shifted so that Grace could walk in front of me. "But that's fucking crazy."

"Oh, I agree," Laura said. We hadn't had time to make Laura a true weapon yet, one for distance between her and the zombies. We'd have to remedy that once we had a chance.

"The other girls didn't believe in Mark's shit either, but they'd learned it was easier to go along with him than to raise a fuss." Her voice was subdued. "Mark liked to take advantage of young women being hydrated and exhausted from dragging that fucking pot all over creation."

I raised a brow. "He . . ."

She nodded. "He never did it with me, I think because of David. The other girls didn't have someone to protect them like I did. But I wasn't too invested in my relationship with David, clearly, because here I am." Shrugging, she walked a little more before speaking again. "I don't miss him. He wasn't my boyfriend or anything. He was just my neighbor."

We walked in silence for a long time, enjoying the sunshine, even though storm clouds threatened us on the horizon. Grace was having the time of her life, sniffing every inch of the road, which went from dirt to gravel to concrete as our feet pounded the ground. We were making fairly good time, even with puppy bathroom breaks—hell, we needed bathroom breaks too, let's not forget that.

The feedstore popped up in our vision after a couple of hours of walking. It was midafternoon by the time we reached it. Owen went to the door and knocked, holding his rifle in his free hand, ready just in case.

No one came.

He grabbed the radio that was strapped to his light backpack. "Aspyn, are you there? Aspyn?"

It took a while, but she finally answered. "Are you here? Really here? Like for real?"

She sounded a lot younger than I'd originally thought. Owen was in his mid-thirties, we were in our upper twenties, Laura was somewhere in between, but Aspyn sounded like she was barely twenty years old. I wondered what it had taken to get her here, alone.

"We're really here," Owen said simply. There were several more moments of static before we heard chains rattling inside the store. They definitely had not been on that door when we'd left; Aspyn clearly had some survival instincts in her.

When the door cracked open, we saw a small, thin young woman with dazzling red curls, bright green eyes, and an extremely worried expression. "Hello?"

I stepped forward. "Hello, Aspyn. Are you ready to get out of here?"

She nodded and started pulling a sled out from behind her. "I packed some things that I thought might be useful where we're going," she said. "There's some food, some water purifier straw thingies, matches and lighters, and a bunch of other stuff."

"Good job," I offered. Grace walked forward slowly, as if she could feel the girl's anxiety, and reached up to touch her free hand with her nose.

Aspyn jumped a little in surprise. "Is this the zombie fighting dog?"

"This is Kiera's dog, Grace," Laura offered. "She was a pivotal member of a zombie-fighting crew during the war."

Her eyes were wide as she examined Grace. "I don't know what I pictured, but this . . ."

Sean nodded in understanding. "It's called her Doge suit. Kiera made it herself after rescuing Grace."

Aspyn peered down at Grace and scritched underneath her raincoat-covered muzzle. "Nice to meet you, Grace." She shut the door behind herself and looked at us with hope. "So now what?"

"Now we go back to the farm, keep listening to the radio, and keep our heads down," Owen said. "If we don't make waves, we should survive just fine until someone figures out what the hell is going on here."

She sighed. "I said everything I'd heard on the radio," she began as we started to walk back toward the farmhouse. "There's government drones, and the city is going to be bombed in two days. Apparently, the zombie population is too big for them to take care of without extreme prejudice."

Laura was walking next to her. "Do they know why people are getting Infected this time?"

Aspyn shook her head. "No, at least no one's told me, and I haven't overheard anything. The only reason I overheard about the bombs was because my radio was on the wrong frequency. After that, I tried every channel I could trying to find somebody."

"What made you go to the feedstore?" Owen asked.

"I remembered going here with my dad when I was little," she explained. "It had all sorts of interesting stuff, camping food, camping gear, sports stuff, outdoors stuff. I thought maybe I could stay here for a while until I figured out what to do, but after the bomb stuff, I got scared."

We chatted back and forth, getting to know each other as we walked. It didn't take a terribly long time to get back to the farmhouse; the sun was setting as we walked into the dirt driveway. The chickens clucked their greetings, and the cows were unmoved by our presence.

"Home sweet home," I sighed. "There's a bedroom no one's taken yet up the stairs to the left. The main bathroom is in the middle of the hallway. Feel free to use any of the rainwater we've collected to do whatever you need to do."

Aspyn unhooked her sled from her body and offered the reins to Owen, who took them silently. "I hope you can use some of this," she said.

He grunted and walked toward the barn. We walked through the wide front door, and I relaxed a little. It felt like coming home after a long vacation: a little sad, but comforting and nice. "Let's get some sleep and figure it out tomorrow," I suggested to Aspyn.

Laura nodded. "Same," she said, and left for her bedroom.

We all went our separate ways, and it was the first time in a long time that I felt like I could sleep. Really sleep, deeply, without thinking about danger on the horizon.

Anger of the Gods

~ Sean ~

We all slept late, likely due to the amount of walking we'd done the previous day. Kiera and I had talked late into the night until we finally fell asleep, and we'd slept better than we had in months.

Things were looking up.

We changed out of our sleeping clothes and Kiera took the pile of dirty laundry, saying she was going downstairs to do the clothes in the basin out back. There was plenty of Borax and washing powder, so we'd at least not smell like heathens for quite some time. It seemed like this could really work out, be a home for our motley crew.

We had time to kill until the next broadcast was supposed to be on. Kiera went off to her garden—with Grace, in her Doge suit, this time—and I tended to the chickens. Owen seemed to like the cows, for some reason, so that was all him. The big bull in the pen next to the cows liked to chase him.

Grace was digging in the dirt next to Kiera when I came up from behind her. "What are you planting now?"

"Oh, I think I have corn, beans, squash, watermelon as a treat, some strawberries, and I have a weird seed that's supposed to be a fruit tree, but I don't know which fruit it is," she answered thoughtfully. She dropped a few small seeds in the hole that Grace dug, and the dog started covering up the hole with her nose.

"How the fuck did you train her to do that?" I exclaimed.

"She did it herself. She watched what I was doing, and then she did it herself. I told you border collies are seriously smart." Kiera wiped a hand across her forehead, leaving a dirty streak.

"Talk about the end of the world; if zombies keep trying to take over, maybe the next world government should be full of dogs," I said, sitting down on an overturned pail next to the garden.

"They can't possibly do any worse than what we're doing now," she said. She gardened quietly, waiting for Grace to make holes—the holes weren't even, of course, since border collies are still dogs and have no use for design—and planting her seeds in whatever order made sense to her.

We made small talk as Grace dug and covered up, and I watched Owen feeding the cows across the field. Laura was in with the chickens, and I couldn't see Aspyn, but I was sure she was around here somewhere.

I didn't need to wonder. She came running into the

field, then rested her hands on her knees gasping for air. "Sean, Kiera!"

Kiera dropped her seed packets. "What?"

Aspyn pointed up. We hadn't heard it over the chickens and the cows; it was a noise that was no longer normal to us, and what it was didn't even register until Aspyn pointed it out. It was a helicopter. More importantly, it was an army helicopter, and it was headed for the city.

Kiera stood up and sighed. "I guess that's it," she said carefully. "Do we need to do anything to prepare for the explosion?"

"I think we're far enough away that we won't get hit too hard," I said. "But I wouldn't want to be back at that feedstore, for sure."

Owen wandered over, whistling to himself, and glanced at the sky. "It's time?" he asked calmly.

Aspyn nodded, near tears. She knelt down next to a rather muddy Grace and hugged her around her neck. Grace tolerated it; she could likely tell that Aspyn needed her, but she wasn't Kiera and was, therefore, burnt toast and discardable.

We stood and watched. We couldn't see the city from here, for sure, but we knew what was happening, and there were many good people left in that city. "God, I hope they evacuated," Kiera breathed.

"We'll never know," I said, feeling solemn. It was hard. That was our home, and we couldn't even save it. We couldn't do anything about it.

But we felt the afterward. The ground shook a little, pebbles dancing against the dirt. I knew that most explosions could be felt for something like fifty miles; this was a much larger blast and a much larger distance. Grace lifted her chin and began to howl. I wanted to howl with her.

It was gone. It was all gone.

Kiera's eyes filled with tears. She sighed, running her fingers through her hair. "I think I want to check out the barn," she said. "Something to keep me occupied. Owen, have you seen much of it?"

"Didn't really look at everything," Owen said quietly. "Just looked for pails for the milk."

"I'll go with you," I volunteered. We walked silently, fingers brushing against each other's, but we said nothing else until we got to the barn.

"We need weapons for Laura and Aspyn," Kiera began.

"Hey. This was a big deal. Are you okay?" I tapped her chin with my fingers, tilting her eyes to meet mine. "Because I'm not okay. And I think you aren't either."

She exhaled slowly, tears finally falling. "It was where we met," she said weakly.

I pulled her down into a bale of hay, holding her with my good arm. "I know," I said. "But we can make new memories here. And we have a built-in friend group. Maybe there's some board games in the closets of the farmhouse that we could play. We could make a life here, Kiera."

I paused. "If you want to."

She was quiet for a long time. "I think so too," she said at last. "I think that this is a horrible thing, and we need to listen for broadcasts, and we need to take care of animals and mind our own damn business. If we keep away from towns and city centers, we should be fine."

We sat in the hay for a little while, just being, existing in a horrible world where blowing up an entire town—and if they were doing it to our city, they were doing it everywhere—was acceptable, somehow. You can bomb citizens if it means getting most of the zombies. I didn't exactly remember my time as a zombie fondly, but I didn't think I deserved to get firebombed into oblivion, either.

Kiera sighed. "Let's keep looking," she suggested.

We found several rakes. Kiera took two. "We can make these into weapons," she explained. She also grabbed the razor wire and duct tape. We peeked through the stalls in the barn, wondering if anyone had taken up residence.

Aside from a small family of nonzombie raccoons, we were alone in the barn. The cows were still out in the field; they rarely came in the barn anyway, only in bad weather. There were a lot of tools I couldn't name, but I put them in the back of my brain to ask Owen about at a later date.

We started back to the house. It didn't take us long to get past the field and to the back door, where Grace was waiting patiently. Kiera and I went into the kitchen to see what kind of weapons we could make for everyone.

"Well, Owen's got his rifle, you've got your cleaver-rod, and I've got my hatchet-mop," Kiera mused. "What if we take the head of the rake off and duct tape . . . mmm, that!" She grabbed something out of the drawer. It was a butcher's knife. That did not look like it would be fun if you got hit by it.

"Laura can have the Meat-Siah. Name courtesy of the

cult we found her in." Kiera looked a little proud at that. "Now we just have to come up with something for Aspyn."

I paused. "Do you think she's . . . like, old enough to have a weapon?"

"She's an adult," Kiera responded. "She's not much of an adult, but she is old enough to fire a gun and vote and do all that shit that we can't do anymore. So she gets a weapon." This time, Kiera wrapped the rake tines in razor wire and added steak knives at each tip. "This will be called . . . fuck, I don't know."

"Rake-inator? Like Terminator but a rake?" I hazarded a guess.

She grinned. "Perfect." We set the weapons by the door near ours and went into the kitchen to wash up. It wasn't more than twenty minutes later that we heard Laura calling for us.

"She sounds upset," I said, surprised. "Let's go check it out."

We rushed back to the living room. The front door was flung open, with Aspyn on the sidelines looking like a kicked puppy. Laura was with Owen, who was lying awkwardly on the too-small couch. And . . .

. . . *that smell. You know that smell. That's the smell of blood, of meat. It's the smell of tearing off pieces of flesh with your incisors and swallowing it whole. Lapping up the blood that's pouring down from the body. Reaching in with your face and your teeth to get the choicest parts of meat, the organs . . .*

Fuck. I cleared my throat. "What happened?"

Kiera went over to the couch and looked at Owen. She

was the closest thing we had to a medic—if you call an at-home amputation medical, that is—and she knelt by his side and whistled through her teeth.

"I did something stupid," Owen hissed. "I got between the bull and the girls, and he wasn't happy about it. Pushed me into the razor wire. I got stuck."

He definitely had gotten stuck: there were flaps of flesh everywhere, oozing bright red blood in no particular pattern. "I didn't know what to do, so I tore my arm out, and . . ." Owen sighed. "Well, this happened."

"Okay. Okay, so we need some first aid. Laura, go into the main bathroom and the master bath and look for any first aid supplies. Aspyn, you check the kitchen and the pantry. Sean, you get me some clean towels and the sewing kit I brought from the feedstore." Kiera was in crisis mode.

Owen was actively bleeding all over the couch as I came back. Kiera was putting pressure on the wounds as best as she could with her hands, but she needed some help. I offered her the towels. "Start ripping them up into strips, Owen's got a knife in his front left pocket," she ordered.

"Aye, aye, Captain," I said before realizing this was a smart-ass thing to say, and this was, perhaps, not the best time to say it.

No one ever said I was smart.

I retrieved the sewing kit from upstairs and handed it to her next. "Sean, I need you to push the edges of the skin together with your fingers."

"You do remember I only have one hand, right?" I swallowed hard. This was so not my forte. I had been drugged to hell and back when Kiera cut my hand off. I'd been a zombie, sure, but I didn't want to think about Owen *like that*. He wasn't a victim. He wasn't.

I put my fingers where she showed me, and she lit a match to sanitize the needle. She started to sew up the flaps of skin, one at a time. She used some strips to bind his arm in a makeshift bandage and the rest as rags to mop up the blood while she worked. "I think that's it," she said, sitting back on her heels. "How does it feel?"

"It hurts like hell," Owen said pleasantly. "But it doesn't feel like I'm bleeding to death anymore, and I'll call that a win."

I looked down at my hands. They were covered in blood. The color—

. . . was the only color you could see, Sean. The red draining from their bodies and moving into yours. Lapping up the blood and eating the viscera. You remember what the liver tastes like, don't you . . . but I know your favorite is the heart. You're not a healer, Sean . . .

—triggered a memory, apparently.

"I'll be right back." Exit stage left to the rain barrel in the kitchen.

~

We all sat in the living room at broadcast time. Owen used his good hand to switch through the channels, one by one. Static. Static. Nothing. Static.

It was infuriating. We had no idea what was happening in the outside world. For all we knew, it really could have been the end of the world. And we'd be dicking around on a farm, doing nothing to help. I sighed, rubbing my stump.

"Wait, go back!" Aspyn said suddenly.

Owen frowned and adjusted the dial. "What am I looking for?"

Aspyn held a hand up. "Just . . . let me . . . stop! Stop right there," she said.

Owen stopped, and through the static, we heard a voice.

. . . bombing cities . . . Government . . . not your friend . . . Exterminating zombies . . . no Cure this time . . . safer to be . . . outside of city limits . . . trust no one . . . trust **no** *one . . .*

"Well fuck," I said after a minute of just static. "So we know they're bombing other cities. We've learned that the government is behind the bombing, which we kind of knew. We know they're exterminating zombies, but we also know that they're killing the Cured, just in case. Now we know there is no second Cure, and it's safer to stay the fuck away from everything."

Owen nodded. "Not much that we didn't already know, except for the part about the Cure. We're on our own out here." He winced, shifting in his seat.

"I say we stay here," Kiera said after a moment. "We're safe here, there's no city around us, no people, just animals. Owen's got his gun for zombie bears, and if those men come back again, all of us should now be armed when we are out of the house, just in case."

Laura nodded. "I like it here," she added. "It feels homey. I think we can stay here for a while, growing our own food and stuff."

I sighed. "Just don't ask me to chop off a chicken's head, please?"

Kiera grinned. "I wasn't planning on it. Wuss."

"You wanna come over here and say that?" I replied.

"Can you two lovebirds tone it down just a bit? We're working on our future here," Owen said.

"Sorry. Right. We have a bull, so we'll eventually have calves, and whoever volunteers can work together to slaughter the cows and the chickens. That takes care of meat. Kiera's growing her garden of vegetables and a few mystery fruit trees, that's Vitamin C hopefully taken care of and fiber in our bodies. I think this could work," I said finally. "I really do."

Aspyn nodded. "What can I do to help?"

Owen snorted. "You can milk the damn cows," he said. "I'm not turning my back on that bull again, not even if he is in his own pen."

"As long as I don't have to be on Team Slaughter, it's good," she said.

Team Slaughter. We had a name now. "Wait, do I have to be part of Team Slaughter?"

Kiera eyed me. "You are one of the stronger ones in our group," she said. "But if you're squeamish . . ."

I shook my head, looking away. "I'd just rather not."

"Okay. So Team Slaughter will be Owen, Laura, and Kiera," she said. "If I can cut off Sean's hand, I can cut the head off a chicken. Except for the cute one, that one's staying."

"You have a cute chicken?" Owen asked.

"I do. She has very flowery feathers and prances around like she owns the place. I've named her Chicken-donna."

"Okay, so we keep Chicken-donna and the rooster," Owen said. "It really does sound like we're set for a while. There's a stream out past the fields, and we're constantly collecting rainwater, so we should be good."

I sat back in my chair. We had a plan. We had a good plan. A few rogue zombie bears or zombie cougars wouldn't take us out, though we did have to spread more of the razor wire around the chicken hutch. "I'll decorate the chickens with razor wire," I said.

"I'll start dinner," Laura said. "Aspyn, would you help me in the kitchen?"

"And Owen, you should rest," Kiera said. "You bled a lot, and I'm a little worried about how deep some of those gashes are. I know you like to go, but now isn't the time."

Owen sighed. "Just one day."

"Kiera? What are you going to do?" I asked.

She smiled grimly. "I'm going to farm the fuck out of this place tomorrow."

Into the Fire

~ Kiera ~

I did, in fact, farm the fuck out of this place the next day. I weeded my crops, watered them plentifully, and did everything a good little farmer should do. I even used cow shit as fertilizer, though it did make me wonder if the vegetables were now contaminated by feces. I wasn't entirely sure how this fertilization thing worked.

We worked all morning, Owen, Sean and I outside and Laura and Aspyn inside. They were turning over the house in an effort to make it more livable: dusting, cleaning rooms that we hadn't been in yet. When we finally got crops from what I'd planted, Laura stated that she knew how to can, so we were all set there.

It seemed like a good thing. We could do this. We didn't need no damn government. We didn't need no damn Cure. We could take care of ourselves, and do a great job of it as we went.

It was about an hour from the next broadcast time before we all went inside, desperate to take sponge baths or bucket-showers. The feeling of being clean after working hard outside all day was awesome. I understood why people felt the need to exercise and the endorphins afterward. Then again, I didn't want to volunteer to run a 5k, so what did I know?

Owen sat down on the couch, hair damp, and winced. He tried to hide it, covering his face in a cough, but I saw his expression before he moved. "Owen, what's wrong?"

"Nothing," he said. "I'm fine." His other hand clutched at his arm.

"Don't lie, we're all in this together. What is it?"

He sighed. "I think my arm is getting infected," he said finally. "But I don't know yet. It feels hot, but there are no lines running up or down, and I used a marker to mark the size of the original swelling last night. I haven't looked at it since, but it's got that too-stretched feeling around the edges."

"Okay." I sat down in the armchair, frowning. "So what do we do? Aspyn, Laura, have you found any medications in the house or anything?"

Aspyn shook her head, red hair flying in front of her face before she brushed it back. "No, I don't think we have anything stronger than ibuprofen," she said thoughtfully. "Would that help?"

"It reduces inflammation and pain and can help with fevers, so yeah, that might be something. Do we have any peroxide?" I asked. I didn't know when exactly I became the medic of this particular experiment, but it seemed as if I was always foisted into this role in one way or another. I guessed once a nurse's kid, always a nurse's kid.

Aspyn retreated to the kitchen and came back with a rather large bottle of ibuprofen. "How many?"

I looked at Owen, at the sweat beading on his brows, at the pained look on his face. "Probably a good three," I said finally. "I usually take two and Owen is bigger than I am."

Owen grunted, downing the pills Aspyn offered and sitting glumly on the couch. "Stupid fucking bull," he muttered.

"Aspyn? Did we have peroxide?" I asked.

"Oh! Oh, yes, I think there's some in the main bathroom. I'll be right back," she said, and scurried off in the house some more.

I walked over to Owen and sat down on the couch next to him. "You're gonna have to show us eventually," I said. "It might as well be now."

"This is so not what I enlisted for," he sighed, and started to unwrap his arm. It was, for lack of a better word, *gooey*. There was pus seeping up through the wounds. There were no red lines radiating up or down, which was good, but it was definitely infected. Aspyn handed me the peroxide and I looked at Owen silently.

"Yeah, I'm ready," he grunted. I held the used bandages underneath his arm to catch the stray peroxide and started to pour. The liquid bubbled up immediately, and Owen hissed between his teeth. "That fucking hurts," he said.

"What did you expect, a day at the sauna?" I said.

"Laura, can you grab me a clean towel and some more bandages?"

"Aye aye, Captain," she intoned, and left the room.

The peroxide was still bubbling, almost audibly. I wondered if there were any other towns nearby that had antibiotics. Surely we could figure this out on our own. It was just an infection, right?

Laura came back, handing me the supplies. I wiped the disgusting mess of peroxide, pus and blood off of his wounds, and started rewrapping his arm. "Thanks," he said finally. "I think."

I tried to smile. "No problem," I said. Really, I was pretty damned worried about him. The amount of pus that bubbled out of those cuts was a little alarming. But I didn't let it show on my face; if I was worried, everyone would worry, and we weren't there yet.

At least, I hoped we weren't.

Owen switched on his two-way radio, and we listened to the static for a while as he flipped through channels. We heard gunfire on one channel; knowing what it really sounded like now, I had a frame of reference for these things. "What the fuck?" I mouthed to Sean.

He shook his head. "I don't know if that's what I thought it was, but maybe we should stay away from that channel."

"Agreed," I said fervently. "Keep looking, Owen."

We all sat in silence as he worked the radio. It took several long minutes before we finally heard something clearly: a voice! Someone else was out there!

Mayday . . . Mayday . . . Mayday . . . This is Wyatt

Hearns, broadcasting from outside of Portsmouth. The government has bombed the city, and there are no survivors that I've found. Please advise, repeat, please advise if you have any new information; we are running out of supplies.

Owen grabbed the radio. "Wyatt, this is Owen Bryant. We're near Portsmouth as well. Are you safe to travel?"

There was static, then the radio squawked to life. *Yes. My party is myself, my wife Anna, and our son Brayden. We're safe to travel if you can give us your location. Is there anything we should bring with us?*

I sagged in relief at the knowledge that there *were* other people out there, and we weren't alone with a bunch of crazy religious fanatics out in the middle of nowhere. "Do you have any food, medications, or tools?" Owen asked.

Static again, then Wyatt came back. *We do have food, negative on medications, and we have a small toolbox in the back of my truck. It's got enough gas in it to give me about fifty miles. Where are you located?*

"Point Peak," I said. "We're outside of Point Peak where the college used to be."

Used to be? said Wyatt. *So they bombed Point Peak, too? Great. How many in your party?*

Owen took over. "Myself, Kiera and Sean came from Point Peak, Laura came from a religious nuthouse out here in the sticks, and Aspyn was hiding in the feedstore off south by southeast. If you follow the highway and walk around the remains of the city, you should find us on the main road."

They kept talking, making plans for Wyatt, Anna and Brayden to join our group. It was such a relief to know that there were others out there. Families, even! We weren't alone. Maybe we could rebuild a community together, away from the cities, and get through this second-wave zombie apocalypse together.

That is, if they hadn't been exposed to the Cure, and didn't turn into second-wave zombies themselves.

I realized that we had to be careful of who we accepted into our little group. It was great to see that outsiders existed, but what would we do if one of them turned? What if the little boy turned, and we had to have Owen shoot him, or worse, he ended up attacking his parents? There were so many unknowns that I could hardly contain my anxiety.

I tuned back in to what Owen and Wyatt were saying. "So you've got the coordinates, and you said your truck can take you, what, fifty miles? You should run out of gas about two miles before you get to our farm. When are you leaving?"

Muffled voices echoed through the line. It took a little while, but Wyatt eventually came back. *We'll leave tomorrow at first light,* he said. *I'll bring the tools that I have and what little food we have left.*

"You might want to stop at the feedstore on your way in," Sean supplied. "They have tons of granola bars and trail mix and things like that. We've got cows and chickens, so we're pretty okay, but it wouldn't hurt to have some more supplies.

Roger came the reply. *We'll see you tomorrow. Over and out.*

"Over and out," Owen echoed, and turned off the radio. "So . . . what do we think about this? I know I kind of bull-rushed it, but the more people we have, the safer we are. I couldn't just leave them there to starve."

Laura sighed. "Are we adopting strays now?" she said warily. "Everyone who comes along can join us? What happens if someone turns?"

"I agree," I interjected. "What is the plan if someone turns?"

Owen thought about it for a moment. "That depends on the last wishes of the person, I guess," he said slowly. "I can put them down no problem, unless they want some other way to go. Do you all agree?"

Nervous nods came from all corners of the room. We didn't want to think about Owen having to shoot us. It was objectively terrifying, and a shiver ran down my spine. I said, "What do we think our chances are, surviving with this many people and not having anyone turn?"

Sean reached across the space between us to hold my hand. "I think we've got as good of a shot as anybody to make it," he said. "We know what the signs are, we have each other to hold accountability, and we have a plan. If someone turns, we'll get it taken care of." He wouldn't meet my eyes.

"Okay," I said softly. "So we've got that taken care of," I echoed. "But next time we run into some survivors, let's hold an actual meeting about this instead of throwing the life preserver straight out, all right?"

"Sure," Owen said. He seemed chagrined. "I wasn't thinking about people turning, I'm sorry."

I shrugged. "It is what it is," I said. "You want to help people. I want to help people. We all want to help people."

Aspyn chimed in for the first time. "I think it'll be good to have more people," she said in her quiet voice. "We can make ourselves a real community here. Maybe we can find enough people to rebuild a little; there are several farmhouses out here for families to adopt."

"I agree," Laura said finally. "I think we can make this work. Especially if the cult keeps going in the direction they were heading, we won't run into any more problems."

I sunk back into my chair, glancing over at Grace, who was asleep at my feet. "I bet Grace will like having a little boy to play with," I mused.

"I'm sure." Sean grinned. "Maybe he can do some of the running around with her so she doesn't drive you and I crazy with her energy."

I leaned down to pet Grace's soft ears. She twitched in her sleep, and I wondered if she was dreaming about chasing rabbits—or if she was chasing zombies. What kind of dreams could dogs have, really? Did she know what we were up against? Did she know that at any moment, my body could rebel against me, and I could become one of them?

Shaking my head, I retreated into my quiet mood. I had the weirdest feeling that we wouldn't all get out of this alive, and I didn't know which one of us was at the most risk.

All we could do was wake up the next day, and be prepared.

~

The morning was busy, but thankfully boring. There were no rogue cults skulking about the house waiting to steal us, we each had a job to do, and it was a nice day outside. I talked to the chickens as I fed them, feeling a little like Snow White with the animals trailing behind me. Grace stood outside of the chicken hutch, because Grace, obviously.

I didn't *know* that she'd eat a chicken, but I couldn't promise that she *wouldn't,* either.

Owen was puttering around the barn, Sean was milking the cows, and Laura and Aspyn were inside canning some of the last of the season's produce that had been bursting out of the seams of the ground when we got here. The house actually had a neat little nook in the kitchen to can from; it made me wonder if the people who lived here had built this house specifically, or had they just gotten lucky and it had been there all along?

Either way, we worked well into the late morning. Owen was sitting in the barn with his radio on and Sean and I were relaxing on some hay bales, watching the cows in the pasture and the clouds in the sky. It was such a peaceful day.

We all went to lunch, eating some of the beef jerky that had presumably been dried here, as it was in plastic baggies rather than a wrap. It went well with the egg soufflé that Laura had made. It was unconventional, yes, but it worked.

"So what time are they supposed to be here?" I asked around a bite of egg.

Owen shook his head. "I haven't heard anything since real early this morning. They're coming, and will radio in when they're trying to find us, I guess."

Laura said, "We should probably tell them not to set up camp in the cult house. It wasn't . . . great. Or clean. Or sane."

"Noted," Owen said.

I sat together with Sean, holding hands. "This really is shaping up to be a good adventure," he mused, as he looked out the window at the so-very-blue sky.

"Aside from the countless people who died in the bombings? Yeah," I said. "Real good adventure."

Sean blushed. "That's not what I meant," he said. "Of course it's a tragedy. But we have to take our safety as a good sign. We have to at least acknowledge that we're tougher than this and have found our way out of the mess we were in. We're helping other people get to safety, we're helping each other, and it's just really . . ."

"Nice," Aspyn piped up quietly. "It's nice, to know we can help people. To know that we aren't alone, that someone else survived the bombings. It doesn't make it any less sad, but it does make us thankful for the warning we'd had."

I sighed. "Yeah, yeah, I get it. Sorry. It's just . . . all this is so stupid. Were there really so many people turning into zombies that it got bad enough to bomb the whole city? Why didn't we notice it?"

Owen spoke up. "Because most of the city evacuated after the war," he said. "They were assuming that anyone who stayed must have been eligible to turn into a zombie, and they weren't prepared to take any chances with an outbreak."

"That's just so barbaric," I said helplessly.

"You're not wrong," Owen said. "It's terrible, but I bet if we'd stayed around and explored a little more, we would have found tens of zombies, if not hundreds, wandering around Point Peak. And I'm not too keen on getting acid spit into my eyes, or anything else they're reported to do."

"What *are* they reported to do?" Sean asked. "Like what kind of zombies are they? I could kind of see their thoughts in the same way I used to see my zombie clan's thoughts, but it was so different from what I'd experienced."

Owen ran his fingers through his hair. "The first step is staring into the sun and not moving. The second step is developing the acid spit and whatever's fucked up in their blood. The third stage is getting fast—really fast. They can outrun any human and move faster than any animal. The fourth stage is Infecting, similar to the zombie war, but here, Infecting usually means killing."

"Lovely," Sean and I echoed.

"So if any of you start finding a real big interest in what the sun looks like today, be sure to let me know," Owen drawled sarcastically.

"I wonder why that is?" Aspyn said.

"Why what is what?"

"Why they look into the sun. It's obviously damaging, does it mean that it no longer hurts zombie eyes?" She looked from face to face, hoping for an answer.

"I think it's more a 'true north' direction-type thing.

The ones I shot, they all seemed to line their bodies up on an east-west type of bearing. For some reason, focusing in on the sun seems to activate whatever causes the acid, like a weird version of photosynthesis or something."

Aspyn grimaced. "That's gross," she said after a few moments. "So that's why Grace is wearing a raincoat?"

I nodded. "She usually fought a zombie by building up speed, running as fast as she can, and slamming the side of her body into the zombie, which usually knocked them off their feet," I said. "She'd bite the zombie at that point, but I've been trying to stop her from doing it. I don't want to know what acid blood can do to a dog."

Aspyn nodded thoughtfully. "She seems pretty impressive."

I smiled. "She really is. I always say that she's trained me more than I've trained her." I leaned down and ruffled the fur between her ears, and she blinked up at me with a yawn.

"Nothing, go back to sleep," I said soothingly.

Laura asked, "Owen, is it about time to start turning the radio on?

Owen was surprised. "Oh, yes," he said, reaching to the table beside him for the radio. "Let's turn it on."

There was static, as we expected, but we let it be background noise as we stayed on the channel that Wyatt had originally found us on. I wondered how they were faring, if they got around the city all right. They might have had to ditch their vehicle due to the bombing, and walk. It could take them even longer to get here.

"We'll just wait until sunset," Owen offered. "See if

they communicate with us in any meaningful way before then."

We sat in simple silence, enjoying the state of being we were experiencing: home, friends, hearth. Owen fidgeted in his seat, rubbing his wounds against the arm of the chair.

"Owen," I began.

. . . On foot, the broadcast began. *We are skirting the edges of the city and working our way back towards 33. We have . . . and . . . Anna and Brayden are with me. How far out from the perimeter of . . . city are . . .*

Owen shushed me. "We're here, Wyatt," he said into the radio. "We're about twenty miles outside the side of the city. With a child, it should take you until midafternoon."

Copy. We brought food, the broadcast said. *. . . have . . . wagon for Brayden . . .*

"You're cutting out," Owen replied. "We'll say an estimated ETA of three p.m., give you enough time to rest and regroup."

Roger, he said. *Wyatt over and out.*

I snorted. "Well, at least we know they're coming," I said thoughtfully. "Though I don't know what they're expecting to find when they get here."

Sean shrugged. "Maybe they just want a place where nobody's a zombie and nobody's going to bomb them. It's not an unreasonable request."

"No," I agreed. "It's not unreasonable. But it does make me wonder what the future's going to look like. It's obvious that the electricity is not coming on anytime soon, especially if cities are reduced to rubble. We're in this for the home stretch, not just a pass-through."

Laura nodded quietly, resting her head against the doorframe. "I think we need to assume that whatever we do, it's on our own. There's no National Guard to save us this time."

"If that's what you want to call it," I muttered. "They're the ones that gave out the Cure."

"And while it does put you at risk, it brought me back to you, unless you've forgotten that," Sean said softly.

I blinked. Sat there for a moment, before realizing I was in tears. "I'm sorry," I said, choked up. "I'm just so fucking terrified that I'll turn at any moment. I don't know what I'd do, what Grace would do, if I turned. Owen would shoot me, I guess, but—Sean, what would you do without me?"

"We'd be down a medic." Sean smiled a little at me. "Grace would survive. I wouldn't let anything happen to her. If you turn, we'll take care of it, and you won't have to worry about being a zombie forever." He hesitated. "And I'd . . . go on, I guess. With Grace, and everyone else."

I nodded, playing with a loose thread on my shirt. "Thank you," I said. "I just . . . don't want to end up wandering the earth forever, alone, I guess."

Sean reached his hand back out to hold mine and I took it. "We won't let you," he said softly.

There was something drastically wrong with me if I considered that to be good news.

Bad Company

~ Sean ~

It was another fitful night sleeping next to Kiera, with dreams that I couldn't shake. I woke up gasping, remembering the feeling of breaking bones beneath my fingers, crushing them in the palm of my hand. I remembered the feeling of my Links next to me, all of us on the hunt to Kill or Infect.

Part of me wished life was that simple.

I sat up against the headboard and watched her sleep next to Grace. She was tossing and turning, clearly fitful, and I laid a hand on her shoulder to calm her. She curled into my hand, resting her chin against my arm, and I sat there like that for a long time, thinking about what it tasted like to lick the sharp end of a bone and remembering the feeling of someone else's skin slipping through my fingers.

Slowly I untangled myself from Kiera and put a pillow next to her for her to hug, and went downstairs.

Owen was sitting in the kitchen eating slightly expired cereal with fresh cow milk. I kind of wondered if luke-warm milk tasted good on cereal, and it made me want to puke to think about it. Wet cereal was not in my future plans.

I slid onto an open stool at the little island in the middle of the kitchen. "So what's the verdict?"

He grunted. "Heard from them at sunrise," he said around his spoon. "They should be here by late morning. I think they made good time."

I nodded, reaching over for the box of corn puffs and pouring myself a little pile on the island. "I think we should keep checking the radio in the evening," I mused. "See if there's anyone else out there. There have to be more survivors than this."

"Before holing up in that apartment, I took a while to wander through the city," he began. "There were not a ton of people left; at least, every building I walked past looked run-down and there were no lanterns or flashlights at the windows. As I started getting towards the food pantry, I found more of the zombies standing in the sun. On my way back, one of them came after me. He was so fast, Sean," he said.

"He tore after me like a bat out of hell, and it took everything in me to get the door shut without letting him inside. I got back to my apartment, found my gun, and shot him clear through the head from upstairs. It was the only way: he was knocking and pounding down my door, and it was only a matter of time before he'd break every door in the building."

I sighed. "Well, at least headshots still work," I muttered.

"They do," he agreed. "But the acid they splattered all over the stoop started burning the potted plants. It melted right through the leaves."

"Great." It was a lot to take in. "So you think there are more zombies than people? Is that what I'm hearing?"

Owen nodded. "I went to the pantry line a few times, and usually counted between seventy-five and one hundred people in line. I looked at how many apartment buildings are in the city, and did a little math: there were hundreds of empty apartments, meaning their original inhabitants fled during or after the war. I saw a zombie approximately every two streets, which meant that there were at least three times as many zombies as there were people, if not more."

He shrugged. "I don't know how many left after the news about the Cure causing zombie-itis, but it's safe to say that of those one hundred people, hopefully most of them left before the bombing."

I sighed. "But we don't know," I said after a moment. "We don't know how many people were turned and how many people were human. And the government just fucking blew it to hell."

"Yeah," Owen agreed. "But we did the best we could with the knowledge we had."

It didn't feel right, surviving this. This was the second of two zombie apocalypses; who the hell survived two? I groaned and stretched my back, listening to the satisfying *pop* as it cracked. "So what are we going to do? Just be homesteaders now?"

Owen nodded. "I guess so," he mused, then grimaced, covering his arm with his flannel shirt.

"You're not okay," I said quietly.

"Don't tell Kiera," he said gruffly. "I'll be fine. Just get that family here and we'll deal with me when we have the time."

"If it's something to deal with when we have the time, why am I not telling Kiera?" I shot back.

"Because I don't particularly want her to cut off my arm the way she did to you?" he said. "I'll live. I've had infections before. I'll be fine."

His face was flushed, and I could see sweat beading up around his hairline. He was not okay. "If you say so," I muttered.

The proverbial ringing of the bell saved me. I could see out the window behind Owen's head, and a man, woman and child were slowly coming into focus in the distance. "I think they're here," I said.

Owen's brows shot up. "They must have started early," he said. "That's good timing."

Laura wandered into the kitchen, yawning. "What's good timing?"

"The family on the radio is here," I replied.

"Oh! Should I go get Aspyn and Kiera?" She hurried off without waiting for an answer.

"Sure," Owen said, and he picked up his gun from its post by the front door. "Just in case," he explained to me quietly.

"Just in case of what?"

"In case they aren't who they say they are."

Owen was paranoid, given, but I couldn't say that he was always wrong, either. We walked out of the house and stood in the front garden, marigolds flowering near the house, and waited as the family grew larger and larger in our view. Finally, I could see Wyatt, a tall, dark stranger, carrying someone who must be Brayden, who was small and pale. Walking alongside was a woman with braided hair who must be Anna. They looked exhausted.

"Welcome to our own special brand of apocalypse," Owen said, greeting them at the front of the walk.

"Thanks," Wyatt said, struggling to readjust a sleeping Brayden. "It felt like it took forever to get around the damn city. Anna and I couldn't sleep, so we started walking." Anna was pulling along a little red wagon behind her.

"I brought food," she offered. I peered in the wagon; there were several loaves of bread, some spices, canned soups and vegetables. Potatoes, which made my mouth water. Corn, even; we hadn't been able to harvest corn yet. "We can just put it in a communal larder, whatever."

Owen nodded. "I wouldn't recommend the house right across the street, but any of the other houses are fair game. Do you want to meet the others or go pick a house?"

"Let's meet everyone and then pick a house," Anna said in her soft, lilting voice. "I think Brayden needs a nap after all that walking, and Wyatt's muscles are probably screaming carrying him for so long."

"Agreed," Owen chimed in.

"Come on in," I offered, gesturing back toward the house.

We walked to the door together, one rambling group, and convened in the living room. Wyatt set Brayden down on the couch and stretched, letting his back pop. "Glad we made it," he said.

Laura came in, glancing over their shoulders and out the window. "What's in the wagon?"

"Food," Kiera supplied.

"Can I."

"Go for it, I said. "We have a lot to talk about here." Wyatt and his wife looked at me, confused. "She's our resident cook. She keeps us from starving to death out here, and I'm sure she wants to make a big dinner, having you guys here."

Anna nodded. "That makes sense," she said softly. Her gaze sharpened and she saw Grace in the corner of the living room, currently residing as a fluff ball rather than a dog. "Who's that?"

"That would be our zombie-fighting dog," Kiera said. "She's actually not bad at it. It's kind of like watching someone bowl without any knowledge of the game whatsoever."

"Neat. I bet Brayden will love her." Anna smiled. "Is she friendly?"

Kiera nodded. "Yes, but she's very much a one-person dog, so Brayden shouldn't feel bad if he doesn't, like, become her best friend."

Laura was leading Aspyn from the depths of the kitchen toward the front of the house. "This is the rest of our crew," I said.

"It's Owen, Kiera and I," I said, gesturing at us

accordingly, "and Laura and Aspyn. We already gave you our stories, so I won't bore you again."

"Nice to meet you," Aspyn said quietly. She rocked back on her heels, looking nervous.

Laura put a steadying hand on her shoulder. "Nice to meet you," she echoed.

Anna twisted her fingers together, perhaps making an attempt at being less intimidating. "I'm Anna, this is Brayden, and this is Wyatt," Anna said. "We've been walking most of the morning."

Laura grinned. "Are you guys ready for lunch? I made extra."

I explained to the newcomers, "She really has a talent, whereas I could burn rice."

"Has burned rice," Kiera muttered, and we all laughed.

We wandered into the kitchen for our meal, feeling a sense of community that I hadn't had before. Sure, I was *with* the zombies in my Hex, but it wasn't like this—a group banded together by a common obstacle, changing their ways of life. I wondered how many more people might wander up this way; if there was anyone else out there.

~

Wyatt, Anna and Brayden took the house kitty-corner to ours, next to the run-down shack that the cultists had taken over. There were a few animals there that had been subsisting on grass, plants and a pond; it was a nice little place, and I wondered if we'd fill up the rest of the houses in this area by the time everything was said and done.

It wasn't more than a day later that Kiera came running into the house. "Sean!" she cried.

I stood up, dropping the sandwich I was eating. "What's wrong?"

"Owen collapsed," she gasped, trying to catch her breath. "We've got to see if we can get him antibiotics, or a doctor, or something."

I followed her to the fields, where we found Owen laying against a water trough. Sweat beaded on his forehead and rolled down his face; he was flushed. Kiera knelt down next to him and started unwrapping his bandages.

. . . tendons, chewy between my teeth . . . ripping into muscle . . . teeth sinking into brittle bone . . .

I shuddered and tried to come back to the present. Kiera was finally done unwrapping Owen, and we could see bright red lines shooting up and down his arm. "He's got blood poisoning," I said.

Kiera nodded. "I shouldn't have listened to him when he said it was healing. I wanted to believe that he'd be okay, but this . . ."

I walked to the back porch by the fields and rang the triangle to get everyone's attention. It took a few rings, but soon, Laura, Aspyn, Kiera, Owen and I were in a huddle. "What are we going to do?" Laura asked.

Owen groaned, his eyes fluttering. He looked like he had one hell of a fever; his hands were shaking and pale.

"We have to look for antibiotics," Kiera said. "We'll check all the houses in this area, and if we have to, we'll go further. We can't let this spread any more; it's too late to even cut off his arm. I never should have fucking listened to him," she said again, closing her eyes.

"It's not your fault, Kiera," I said. "Owen's the kind of

guy who thinks he can take care of everything. Now he knows he can't. But in the meantime, we need to take care of him."

Aspyn sat down next to Owen, pushing the hair out of his face. She let him rest his head in her lap, and she looked up at us. "He's so hot."

Owen was mumbling, talking to someone or something we couldn't see. I half wished for a fucking zombie bear; at least that I knew what to do with. This was out of my scope of practice by far.

Laura offered, "I read somewhere that many people can survive sepsis. If we get him the right meds, there's a chance we can beat this thing before it takes him."

"Right," Kiera said, standing up and dusting the dirt off of her pants. "Laura and I will take all the houses on this side of the road. Sean, you ask Wyatt for help and take all the houses on the other side. There's about five houses apiece, so it shouldn't take us long."

"Where's Grace?" I asked.

"She's inside eating." Kiera offered a brief smile. "She's safe, don't worry."

We split up, and I went to knock on Wyatt's new door. It took a while to get a response, but when I explained to him what was going on, he shut the door behind him and followed me. We went into the cult house first, wanting to get it out of the way.

The walls were painted black. There was blood, or syrup of some kind, decorating the walls. I saw the big burned area in the middle of the living room, which must have been where they'd started cooking before they took their road show outside. I offered to take the upstairs, Wyatt the downstairs, and we went to work.

I went through each bedroom and bathroom, tearing through drawers and medicine cabinets, but this house had been pretty ransacked. The whole thing was stripped; they hadn't left anything behind. As I met Wyatt downstairs, he reported about the same thing. "There's a dead pig in the backyard," he said. "But I don't know if it was a zombie pig or a regular pig." Shaking his head, he sighed. "Lotta good pork going to waste."

That was a mystery for another day. "Let's go," I said.

We hiked to the next house on the list; it had blue trim and a broad white porch. There was even a swing on the end of the porch so that you could see the sunset. It would have been beautiful, had we not been on a mission.

"Same routine? I'll take downstairs?" Wyatt asked.

"Same routine," I echoed. I leaned on the stairway railing, feeling overwhelmed. This was such a heavy subject: Owen possibly dying. Owen, who had rescued us from a zombie bear, Owen, who had come with me to get Kiera back. I felt so small in the grand scheme of things. Who was I to change the fate of a man?

I dug around through the medicine cabinet, frowning. There were three different kinds of cough syrup, a bottle of ibuprofen, which I pocketed, and some miscellaneous psych meds. The name on the label was *Kim Janeth*, who I assumed was the wife before all went to hell in a handbasket.

No antibiotics, though.

We met downstairs, both of us looking more serious the more time passed. "There's nothing there," he said.

"Let's check the other two houses, and if we don't find anything, we'll make a plan. I know that there's a reservation maybe fifty miles down the road; maybe they have a doctor that can help Owen," I said.

I had to break the door down on the third house, and it was the same there: a few random prescriptions but nothing useful. Wyatt and I were running out of places to look, and Owen was running out of time.

"Last house," I said, panting a little from going up and down so many stairs.

I went upstairs, my legs feeling heavy. If there wasn't something in here, we'd be sunk. "Hey," I called. "Do you know what vancomycin is?"

I heard him running up the stairs. "That's an antibiotic," he gasped. "Holy fuck! Hopefully, we found it in time. Let's go!"

We ran out of the house and towards our little farmhouse, out towards the backyard and fields where we had left Owen with Kiera and Aspyn. I gave her the little bottle, and she shook out two pills. "Go get him some water," Kiera ordered.

When I returned with the water, I saw her tilting his head back and putting the pills in his mouth. She carefully poured the liquid down his throat, making him swallow, and sighed. "I don't know if this will help," she said carefully. "He might need something stronger, or a combination of things to beat this. We might not be out of the woods yet."

I nodded. "Wyatt, let's get Owen into bed. You carry his head, and I'll carry his feet." We hefted up the not-very-small man between us, maneuvering awkwardly as we carried him inside the house and toward his bedroom. "Where's Anna and Brayden?" I asked.

"It's Brayden's nap time," he explained, huffing and puffing beneath Owen's weight. "She brought three or four storybooks to entertain him with. Stories get him to fall asleep quick, every time."

We bumped Owen's head against the doorframe, and he groaned. "Sorry," I whispered, before we righted ourselves and dropped Owen on the bed fully clothed and dirty. "Do you think we should clean it again?"

"Can't hurt," Wyatt said. I ran to get the bottle of peroxide and we poured it onto the cuts, wincing as it audibly popped and snapped. I used a spare handkerchief to wipe the pus away and noticed how swollen his arm was. Hell, maybe this *was* a cut-off-the-arm situation. We'd done it before, and it had bought me some time. Maybe it would buy Owen the same.

"What are we going to do?" Wyatt said as we sat and watched the wound bleed freely, finally, with no pus.

"I guess give him the antibiotics as it says on the bottle, and if that doesn't work, we'll go on a field trip," I said quietly. "I don't know much about the reservation. I don't know if they'll be welcoming outsiders at all, or if it's a moot point."

He sighed, rubbing the dirt away from his eyes. "Understood," he said warily. "I guess a trial by fire is the best way to get acclimated to a new community. Well, I'm going to go back to Brayden and Anna. Ring the triangle again if you need me?"

"I will," I said, and watched him disappear down the stairs. I sat next to Owen as Laura came trailing in with new bandages and some Neosporin. "Do you really think this is a Neosporin situation?" I asked her.

She shrugged. "Antibacterial ointment can't hurt at this point, so why the fuck not?" She slathered a layer of gel across the angry red wounds and rebandaged them tightly.

"Do you think we should cut off his arm?" I asked.

She blinked. "I can't say it's occurred to me . . ." She looked at my stump. "Then again, you do have experience in these things. Maybe we should ask Owen when he wakes up."

Owen was calling out in his sleep, or his passed-out state, whichever. His eyes were twitching beneath the lids, and his hands clasped and unclasped rapidly. He sat up all at once and took a deep, gasping breath. "What the fuck happened?"

I put my hand on his shoulder to steady him. "You collapsed in the fields," I told him. "We found some antibiotics and are hoping this is all we need to patch you up."

"Great," he mumbled, rubbing his eyes with his free hand. "So it is as bad as it looks, then?"

Nodding, I sighed. "It's as bad as it looks, according to Kiera, and random internet knowledge in the back of our collective brains. I do have to ask . . ."

"What?" Owen groaned and sat back against the headboard.

"Do you think we should cut your arm off?" I asked in a rush. "Or should we push for the reservation and see if they have any doctors there?"

He blinked. "It would be very hard to shoot people with one arm," he said after a moment. "I vote no on the cutting-my-arm-off thing, and yes to the reservation."

"All right," I said carefully. To be honest, looking at the red streaks, I didn't know if amputation would fix anything or not. It hadn't kept me from turning into a zombie, it just bought me some time to come to terms with it. Owen was a very gung-ho sort of guy, and I knew if he couldn't protect himself from zombies in the manner to which he was accustomed, he wouldn't be happy.

"Let's let him rest," Laura said after a few moments. Owen sunk back against the bed, freshly bandaged and exhausted.

We walked downstairs quickly, reconvening next to the triangle outside. "He's resting now," I reported. "And he doesn't want to consider amputation."

"I don't even think it would do it at this point," Laura added. "The antibiotics need time to work."

"We'll give it three days," Kiera said finally. "If he doesn't make some kind of improvement in three days, we'll truss up one of the wagons and pull him behind us. If we take turns, it shouldn't be too bad." She paused. "That being said, who's volunteering to go? I don't want to assume that all of you are on board with this plan."

Laura raised a hand. "If I have to stay here, I'll go stir-crazy," she said. "I'd rather be helping than holding down the fort."

"So that's what, me, Kiera, and Laura," I said thoughtfully. "Aspyn?"

She shook her head shyly. "I think I'd like to stay behind and watch the little boy if they need me," she said. "That's much more up my alley than traipsing around the countryside trying to find a miracle cure."

"Noted," I said. I rang the triangle again, and we waited. It took several moments for Wyatt to get to the back field.

"What's up?" he said. His dark hair was blowing into his face in the wind.

"We're giving him three days on the antibiotics, if he doesn't get any better we're pulling him in a wagon behind us, and we wanted to know if you'd rather stay here or come with." I picked at the dirt underneath my fingernails, knowing that I was asking a lot. "It's just me, Kiera, and Laura, and I don't know how long they can pull him without being tired. I really need someone else to help cart him around."

Wyatt thought about this for a moment.

"I'll stay to take care of your wife and your little boy," Aspyn volunteered quietly. "We can watch over the animals and take care of the crops. You've got a nice pigpen behind your house, I'm sure Brayden would love feeding them."

He smiled a little. "No, I agree," he said, looking troubled. "I definitely think you need more than the three of you to go on this little jaunt. Let me talk it over with the wife, and I'll get back to you about it tomorrow?"

I nodded. "Sounds like a plan, sir. Thanks."

He disappeared toward the front of the house, and we collectively sighed. This was a lot; an adventure of this magnitude required planning and foresight that we were seriously lacking, not knowing what the terrain looked like or what we'd face, even if we followed the roads.

"Let's get some dinner and regroup," I said finally. "Laura, what's on tap for today?"

"Chicken and beans," she offered. "First time we'll have meat in a while."

I chose not to think particularly hard about what that meant for the poor chicken. Being removed from our food sources kept much of this country sane, and knowing that some chicken had gotten its head cut off because of me didn't sit well in my soul. "All right," I said.

I took Kiera's hand in mine and led the way inside the house, Laura trailing along behind us. We could do this; we could save Owen. We just had to give him the pills and he'd be fine.

~

It was day three of the antibiotics, and Owen wasn't improving. He was pale, ashen gray, and clammy, and we couldn't wait any longer. Laura, Kiera and I staggered down the stairs with Owen in our arms (arm and a half for me, really) and loaded him into the larger of the two wagons. He didn't quite fit, but it was better than nothing. Wyatt met us at the front of the house as I pulled Owen behind me.

"Is Anna okay with this?" I asked curiously.

"She thinks that we should help anyone that fought for us to get to safety," he said after a moment. "Owen was the one who found us and brought us here, so if I can return the favor, I will." His longish hair was pulled back in a small braid and he wore a green *Avengers* shirt. I had to give the guy an A-plus for effort.

Our backpacks had been packed for two days. We weren't quite confident that the antibiotic wouldn't work, but it seemed as if Owen was going to need some help that we couldn't give him.

"So how do you know about this reservation, anyway?" Wyatt asked.

"I used to ride my motorcycle down there with a friend," I answered. "Before Kiera, anyway. There's some awesome views out there, trees and lakes and shit."

"Sounds nice," he said, and we started to walk.

I thought about my motorcycle; I hadn't, not since Kiera cut my hand off. I wondered where it was now, if someone had driven it to safety. I didn't usually find myself getting so maudlin with inanimate objects, but riding my motorcycle was a big deal before I found Kiera. It was my first taste of freedom at eighteen. I hoped that wherever she was, she was being taken care of the way she should be.

Owen was half collapsed, half sitting up in the wagon. It was a fairly deep wagon, made for keeping more than one child inside. I wondered where Wyatt and Anna had gotten it; they only had one child. Or did they?

"Where'd you get the wagon?" I asked after a moment.

"Baby shower present," Wyatt answered softly. "Turns out we didn't need it for its intended purpose after all."

Oh. *Oh.* "That sucks, man," I said lamely. "I'm sorry to

hear that. How old is your son?"

"He's three," he replied, hefting his backpack over his shoulder. "Just old enough to have opinions but not know what to do with them."

I chuckled. "That sounds about right," I mused. We walked in silence down the road together, the four of us, with Laura behind the wagon to keep watch over Owen. Kiera was beside myself and Wyatt, and we were making pretty good time, as far as I could tell.

I wondered if Kiera and I would ever have kids. Hell, if I *could* even have kids, after being a zombie. It wasn't something I'd ever given much thought to, but it was a talk that we should probably have eventually. I looked over at Kiera, who was deep in thought with Grace trailing next to her. Because of course we brought the dog.

Kiera would have killed me if I'd left Grace behind.

The first day was pretty uneventful. We fed Owen his antibiotics and he came in and out of consciousness, sweating profusely and shivering. It was almost like the antibiotics were trying to help, but they just weren't strong enough. I hoped that whoever we met on the other side of the river would be friendly and willing to help.

The next day, we refolded our little tents and stashed them in our backpacks. We ate some beef jerky that Laura had packed for us, and we continued on, trying to save our friend.

It was a long-ass walk. Most of the bottoms of our backpacks were dedicated to water, though we had those big straws you could purify water through. We wanted to save them for last, since we couldn't exactly replace the filter in three months or anything. We set up camp that evening, with Owen still shivering in his sleep, and I put my spare blanket over him and pushed the wagon near the fire to warm him up. Laura gave him his pills, and we sat beside each other around the fire, quiet for a long time.

"So we're about halfway there," I said thoughtfully. "If we don't take too many breaks, we should be there tomorrow night."

Laura nodded, spooning a bit of rice and beans into her travel bowl. "How sure are you that these people want anything to do with us?"

I swallowed around my spoon. "Not at all," I admitted. "I had a buddy up there for a while, but we lost touch. I only know they have a doctor on the reservation because it was his uncle."

"Makes sense," Wyatt said. "If I were living on a reservation, I wouldn't want to bring in outside doctors either. I'd want to stay as true to my way of life as I could, and fuck everybody else."

I agreed. "I think once they see Owen and hear our story, they might be more amenable to helping."

"What is our story, exactly?" Laura asked, taking another bite.

"We figured out that staying in Point Peak was a really fucking bad idea and made our way to a farm village," I said after a moment. "We have me and Kiera, Wyatt, Anna and Brayden, and Laura and Aspyn. Owen's the one who got us there and saved us from a zombie bear. So we owe it to him to try to help him, if we can."

"Speaking of zombie bears, does it seem a little too quiet to any of you?" Kiera said in a stage whisper.

I blinked. "It kind of does," I said slowly. My eyes scanned the tree lines on each side of us, trying to find what had made the woods so damn silent.

Wyatt tensed, looking out over the fire. Laura grabbed her flashlight and started shining it on the groups of trees, and Grace started growling, low in her throat, her posture ready to pounce. She, of course, was wearing her Doge suit.

It took us a while to find it, but when we did, a chorus of "fuck"s echoed throughout the clearing. What we found was a giant buck, with huge antlers, and it was running in that lopsided, too-fast way that we'd become accustomed to with zombies.

"You've got to be kidding me," Kiera said. She stood up and freed her hatchet-mop from her backpack. The rest of us got our weapons out as well; Wyatt had made a machete-rod with some duct tape, so he was in good company with the rest of us.

The buck reared back and growled, a hissing sound that didn't feel natural. I could see him tossing his antlers back and forth, scraping at the dirt, almost as if he was daring us to charge him.

"Don't approach him, but if he comes here, let's fuck him up," Laura said.

"I don't think we're going to have a choice," I said as the buck reared back and charged.

We formed a circle around Owen and Grace bared her teeth. She took off running at the buck, body-slamming it in the side with her Doge spikes, then quickly shook herself free, bouncing back toward the circle. I swatted at the zombie with my cleaver-rod, and managed to hack off a good chunk of the side of his body.

As the deer moved, it circled into Keira and Grace's territory. Grace stayed behind Kiera as she swung hard, and I could hear the meaty *thunk* as her hatchet found purchase in the buck's neck. She had to haul the hatchet-mop out from the buck, making sure it didn't get stuck in a rib.

The zombie buck howled: it was a sound that I'd never experienced before, not even at a zoo. He threw his head back and he howled, and all of a sudden, there were two more zombie deer in the area. One female and one younger male.

Fuck.

"Kiera and Grace, take the female. Wyatt, you take the younger male. Laura and I will stay on the buck," I called. It was a dizzying array of weaponry and antlers, with a *crash* every few moments as the deer charged only to be met by our makeshift weapons.

Kiera and Grace squared off with Bambi's mom, and I stood next to Laura and her Meat-Siah as the buck reared back and charged again. I felt the impact of my cleaver-rod against its chest before he opened his mouth.

It took everything in me to pull back and get out of the way before he spit on me. The acid stuck to the dirt, sizzling and burning what little grass there had been. "So now we have acid-spitting zombie deer," I muttered.

"Not the time, Sean!" Laura crowed as she drove the Meat-Siah into the flank of the deer. With a shuddering sigh, he finally fell, the ground vibrating when he lay down for the final time. He had been one hell of a buck, that was for sure. It almost made me sad, except for the part where he had tried to spit acid at me.

Kiera and Grace were tag-teaming the mom. Both circled around her, one on either side, then attacked. Bambi's mom didn't see it coming, and her head was sliced cleanly off underneath Kiera's hatchet-mop.

Wyatt was having trouble with the young male, but Laura was faster than I was. She heaved her Meat-Siah and hacked into the neck of the young buck. It fell hard, taking her with it, and she wrenched her weapon out from between its vertebrae, only to quickly stand up.

"What is it?" I asked.

She was jumping and tearing off the sweatshirt she was wearing over her T-shirt. "I got some acid on me," she exclaimed. We rushed to her aid, but it hadn't gone through the T-shirt; she was safe. For now.

"So that was an adventure," Kiera said mildly. She reached into her backpack and got some Lorna Doones for Grace, a crowd favorite for sure.

Owen was still lying in the wagon moaning, but I wondered if it had been his scent or his voice that called to the deer family. "Should we move on? I know we didn't really sleep, but . . ."

"But we don't know what the fuck else is in those woods," Laura supplied. "Let's go. I'll take a turn with the wagon."

We all slung our weapons through our backpacks and started off again, into the dying light of midnight. Owen was calling out quietly; I heard the name "Susan" pass his lips more than once. I wondered if that had been his wife or girlfriend or something. Truth be told, we really didn't know much about Owen and what his life was like before he joined our little troupe.

Kiera sighed, leaning toward me and bumping me with her shoulder. "How are you holding up?"

"Glad I didn't choose the crowbar," I said blithely. "I didn't want that fucker anywhere near me."

"Me either," she chuckled. We kept walking until early in the morning, where we finally found a run-down diner in the middle of the dirt road. I broke the door with my crowbar and we set up watch: Laura was on first watch, I was on second, and Wyatt was on third. Kiera was on breakfast duty, even if that meant just passing out more disgusting beef jerky.

I settled down across her in one of the booths. We moved the table so there was nothing between us. "Can't anything ever go right?" she complained.

"No," I said solemnly. "No, it can't. Because this is a fucked-up world we live in with fucked-up creatures and fucked-up humans that bomb cities and toss around Cures that can get you killed. We're on our own, Kiera. And that means nothing will go right until this is all over."

"Over?" she echoed. "I don't know that it'll ever be over."

I nodded, resting my head on my arm. "Let's get some sleep," I said finally. "Things will look better in the light of the morning.

Trips and Traps
~ Kiera ~

We headed out at first light, pulling Owen behind us as we went. Laura had made oatmeal for breakfast, and somehow, she'd managed to make it taste pretty good. It wasn't too far of a walk to the reservation, but it took us most of the day to get there, with us trading Owen back and forth so we could have breaks.

Owen himself was miserable. He did not want to be carted anywhere; he did not want to be seen as vulnerable, or that was how I read his disgust. He said very little as we hauled him up the freeway, passing two exits and finally hitting a small sign on the side of the road.

—Chantigua Reservation—

It was Sean's turn to pull Owen, and we veered in the direction of the reservation. It was so quiet, now that cars weren't really a thing anymore; Wyatt had said he hadn't seen a single car on his way up to the interstate. We walked through a small passageway between trees and ended up at a wooden gate with the same sign on it.

"Should we, like, knock?" Laura asked cautiously.

"They know we're here," Sean said mildly. "They have cameras and shit all over the place, I know they have solar panels and stuff like that."

As if he had summoned someone with his voice, the gate opened, and a man stepped out. He had long, braided hair and wore a button-up shirt and slacks. He was taller than any of us; I felt like a dwarf as he came up beside us.

"Sean. I recognize you. What are you doing here? Why do you have so many people with you?"

"Hey, Brandon. We have a problem. We had to leave and then they bombed the city, so we couldn't go back, and we chose to hang out on some of the farms just south of here. We were doing fine until Owen had a run-in with an annoyed bull and some razor wire, and now he's dealing with one hell of an infection. I can't imagine that there are any doctor's clinics besides yours anywhere in the area," Sean explained.

Brandon nodded. "And who are your friends?"

Sean smiled and pulled me up toward him. "This is Kiera, my fiancée. The man on the wagon is Owen, our resident sharpshooter and cow-carer person. Laura and Wyatt are behind us; we picked them up off the radios when they were trying to get out of the city."

"Well, I'm sure Jax will be happy to see you again. He loved that motorcycle," Brandon said. "Come on in, we'll see what Doc can do."

We followed Brandon down the dirt path, and I was surprised to see some pretty big log cabins built on either side of the road. I didn't know what I'd expected, but I hadn't expected this. They were expertly made as far as I could tell, and they definitely looked modern.

Brandon stopped us about halfway down the main road and gestured for us to wait. He knocked on the door, and a man with long, gray hair let him in. We couldn't hear what they were saying; all I could do was hope that Brandon was the right guy to introduce us to his doctor friend so that we could get Owen treated.

"Let's bring him in," a gray-haired man said, popping his head out from behind the door. "What exactly happened to him?"

Wyatt and Sean struggled to lift Owen, getting him on the metal table in one of several different rooms. I didn't know what kind of things this doctor normally saw, but surely a rogue cow wouldn't be beyond his skills.

"Hi, I'm Kiera," I said to the gray-haired man.

He grunted. "I'm Saphi. What's wrong with your friend?"

"He turned his back on a bull," I explained. "Ran him right into the razor wire fence. It's pretty infected; we luckily found some vancomycin, but it hasn't brought down his fever or gotten rid of his infection."

Laura nodded. "He said he only turned his back for a second, and here we are. He was instrumental in rescuing me from a zombie cult, and I'm a little worried about him."

"A zombie cult?" he chuckled. "That's a new one. Tell

me about this zombie cult," he said as he rolled Owen's sleeve up.

"A bunch of crackheads are boiling zombie flesh and feeding it to their people. They are awaiting the call of the messiah, or at least that's what I was always told. I have some rather unpleasant memories regarding the boiling of the zombies," Laura said quietly.

"Understood," Sachi said. "It's interesting that boiling zombie flesh seems to negate some of the acidic properties of the Infection," he mused thoughtfully. "I've seen a bunch of animals come down with it, and I wouldn't have thought to boil them for food."

He assessed Owen's arm with a sigh. "This is very infected," he began. "I'll have to clean it out and debride it, and we'll put him on some IV antibiotics to hopefully get this thing cleared. You." He pointed to Sean.

"Oh, sorry. I'm Sean," he said. "This is Wyatt."

"Either way, you two, carry him to the room back by the left. There's a more comfortable chair to sit on while he gets his antibiotics that he won't fall out of."

Wyatt nodded. "Aye aye, Captain," he said, and he took Owen's legs as Sean took his arms.

"I really think that I could walk by myself," Owen said weakly. Sean almost dropped him; it was the first thing that he'd said in miles.

"No, you couldn't," Saphi answered. "You've got blood poisoning, sepsis. Let them carry you. It'll be fine."

Owen sighed heavily and seemed to drift back off into sleep. Wyatt and Sean got him into the puffy green recliner, and Saphi sat down next to him on a stool with a small table of tools. "Brandon, why don't you see if we can feed these people? They've come a long way, and this will take me a while."

Brandon nodded. "All right. Everyone not involved in treating Owen, follow me." He led us out of the doctor's office and through a maze of streets; if someone asked me how to get to the heart of this village? Town? City? I would never be able to tell them where to go. The streets were all dirt, and I saw more than a few animals.

"I'm glad you remembered me," Sean offered to Brandon as we walked.

"How could I forget? Jax talked about his motorcycle rides with you for an entire year. He was upset when you stopped coming."

Sean blushed sheepishly. "Can I blame the woman for that one? I suddenly had a lot more to pay attention to than the motorcycle."

I smacked his shoulder. "You didn't come back because of me?"

Sean nodded. "It just got so busy with school and work and everything. I didn't really go on joyrides anymore."

Wyatt interjected. "I can vouch for that," he offered. "Women are by far the biggest distraction that you'll ever have."

Laura and I scowled. "Thanks, I think," I said. "But it's not my responsibility to keep you in contact with your friends."

"Ouch," Brandon said mildly. "She's got you there."

Sean sighed. "You're not wrong," he said finally. "I'll apologize to Jax. If we ever get to a place where motorcycles are a thing again, I'll take him for another ride."

Brandon smiled. "He'd like that. But I don't think we have much of a chance for motorcycles to 'become a thing again.'"

"What's been your experience with everything that's gone on?" Wyatt asked him quietly as we were led into one big common room with a neglected TV, a pool table, and ping pong.

"They didn't bother to give us the Cure," he said after a few moments. "So we're seeing two types of zombies now: ones that are from the original war, and ones that are newer, faster, and more dangerous. We don't usually see people Infected, but I sure as hell have seen some zombie moose that I don't want to make trouble with."

"Did the first war result in a lot of zombie animals for you guys?" I asked.

Brandon shook his head. "Not really, no. I don't think it was transmissible to animals originally. Whatever they did to cured people, that's what led to having the animal zombies."

"It seems like you guys are doing all right," Laura chimed in. "Without electricity, without everything we're missing."

Brandon snorted. "We have to," he said. "The electricity wasn't always great in the first place, even with the solar panels, so we're semiused to dealing with lanterns, fires, and wood stoves. It wasn't a far stretch of the imagination for us to live like this."

Sean plopped down on one of the couches in the

common room, and I followed suit. We all sat down around a big, custom wooden table, made out of a tree so wide around that I couldn't even imagine it. I wondered how the hell they had made such a tree into something like this.

"So what's going to happen to Owen?" I asked finally, reaching down to pet Grace.

"Doc'll give him IV antibiotics and probably steroids," Brandon said. "Gotta perk him up a little bit, with how low his energy is."

Laura asked, "Do you think it's going to work? Like, we can save his arm?

Brandon thought about it for a few moments. "I think so," he said finally. "Doc has saved patients farther gone. I remember one man was attacked by a zombie bear, and had similar injuries, just deeper and longer. He recovered after a while; I think Owen will be okay eventually, but it might be touch and go for a little while."

"So what kind of defense do you have here against zombies?" Sean asked. "We're on plots of farmland south of here. Nice little community of houses. It'd be nice to know what we can do to make it safer."

Brandon nodded thoughtfully. "We have a perimeter fence, as you saw. We don't get *many* zombie animals, but we do have a loose guarding schedule mapped out. We've had two zombie moose, I think? And several deer. Sometimes we get a person coming in from the interstate, similar to the way you got here; we're not exactly out by the road where people can get direct access to us."

"Gotcha," Sean said.

Wyatt chimed in. "So what would you recommend we do to secure our farmhouses and land? We've got a bunch of animals between the two houses we're currently using."

Brandon had to think about that for a moment. "Definitely mark the borders with razor wire," he said eventually.

"We've got razor wire. I'm not sure how much, but we do have some," Sean said.

"I'll give you some when you leave, we've got coils and coils of it. Running fence line around your property laced with razor wire keeps the majority of the animals and people out; it just slices them up until they can't move anymore." Brandon shrugged. "Easy."

"Definitely have to fence in the field in back," Laura said. "That's where we saw the zombie deer."

"Zombie deer are certainly a threat out here," Brandon said. "I've seen about a dozen of them. I don't know where they came from or how they got Infected, but I know there was a group of hunters out in the woods when everything started back up again for the second round of the apocalypse. Maybe the acid-spitters got to the deer, who knows?"

I nodded, thinking for a while. "Have you had anyone on the reservation become Infected yet?"

Brandon sighed. "Yes," he said simply. "We had a few people who went to the city and were exposed to the Cure. It wasn't all of them, but a good bit of them started showing signs of being zombies pretty early on, maybe two months ago. They were staring into the sun, staggering, but they were quick."

Sean nodded. "I was turned during the war," he explained quietly. "I can't exactly read the zombies' minds like I could before; it's just a jumbled mess. I don't know what's so different about these zombies that they aren't thinking the same way we did."

Brandon blinked in surprise. "You were a zombie?"

Sean held up his stump. "Didn't get to chop the arm off in time," he said mildly. "We tried, but I turned, and Kiera had to throw me to the wolves."

I cringed. I really didn't like hearing about how I'd practically abandoned Sean to the zombies once he started turning. I knew that it had to be done, but the reminder hurt all over again.

I said, "So you have both types of zombies here?"

He nodded again. "We've got some that wandered onto our property from the first war, locked up in a shed about half a mile down the road. We don't really know what to do with them, but they're there in case we need to study them or anything."

Sean swallowed hard. "They probably can think," he added quietly. "They have thoughts and Links to each other. It's probably torture to stay in a shed by themselves, not allowed to be out in the world."

"Really? Your experience was that you could think as a zombie?" he asked.

"Yeah," Sean said. "It was difficult, and different, but I had thoughts and feelings. I could feel my Hexmates—the zombies that were in our little mental telepathy group—and they at least had rudimentary thought, if not almost full ability to think."

Brandon was pale. "What should we do with them?" he asked finally.

Sean shrugged. "There might be a chance that they'll get exposed to the Cure eventually," he said. "You could keep them in an open enclosure, give them some room to think, and keep the rest of the reservation away from them."

Brandon nodded. "I'll get on that right away," he said. "I didn't realize they could think. They must be in a frenzy being locked in a shed."

"It wouldn't be fun," Sean explained. "There's such an intense drive to Infect and kill. I remember trying to think about what I was doing, to internalize the actions I was completing. But I couldn't, no matter how hard I tried; I wanted to reconcile how I felt about killing humans with my new drive to Infect or eat them, and I couldn't."

"Thanks for letting us know," Brandon said. "If you don't mind, I'll step out now and take care of that."

Sean nodded, and so did the rest of us. It took a little while before anyone tried to speak. "So your experience as a zombie was . . . different?" Laura asked, hesitating.

"Yeah. I was at least partly cognizant, I wasn't mindless like the new, acid-spitting zombies seem to be."

Wyatt exhaled slowly. "Well, it's good news that the new zombies don't appear to be sentient," he offered. "I haven't seen many of them together, so I don't know if there are any added benefits of a group, but the ones I've seen so far were purely reactionary, spitting and ripping with their nails."

Sean nodded. "That's what we've seen," he said. "They

have the same drive to kill, but I don't think they're trying to Infect anyone. The acid doesn't turn you into a zombie, it just melts you, so I think we're in the clear on that one."

"Right," Wyatt said. He leaned back in his chair and sighed. "This is such a fucking mess."

"Agreed," Laura said. "But at least we know Owen is in good hands, and you've been able to free the possibly sentient zombies, Sean. We can count that as our good deed for the day."

Sean just nodded, looking disturbed. I made a mental note to ask him about it privately when we set up to sleep. He wouldn't meet my eyes, and I frowned.

"So what's the plan here?" I said abruptly.

"I guess we wait here until someone comes to get us," Laura said finally.

"At least it's indoors, relatively warm, and safe," Wyatt said.

"It's probably the safest we've been in a while. No zombie deer getting past the razor wire and the guard." Sean slid his feet under him and sat crisscrossed. "But I could really use something to eat."

Laura smiled. "I don't know what they have," she said. "But the next time someone comes in to check on us, I'll see what I can do."

"You're such a great cook, Laura—where did you learn that from?" Sean asked.

She shrugged. "My grandmother cooked a lot," she explained. "And I was always in her kitchen causing mischief, so eventually she put me to work."

We started talking about potential recipes with the meat,

eggs and produce we were working on back "home." It was nearly dark out when Brandon came back to check on us.

"Are you all okay?" he asked.

Wyatt nodded. "We're a little hungry, though, do you have a kitchen or something?"

"Oh, shit, I totally forgot," Brandon said. "Yeah, there's a kitchen through the double doors on the other side of the building. Help yourself to anything you want. They're gas stoves, so you can just light them with some of the matches we've got. Feel free to make yourselves at home. What are your plans for tonight?"

Sean shrugged. "I thought we were going to be making camp," he said.

"Well, you can stay here," Brandon offered. "There's blankets in the closet behind you, and the furniture is pretty comfy. I'll go check on Doc and Owen."

He left us to our own devices, and Laura and Wyatt disappeared into the kitchen, followed by some banging of pots and clanging of pans. I didn't know what they'd found, but I was excited to find out.

"Are you okay?" I asked Sean.

He shook his head. "I just . . . if I had been shut in a shed like that, I don't know that I would have come out of being a zombie okay," he said. "It's such an intense need to Infect and kill. I wouldn't be surprised if they're frenzied at this point. I'm going to ask Brandon exactly what he did with them in the morning."

I nodded, reaching over and lacing my fingers with his. "Well, now they'll be free, hopefully."

"Yeah," Sean exhaled. "At least there's that."

~

Brandon came back for us in the morning. Sean was true to his word, and cornered him immediately, asking, "What did you end up doing with the zombies?"

"We made a makeshift, fenced-in field for them in the woods west of here," he explained. "There's a lot of game there, they can Infect zombie bears, maybe. Depends on how the virus evolves, I guess."

"Thank you," Sean said simply. "I couldn't imagine being locked in a shed for . . . how long now?"

Brandon grimaced. "About six months," he admitted.

Sean closed his eyes briefly. "That sucks," he said. "But at least they're better off now."

Brandon nodded. "I see Laura and Wyatt commandeered the kitchen early," he mentioned. "What are you all going to have?"

"Eggs and toast," Laura called from the kitchen. "With strawberry jam."

"I haven't had jam in a long time," I admitted. "Lots of peanut butter, but no jam."

"It'll be a nice change," Sean said. He still looked bothered. I made a note to ask him about things the next time we were alone.

We all sat around the large table, eating our breakfast with Brandon. "Doc says that Owen's started responding to the antibiotics," he said. "It'll be another couple days before he's safe to travel, but he's on the mend."

"Oh, good." I sagged in my chair with relief. "So we got here in time."

"Seems like it," Brandon said. "Sean, Jax asked about you. He's at my house, if you'd like to visit him."

"I'd love that," Sean replied. "He's a good kid."

Brandon stood up and slapped his hands against his thighs. "Well, let's go, then. What are you guys going to do while we're gone?"

"I have no idea," I answered honestly. "But we'll come up with something."

Sean and Brandon disappeared out the door, and Laura, Wyatt and I were alone. I sighed, briefly closing my eyes. "At least we have a home to go to," I said, reaching down to pet Grace's head. She leaned into the contact, and I wondered if they had anything for her to eat; we'd packed dog food, but she was such a good dog and deserved so much more.

"Laura, what can we give to Grace for breakfast?" I asked.

She thought about it for a moment. "She can have the rest of the eggs, and I thought I saw some venison in the larder," she replied. "We can give her some of that, too."

Laura went off to grab the food, and Wyatt and I sat in the common room together. "So there was a zombie cult, huh?" he asked finally.

I nodded briefly. "They fed people zombie flesh. They fed *me* zombie flesh. It was horrible."

"I wonder why it didn't Infect you," he mused thoughtfully. "I don't know much about this new breed of zombie."

"What we'd heard was that people who were exposed to the Cure were gradually changing into acid-spitters; not all of them, thank God, but enough that it's a concern."

I shrugged, trying to seem casual. "So I'm definitely at risk."

Wyatt winced. "I didn't get exposed to the Cure," he admitted. "We were outside the city the whole time that was going on."

I nodded. "It's okay," I reassured him. "Sean knows what to do if I become a zombie."

"You put that on him?" he asked.

I frowned. "What do you mean?"

"I mean he's your—fiancé, husband, whatever he is—and he's the one who has to put you down?"

I sighed. "I had to cut his arm off and shove him out of the door when he became a zombie," I explained. "It was the hardest thing I've ever done in my life. I didn't know when I'd see him again. *If* I'd ever see him again. There was no Cure when I turned him loose in our apartment building. I guess we want to 'keep it in the family,' so to speak."

"I guess that makes sense. But damn, I don't know what that would do to a person, having to put down their significant other," he added. "How worried do we need to be?"

I shook my head. "I don't know," I admitted. "It doesn't seem like an across-the-board thing. Some people that were exposed to the Cure, and weren't original zombies, are turning, for sure. But I can't say it's, like, fifty percent or something. The government started bombing things before we could make sense of it."

"I wonder how many cities they firebombed," he said. "The radio only reaches so far. We had heard about another group of survivors in the city, but we don't know if they'd gotten out in time. It was kind of horrifying to think about."

Nodding, I sighed. "It's just a big fucking mess," I said. "But we do have somewhere to go, when we leave here. We're safe at the farm. I know we can make a go of it there, at least."

"It seems we've stumbled onto a pretty good setup," he said. "I wonder how Anna and Jax are doing with Aspyn?"

"I have no idea. Aspyn is very young. I'm surprised she survived on her own, getting to the feedstore before the bombing. I don't know if I'd have been able to do that at her age."

"Same," he said. Laura came back with a little plate of meat and eggs and Grace started wolfing it down. Wyatt added, "Where'd you get the dog, anyway?"

I smiled. "I found her in our apartment building. She was barking behind a closed door, so we forced the door open and found her."

"Who's we?" Laura asked.

"Me and Brett," I said, a little sadly. I still didn't know how I felt about Brett's death. It was so sudden, and he had meant a lot to me in the short time we'd been together.

Laura seemed interested. "What happened?"

"I had an inside source, Callie, for the war. She was working with the National Guard when they stormed the city. I don't really know how Sean's zombie cadre got there, but we made our way into the college where the National Guard was, and had to kill a lot of zombies to get there," I explained. "I wonder what Callie's doing now."

Wyatt snorted. "If she's working with the National Guard, she's probably bombing innocent civilians," he said. "I don't know how many people were left in Point Peak when they bombed it, but there had to have been at least a few hundred people."

"I just don't understand why they did it," I blurted out. "Were the zombies really hurting anyone? What was the method to the madness?"

"They're fast, and when they're together, they seem to coordinate. They were dangerous. I don't know why they chose bombing to take care of it, but there was definitely a chance of them Infecting the rest of the city and growing from there," he said.

"Sean said he could kind of hear one of the zombies," I said. "I don't know if he can hear zombie animals, though. I'll have to ask him about that."

Wyatt nodded. "I don't know how animals think, but it could be interesting. Grace was exposed to the Cure as well, wasn't she?"

I leaned down, petting Grace to comfort myself. "I don't know," I admitted. "I don't know if she was exposed to the Cure. So she could turn into an acid-spitting dog at any moment."

"Why do you keep her around?" Laura asked quietly.

I struggled to find the words. "Because I love her," I said simply. "She's saved me in a lot of different ways. Either by being emotional support, or attacking zombies, or just by lighting up the dark times. It's worth the risk, to have her with me."

"I was surprised when you didn't leave her at the farm," Wyatt said.

"Why?" I asked.

"Because she'd be safer there," he explained. "And Aspyn and Anna could have taken care of her."

I shook my head. "No," I said finally. "She's better off with me. We know each other. We take care of each other. She's been by my side through the hardest shit I've ever been through, and I'm not going to leave her behind."

"Fair enough," Wyatt said. He looked down at Grace, who was licking the plate clean. "She's a pretty good dog. I have to say, I never would have thought to teach a dog how to hunt zombies."

I smiled briefly. "Yeah," I said. "It just made sense at the time. She was all I had, after I lost Sean. There was no way I was going to leave her behind. Besides, she's pretty good at it."

Wyatt nodded and Laura chimed in. "What are you going to do if she turns?"

I swallowed hard. "I don't know," I admitted softly. "Set her free in the woods, maybe. I know she wouldn't want to hurt us, but I don't think that can be helped." My mood turned morose, and I settled back into the couch, staring at the raindrops on the window.

"Sorry," Laura said after a moment. "I didn't mean to kill the mood."

"It's fine," I said. "It's something I need to think about

anyway." And I also needed to think about what would happen to Grace if I turned.

I shuddered. Turning into an acid-spitting zombie was not high on my "wants" list. I reclined, watching Grace wag at some very wet squirrels out the window. *We would make it,* I said to myself. *We can do anything together.*

At least, that was the thought that came to me when the fear rose in my body. We would do it together. I had Sean and Grace, and Aspyn, Wyatt, Laura, Jax and Owen. We had a team. We could do this, together.

Old Friends

~ Sean ~

I followed Brandon back to his house; it was a nice little cabin. "Did you build this place yourself?"

Brandon nodded. "We all did, in the beginning," he said. "We built the cabins and the common room together. This was years ago, when there were more of us," he admitted quietly. "We don't have so many here now."

"Why not?" I asked.

"Healthcare, mostly. Doc can only do so much, get so many supplies. People die in stupid ways and there's no way to save them. We had a lot of elders die of pneumonia a few years before the zombies came. Not so many children were born, either. So we're kind of in a precarious position." Brandon opened the door; it was unlocked. I wondered if they ever locked their doors here.

Jax was sitting on the couch, doing something that looked like knitting. "Jax?" I said.

He stood up abruptly, spilling the yarn out of his lap. "Sean!" he crowed. "I thought I'd never see you again!"

He had to be at least Aspyn's age now. We shook hands, and I smiled. Brandon grinned at us and wandered into another part of the cabin. "I'm sorry that I don't have the motorcycle anymore," I said. "It went down with the bombs."

"It's okay," Jax said simply. "It's just nice to see you after all this time."

"Agreed," I said. I looked around the cabin: it was comfortable, with a ladder holding several quilts near the corner, and a defunct TV sitting against the wall with another one of those tree-trunk tables, though not as big as the one in the common room. "What have you been up to since I saw you last?"

"School, mostly," he admitted. "I graduated high school last year, before everything went down."

"Congratulations," I said. "I guess asking what you want to do with your life isn't really an appropriate question anymore."

He snorted. "I guess not," he echoed. "But I do handyman stuff. Keep the cabins in shape, cut firewood, dig rows for crops. It's a job, anyway."

I nodded. "It seems like a very worthwhile job," I added.

"Thanks," he said, beaming. "So how have you been?"

I exhaled slowly as Jax led me to the recliners in the living room, next to the quilts. "I fell in love, turned into a zombie, got turned back into a human, and now I hear the zombies in my head. They're not the same kind of zombies I was, though. There's something different about them."

"Fell in love?" He sure knew how to capitalize on the information I'd given him. "Where is she? You were a zombie? How are you okay?"

"She's at the common room with some other members of my little community. You can meet her today, if you want. Her name is Kiera. We met at the sporting goods store I used to work at; she was looking at archery equipment, for some reason. I never got a good answer out of her as to why." I shrugged. "We have a man down, though. Owen. He's got a majorly infected wound or three, and your doctor is taking care of him now."

"And the zombie situation?" he pressed.

"Yeah, I turned," I sighed. "Hive mind and all. I remember everything: every moment of being a zombie. It's not a lot of great memories, I have to admit."

He winced. "Sorry. But you're safe now, though, right?"

I nodded. "It appears that former zombies can't catch this new zombie plague," I explained. "So now I just have to worry about everyone else that was exposed to the Cure. Including Kiera."

"That sucks, man," he said finally. "At least none of us were exposed to the Cure out here. It may not look like much, but it's home, and we work together pretty well."

"That's great," I said, and I meant it. "We aren't staying for the long term, we've got some other people waiting for us back at some farmhouses we've taken over. I just wanted to see you before we left, see how you were doing. I miss talking to you."

Jax smiled. "I missed you too. It was awfully quiet around here without you to ride around with."

"Aren't there other kids your age?" I asked.

"No, they're all older or younger," he explained. "The closest are a sixteen-year-old girl and a twenty-two-year-old man. Close, but not exactly in my age group. And they aren't interested in what I do, like you were."

I nodded. "I've always been interested in what you're doing, Jax. I'm really glad I got to see you again."

"Can you stay for a little while? Catch up, talk about zombies, I can show you the things I'm working on?" Jax asked.

"Sure," I said. "I'd like that. What are you working on now?"

"A drainage system for the crops. I have a bunch of pipe fittings from when they originally built the place, and I'm working on irrigation. It takes a while to cut holes in the pipe without a drill."

"That's awesome," I said, and I meant it. "You came up with that all by yourself?"

He beamed. "Yes. I'm the best handyman around here. I can fix anything."

"Can you take a look at my wagon? We'll have to cart Owen back to the farmhouse in it, and I just want to make sure it's sturdy and ready for another trip. If you've got tools, I'm sure you're the right man for the job."

"Of course," Jax said. "Lead the way."

"Actually, I'm not that great with directions," I admitted. "Your dad led me here. Can you take point on this one?"

He chuckled. "Of course," he echoed, and we went back outside. It had started raining at some point; there were chickens in an enclosed yard next to his cabin that were clucking quietly, complaining about the rain.

"So what was it like?" Jax said as we walked.

"What was what like?" I replied.

"Being a zombie."

"Oh." I hesitated. "It was . . . complicated. I'm sure you've heard of the hive mind theory; it was true. We really did communicate with each other, kind of telepathically. Most of the zombies I met were all emotion and action; there were only a few that had really concrete thoughts like I did."

"Do you remember being a zombie well?"

. . . the gun clattered to the floor as I dug my teeth into the tendon of his neck. Blood dripped down the front of his shirt as he screamed. I silenced him with one bite, ripping his throat to shreds with the dullness of my teeth. It tasted so good, I thought. I wanted more. I couldn't Infect him, not now, but that was okay—I was perfectly content to tear him limb from limb. I bit down on his shoulder, yanking his arm out of the socket and working at the muscles the . . .

"Yeah," I said briefly. "I do."

Somehow he knew that I didn't really want to talk about it. "Hey, we're almost at the common room," he said, just to have something to say.

"Great." I was still trapped in my thoughts. We entered the low door and I saw Kiera petting Grace on the couch. Wyatt and Laura were deep in conversation, and I could hear the rain hitting the tin roof, making little happy sounds as the droplets fell.

"You're back," Kiera said simply.

"I'm back," I said. "This is Jax, Brandon's son. Brandon, this is Kiera, my . . . I guess we've been through a zombie apocalypse together, we're probably common-law married by now. This is my wife, Kiera," I said, and her face lit up.

"Nice to meet you, Jax. This is Grace." The aforementioned Grace jumped up onto the couch beside Kiera, and I smiled.

"You have a dog in the zombie apocalypse?" he asked, confused.

"It's a long story," Kiera and I said together. We laughed, and I shook my head. "She's a zombie-hunting dog."

"That's pretty damn cool," Jax said. "Nice to meet you, Kiera."

"Nice to meet you too. Wyatt and Laura are over there in the corner, contemplating their navels or something," she said.

Laura glanced up and waved. "I'm Laura," she introduced herself. "You're Brandon's son?"

Jax nodded. "Sean wanted me to come look at your wagon to make sure it's shipshape for when you leave."

"It's next to the door," she offered. "We pulled it in when it started raining."

Jax went over to the not-very-small wagon, inspecting it carefully. "I think we could make a few improvements," he said slowly. "I've got some WD-40 for the wheels. Not much of it's left, but this is a good use for it. And I can weld the handle a little better; it looks loose."

"Sounds like a plan. What do you need from us?" I asked. "We brought a lot of jerky, chicken mostly. We could only take things that traveled well."

Jax shook his head. "We don't need anything. I'll be back in a few minutes, I'm going to go get the WD-40 and my welding supplies. I also have a relatively unused dog bed that you could prop Owen up on, if you want it?"

"Sure," Kiera said. "That would be great."

Jax smiled. "Be right back," he echoed, and disappeared through the doorway.

Kiera looked up at me, worry etching lines around her eyes. "Are you okay?" she asked softly, too softly for Wyatt and Laura to hear.

I sat down next to her and sighed. "Not really?" I hedged. "I had another flashback while we were walking back here."

She laid her head on my shoulder. "Was it bad?"

"Yeah. I could feel the meat in between my teeth." I shuddered, staring out the window to replace the images of blood with one of rain rapidly falling.

"I wish I knew how to help you," she complained. "I can't take the nightmares and flashbacks away from you, no matter how much I want to."

Smiling a little, I said, "I know. And I know you're having them, too," I added. "Don't think I haven't noticed you waking up in the middle of the night."

"So we're both haunted," she sighed. "That's great. At least we're in this together."

At least we're in this together, I thought. *For as long as it takes.*

~

It took a little while for Owen to fully respond to the antibiotics, but we were hauling him into the wagon before we knew it. He was still too weak to walk, but he was definitely on the mend. A few days after we'd arrived at the reservation, I was taking my turn pulling Owen in the wagon, and Kiera walked beside me, with Wyatt and Laura in front of us, talking about improvements we could make to our little farm community.

"It'll be nice to be home," I said.

Kiera smiled slightly. "It's home now?"

I shrugged. "It's as much home as our apartment was home. I like the farmhouse. I keep wondering what happened to the family that lived there, though. Did they turn? Were they driven out of the community? Why are there five empty houses in one community?"

"I wish I knew," Kiera said. "Grace, come back here." Grace was currently chasing a nonzombie squirrel, but she came back to Kiera immediately.

We walked on, back towards our farmhouses, and it was a relatively uneventful day. We made camp about halfway back, pitching our tents off the dirt road. Kiera and I climbed in to sleep while Wyatt and Laura took first watch.

It seemed as if we'd only been asleep for a minute when I heard Laura holler. "What the fuck is *that?*"

Kiera and I stumbled out of the tent, grabbing our weapons that we'd leaned against the poles. She put Grace behind her, since she wasn't in her Doge suit, and told her to stay.

"What is it?" I asked Laura.

"Fucking zombie moose," she said. "A fucking zombie moose."

The moose was fast. Too fast. It came running, head down and antlers at the ready. I swung my cleaver-rod hard as he passed by and caught some skin. He was bleeding now, big black droplets staining his brown coat. He was huge, taller than any of us, and his girth was massive.

We were so fucked.

Kiera took a swing with her hatchet-mop and managed to hack off about a quarter of the moose's face. His eyeball slipped out of its socket, dangling down to his mouth, the bundle of nerves not enough to keep it in place.

Wyatt swung with my crowbar and made contact with a solid *thunk* into the moose's chest. He dove out of the way, rolling into a crouch. I made a mental note to ask him where the hell he learned that move from.

"He's too big," Kiera said, out of breath.

"We have no choice," I shouted. I swung my cleaver-rod and hacked into the moose's neck, with a thick, meaty noise accompanied by a spray of blood. The moose reared back and spit the yellowy acid, and I barely dodged the liquid. It hissed behind me, killing the grass and anything else that lived there.

It took a little bit to maneuver the cleaver-rod out from between the vertebrae of his neck. His head was hanging to the side, but he was still coming. He reared back, hooves in the air, and all I could do was shield myself with my weapon.

Before he fell into me, Laura was there with her Meat-Siah, slashing at the side of the moose's skull. That was the final blow that put him down; gray matter splattered across the grass, and blood pooled in the dirt, as the great beast finally fell.

We were all panting and dirty by that point. I knelt down near the ground, trying to catch my breath, holding my cleaver-rod with my one good hand. "Well, that was an experience," I said.

Wyatt collapsed himself on a fallen log we'd rolled over to the fire. "I'd always heard there was moose up here, but I sure as hell never thought I'd see one, much less a zombie moose."

Laura nodded, her chest rising and falling rapidly as she put her Meat-Siah next to her tent. "I can't say I ever expected to find one, either," she said.

Kiera was sitting with Grace, who had stayed like the good girl she was. "Do we dare go back to sleep? I'm awake now, so if Sean doesn't mind, we can keep watch this time."

"Laura and I can get some shut-eye," Wyatt said simply. "I'm exhausted. And dirty as hell."

"Agreed," Laura said, and folded herself back into her tent, zipping up the door.

Kiera and I sat on opposite sides of the fire, both of us more or less back to normal after our Sudden Event. "That was unexpected," she said mildly.

The moose was about ten feet behind Kiera. It lay

there, acid and blood pooling in a sickly mixture in the dirt. "I thought it had me when it spit," I admitted.

"I'm glad you dodged it," Kiera said softly. "I remember what it does to skin. I'm not a fan."

I chuckled, and we both settled in on our logs, Grace lying across Kiera's feet by the fire. It was a mostly uneventful watch, except for some rabbits that Grace really, really wanted. Kiera let her catch one, and Grace tossed it in the air and caught it in her mouth.

I hoped it wasn't a relative of Bugs Bunny.

Watching the stars was rather peaceful; there was nothing we needed to mention, except for the moose in the "room." I would have sworn I saw a shooting star jetting across the sky, but when I pointed it out to Kiera, she didn't know what I was talking about.

We passed the night that way, watching stars until the sun began to climb into the sky and it was time to wake Laura and Wyatt. Owen, of course, got to sleep through all the fun.

Owen opened an eye and looked at me. "I'm sick of the damn wagon," he said. "Let me walk."

"Sure," I said. "Should we keep some moose meat, now that we know that zombie flesh isn't catching?"

He thought about it for some time. "Might as well," he said. "If nothing else, Grace can eat it."

We made our way over to the steaming pile of moose. It was a cool morning now that the fire was out. Owen began to teach Wyatt how to field dress a moose, and I watched.

It was disturbing. Seeing the tendons snap as they

were cut, the muscle opening to the knife. There was so much blood.

. . . so much blood pooled beneath me. I sat on the floor in the puddle, gnawing on the girl's arm. She was still breathing, but barely. The toned flesh of her arm slid down my throat and I reveled in it, reveled in the blood coating my face. I went for her throat to finish her off and felt the way my blunt teeth bit into her skin, hard and then harder, freeing her pulse in a rush of blood . . .

My vision refocused on the moose meat that was being neatly piled in the wagon. It was a disaster; the entire chest was open, and I could see its intestines in a slimy pile. The heart, of course, was huge and Owen put it in the wagon without any further dressing. "I bet Grace would like the liver," he mused.

I wanted to throw up.

I stared at Kiera, who was cooking breakfast: oatmeal, of course. "Are you okay?" she said quietly.

"No. I am pretty not okay." I shuddered, closing my eyes against the sight.

"What's going on?"

"I keep getting flashbacks," I explained. "I can feel them. They're so real, Kiera. As real as when I did the stuff I see. It just . . . zaps me back there, feeling my mind going, tasting the human meat and playing with the veins."

"I have some too," she offered. "The sound it makes when a hatchet connects with a person's neck or torso. The way Chen looked at me before he died. Hell, the way Brett looked at me before *he* died. There's just so much death and darkness that I don't know how to walk with it."

Nodding, I started packing up our tent. It was an easy setup, you just had to twist the top and it popped down. We'd gotten it from the first trip to the feedstore. "I just don't know what to do," I admitted quietly.

Kiera sighed. "The most we can do is learn from it," she said finally. "Remind ourselves why now is different. There are less zombies now, but they're more powerful. We have to be able to defend ourselves, Sean. There's just no two ways about it."

"I know," I replied as Wyatt and Owen came back with a wagon full of meat and parts. "I just wish it didn't hurt so much."

Laura had packed up after breakfast, and we were pretty much set to head back down the road. "I wonder what Aspyn, Anna and Jax have been doing," Wyatt said quietly. I'd been watching Wyatt during this trip; he was a fairly quiet guy with a serious streak, but he was good in a fight.

"I don't know Aspyn that well yet," I admitted. "But she seems schoolteacher-ish. Maybe they're playing school."

Wyatt nodded. "That would be fun for him," he said. "He never got to go to nursery class. By the time he was old enough, the war was on."

"It must be hard to raise a kid through a zombie apocalypse."

"It is," he replied. "Do you and Kiera want to have kids?"

"I don't know. I don't know if I can, I mean, after being a zombie. We haven't really talked about it. But I can't imagine bringing someone else into this fucked-up hellscape with zombie moose and cults and everything else," I said.

"Fair enough," Wyatt replied. "We had Brayden before all this shit happened, so we didn't exactly get a choice. But he's been adapting well: he doesn't know anything other than what we've been doing since the war, so he doesn't miss the toys, the electronics, the conveniences. He's used to Mom washing clothes out back in a tub and hanging them up for him to run through on the clothesline."

Wyatt grabbed the wagon and started pulling it behind him as the rest of us finished up closing camp and repacking our stuff. We followed along in a little duckling line, each of us lost in our own thoughts, and it was quiet for a long time.

We finally crested the hill and saw the farmhouses on the downslope. It felt like a blast of fresh air: the relief of knowing we were home, we were all safe and sound, and we even brought back food. "We did it," I said to Kiera.

"We did," she agreed, and we walked hand in hand back to the farmhouses. It was a good day.

Not for Long

~ Kiera ~

It was relatively uneventful, making our way back into our normal lives. It made me laugh a little, thinking that this was normal now; how very different it was from what we'd done before. Before the war, before the zombies. Just before.

Grace was currently eating moose meat on a plate at my feet in the living room, and I sighed. "At least I've still got you and Sean," I said mildly. "I don't know what I'd do without you two."

We were back, and we were safe. We hadn't lost anyone this time. Not like Chen and Brett. Not like Sean's zombies. We were all together, most of us in one house, and the Hearns across the way. The chickens were clucking, the cows were mooing, and everything was all right with the world.

We cooked moose on our wood stove, and while I admitted it wasn't as disgusting as I'd thought it would be, it still gave me the heebie-jeebies and flashbacks of eating the zombie man.

. . . he thick, meaty flesh in my mouth; dripping with blood. Coughing as they shoved it in my mouth; crying as I swallowed . . .

Damn it.

It was different. This was voluntary. This was meat, just meat, like you'd buy from the grocery store. Laura and Wyatt had cooked for all of us. We were having dinner out back by the fields, with a festive atmosphere that I couldn't get into.

I ate in silence, wondering when I'd stop being a haunted house. I watched Laura laughing with Aspyn, Anna and Jax were drawing pictures in the dirt. The cows were singing the song of their people and the chickens were fine, we were all fine, here . . . just fine.

I was not fine.

It wasn't the most smooth exit in the world, but I absconded away from the fields and walked toward the front of the house. I sat on the porch and got out Owen's radio. We hadn't listened for broadcasts since we'd been gone; I wondered if anyone was on the radio at all.

I repeat, stay in your homes. The National Guard will be going highway by highway to pick up anyone who has found themselves displaced by the new zombie wave. Again, there are more of them than there are of us; we won't be able to get everywhere. Please stay inside and do not engage with the zombies.

Fuck that, I thought. I turned the radio off and wandered back toward the field, feeling a little better now that

I had something to contribute to the conversation. "The National Guard is coming," I announced.

Laura stopped in her tracks. "What, here?"

"By the interstate. I don't know if they'll go down dirt roads. Probably not, I would think?" I squinted in the low sunlight. "I don't think we'll see them here."

"How did you find out?" Wyatt asked.

"I turned on the radio. The feed is a loop, it just plays over and over again. I guess they're sick of telling people that the Guard is coming," I mused.

"Well, that's great," Sean said, using his free hand to make a sun visor for himself. "Fat fucking lot of good they've done us every other time."

"They said that the zombies outnumber us," I explained. "That it's turning very quickly into a war situation. At least, that's what I gathered from it."

"Great," Owen scoffed. "Another fucking zombie war."

"We shouldn't have to deal with it out here," Aspyn offered softly. She was sitting on the ground near Brayden, playing some incredibly intricate drawing game in the dirt with him. "The National Guard won't bother us."

She was right, most likely. They didn't have a reason to pound down dirt roads looking for random farmhouses. We were safe, for now.

"I'm going to go take a rainwater bath," I said finally. "Grace, come on."

I took Grace into the house with me, then filled up her bowl with water to drink while I went to the bathroom and used the barrel next to the toilet to wash my face, my body. We had a minimal amount of soap, but I thought that a zombie moose was probably a soap occasion. I didn't feel as refreshed as a shower would have gotten me, but I definitely felt cleaner.

We went back down to the living room and I sat in my favorite armchair. It was overstuffed, green, and fluffy. Grace looked at me plaintively and I smiled. "You want your Doge suit off, Gracey?"

Grace huffed and puffed and pawed at the floor. As I went to go to take her suit off, I heard something out front. "Stay here," I hissed.

She was the goodest girl, so of course, she stayed in the living room as I crept toward the front door. I heard yelling; I looked out the front window and saw honest-to-god torches raised as a group marched down our streets.

I ran to the back door and stuck my head out. "I think the cult is back," I gasped.

Everyone moved in a hurry. Anna brought Jax inside our house, and the rest of us circled around the outside to meet the mob that was looking pretty fucking creepy in our front yard. "What do you want?" Sean hollered.

"You took our women," Mark said. "We're here to get them back."

Owen, bless him, had his gun strapped on him from the moment we got back. "I think you'll find that they disagree with your assessment," he said calmly.

"Suit yourself," he said. He opened the ranks and I saw zombies. Zombies everywhere, held together by a limp chain around the outside. He dropped the chain, and the zombies started moving. They were fast. They were *fast*.

We always kept our weapons in arm's reach just in case

of a zombie deer, but I'd never been more grateful for my hatchet-mop than I was at that moment. We all got in a line, all of us: Owen, myself, Sean, Laura, Wyatt and even Aspyn were out in force. We were ready for this. This was what we had trained for: protecting our community, especially Anna and Jax, inside.

I realized at that moment that we'd never really trained in the first place. Oops.

The zombies reached our line and you could hear the slick chunking sound of meat meeting blades and tenderizers. Aspyn's Rake-inator tore through a zombie, the steak knives making quick work of his throat and chest. She looked surprised at herself, and I called, "Don't celebrate yet. We have more."

The zombie in front of me inhaled and I knew what was coming. I ducked as he spat where my face had just been; the acid sizzled behind me, and I thanked God for any reflexes I'd ever been given. I whacked at him with my hatchet-mop and he fell with the hatchet stuck in the side of his neck. I stepped on his chest, pulling hard, and blood blossomed onto my shoes and ankles as I retrieved my hatchet-mop.

Sean was ducking and weaving as well, his one-handed style with his cleaver-rod really showing off how much he'd strengthened his arm muscles. I was impressed. I realized I didn't have time to be impressed as his zombie, a young woman, spit at him. It caught the edge of his shirt and he backed off, tearing the shirt off as quickly as he could.

"Did I get it in time?" Sean panted.

I inspected him as closely as I could, what with the zombies coming at me and everything. "I think so. On your left!"

He fell back into the fray, and I hit another zombie in the chest. I yanked my hatchet-mop out and saw his heart beating. He kept coming.

"Fuck this," I whispered. I wished I'd let Grace out for her to do damage control. The man in front of me reached for me, almost dancing his way across to me after I'd pushed him back.

The blood was thick and almost black. It was a little oily, actually. I'd never noticed that before; the little rainbow sheen that caught the sunlight. I dashed back a few feet, waiting to see if the zombie would fall. Then I swung my hatchet-mop in a wide arc and felt the blade cut through his vertebrae; his head rolled off of his body, tumbling down the small hill in the yard and landing at my feet.

I kicked it out of the way and moved past his body. There was another female zombie ahead of me. Laura and Aspyn were tag-teaming a male, the Rake-inator and Meat-Siah formidable together. Blood ran in rivulets down the dirt and grass, staining our shoes a permanent black-rust color.

Owen was behind us all, shooting between our bodies. The hard *thunk* of each bullet into the chest of a zombie was loud, louder than the moans of the zombies themselves.

. . . I dodged Grace's attack on the zombie, turning around and going after it from the back. We hacked into her together, Grace running into the zombie full-force

and me slicing the zombie's face with my hatchet-mop.
We whirled together, and it was beautiful . . .

Not now!

I shook my head. There were at least five more zombies. Sean was cleaving everything in sight with his cleaver-rod. He was hacking at zombies harder than anyone, even with a missing arm. Wyatt had a makeshift staff, and he was using it to keep our perimeter as free as possible; he had to dodge acid spits, though.

The blood didn't seem to hurt anything, which was a relief, considering I was ankle-deep in it. I swung low as Laura swung high and we knocked a zombie off his feet, with Laura using her Meat-Siah to cut his throat and vertebrae. He didn't get up after that.

There were only four zombies left, but I couldn't see the cultists. I could hear them, though: they were howling at the sky, and I wondered what they'd do after their pet zombie horde disappeared.

I had plans for them.

Laura mowed down another zombie and Sean was cornering the last female. Aspyn and Wyatt had the other male, and I watched as Aspyn sliced through his throat with her steak knives. That had been an interesting weapon to build; I was glad it worked so well.

I blinked, coming back to the present, and realized that all the zombies were accounted for. I left my merry band of mischief makers behind, storming up to the yard where the cultists were setting fires and dancing.

"What in the FUCK do you think you're doing?" I screamed.

David wandered over as if he had all the time in the world. I bared my teeth at him. "Get the fuck away from me," I hissed.

"Or else what?" he drawled. "What are you going to do, pretty little lady? You've got a mighty big knife there. Bet you don't know how to use it."

I had a split second to think about what I was doing. I had to commit to it; had to stop second-guessing myself. When he came at me with his torch, reaching to grab my arm, I brought the hatchet-mop down and cleaved his chest in half. He sputtered and gargled blood, and fell to the ground.

"Oh fuck," I gasped. I had killed a human. *A real human.*

Sean ran up next to me, looking from me to David to the rest of the cultists, who stood there staring at me like I was the anti-Christ. Well, maybe to them, I was.

Oh fuck oh fuck oh fuck

"Kiera?" Sean said hesitantly.

"Yes?"

"Did you kill the cultist?" he asked.

"Yes." My voice was flat. Empty. Just like my soul.

"I think you need a minute. Aspyn, take Kiera to the house," he hollered. I walked, shaking, following Aspyn's lead and coming back to myself when I felt the carpet under my squelching shoes.

"Shit," I mumbled. I slid my shoes off and got rid of my blood-soaked socks, leaving them at the door. I saw Anna pulling Brayden away from the window and back toward the kitchen.

Aspyn led me to the big couch, where Grace was waiting for me. She looked as happy as ever. I thanked God I hadn't brought her out into that fight.

"Aspyn?" I said finally.

"Yeah, Kiera?" Her voice was soft and light. Like a kindergarten teacher's voice. I knew she'd be really good with kids.

"I did something bad," I whispered. Grace climbed into my lap and rested her head on my shoulder. I was covered in blood and dirt after my rainwater bath. I felt disgusting. I felt like ripping my skin off, tearing apart my own flesh and climbing out of my body. I was shaking so hard.

"It's okay," Aspyn said soothingly. "You didn't mean to. You were in the middle of a zombie battle and . . . just . . . you carried on."

"I carried on," I echoed. "I did. I hit him with my hatchet-mop. Oh, God, I killed him with my hatchet-mop. I'd only ever used it on zombies, I promise," I said, retching over the side of the couch.

Aspyn sat down next to me and rubbed my back in small circles as I threw up moose meat. "I didn't mean to," I said plaintively through bouts of vomiting. "I didn't mean to."

"I know," she said. "Just rest. Let the others take care of the rest of them."

Sean came barging in the door, covered in blood. He looked down, realized I'd taken my shoes off, and followed suit. He unlaced his boots that were nearly black with the oily blood and slid out of his socks, coming to sit in the chair opposite me and Grace.

"Are you okay?" he asked.

"I'm f-fine," I stammered. I was still shaking. I couldn't stop. "I just . . . I just . . ."

"Owen's out there with the rest of the cultists giving them the good ol' what for," Sean said, trying to sound a little jovial. "He's threatening them within an inch of their lives not to bother us again. They're moving north towards the highway."

"Okay," I said in a small voice. "Sean?"

"Yeah?"

"I did a bad thing," I said again.

He leaned over and hugged me around Grace. "I know," he said quietly. "But you didn't mean to."

"He's still dead, no matter how much I didn't mean it. I did that. I caused that." I shuddered with one final bout of vomiting. Aspyn started to clean up after me and I felt guilty.

I laid my head on the chair and Grace put her paws on my shoulders, licking the blood off my face. "What do I do now?"

Sean had to think about that for a minute. "Go to bed," he said softly. "I'll take care of everything. Don't worry. Just go to bed." He paused. "Maybe take another bath," he added as an afterthought.

Aspyn helped me up the stairs and into the bathroom. I went through the motions of bathing again without really feeling it; I knew what I was doing, but my body was on autopilot. Aspyn helped me dry off and found some clean clothes in the closet of Sean and I's room. She stayed with me while I dressed, and Grace followed us into the bedroom.

I slid underneath the covers. I felt small. The world felt so big.

"Thanks, Aspyn," I said finally.

"Sure," she said. "I'll be downstairs. Yell if you need something or if you have bad dreams, okay?"

I wondered where Brayden was during all of this; he had been near the picture window. Had he seen me kill someone? I rarely interacted with the little boy, but suddenly his view of me mattered.

I closed my eyes. I could see him falling every time. He fell over, and over, and over again.

It took me a long time to finally fall asleep.

Dear God, please don't let me dream . . .

~

I avoided Sean the next morning. Hell, I avoided everyone. I went out into the chicken coop and fed them first thing, giving myself something to do with Grace following faithfully behind me. She was interested in the chickens, but I didn't think she'd eat one, now.

How was I just supposed to go on with my life like this?

I heard Wyatt's pigs rooting around in his backyard. It made me smile a little; they were cute, even if they were food. I treated that man like he was no better than a sack of meat.

Fuck.

Owen was walking into the barn when I passed by, and he stopped me. "You'll deal with it," he said simply.

"What?" I said, feeling stupid.

"Killing someone. You'll deal with it. It compartmentalizes eventually, and it'll just be another thing you did to survive," he offered.

I exhaled slowly. "I take it you have a lot of experience in such things?"

He nodded, reracking his gun behind him. "I spent a lot of time overseas and did a lot of things I'm not proud of. But I survived, and that's the most important thing. I survived and so did the rest of my team. We may have done the unimaginable, but we did it together, and we did it so we could all go home."

I thought about this for a while. "I guess you're right," I said finally. It still felt like a hole in my soul. I was still ashamed of myself. But as Sean started to dig a grave in the side yard, I didn't want to throw up anymore.

I went to Sean. "Do you need help?" I asked softly.

"I don't think it's quite six feet, but it should do the job," he replied. As he went to drag the cultist—David—into the grave, I grabbed his feet and helped him. He was ripped apart on his chest. My hatchet-mop had hatchet-ed right through his rib cage.

"Are you okay?" he asked, a little out of breath.

"I think so," I said finally. "I had a talk with Owen and it helped."

"Owen would probably be the best person for that particular conversation," he acknowledged. "We have to do laundry today. I'm running out of shirts."

It was a simple, daily task. It was easy, and I could do it without judgment. "I'll do it," I said, and started walking back to the house as Sean started filling in the hole with dirt.

It was nice to have a mindless thing to do. I soaked the clothes in one tub, washed the soap out in the other, and ran them through a hand-cranked dryer. It was rhythmic and soothing. It gave me time to think.

I realized how nervous I was, thinking that I was going to turn; I was already panicked about killing David, so why not add to the list? It was always in the back of my mind, no matter what I was doing. Did that heartbeat feel wrong? Did I suddenly have an urge to stare at the sun? Every movement was questioned. It was awful.

"I can't live like this," I said to myself. I washed all of my and Sean's clothes, and started hanging them up to dry as I thought about it. *I did what I had to do to survive,* I told myself.

Did you really? my brain said back.

The trouble was, I didn't know. I had thought he was coming at me with a torch and he was trying to grab me, so I swung. *It was necessary,* I thought.

I had to live with what I'd done. There was no way around it. I'd killed someone, and he wasn't even a zombie. A crazy cultist, yes, but not a zombie. I would have to live with that forever.

Grace chuffed at a squirrel that was running along the fence line. I tried to smile, but I just couldn't. I knew this would haunt me for a long time. I wondered what Sean thought of me; he wasn't acting any different, but he might have strong opinions, for all I knew.

I finished hanging up the laundry and Grace ran through the wet sheets that billowed in the wind. This time, I did smile. She was one of the highlights of my life, and I had to focus on those now. Sean was another: he was the brightness that kept me going, even when I was terrified that I'd turn. And that fear, coupled with what I'd done, was threatening to devolve me into goo.

In the barn, I tried to find some stuff I could use to build Grace an agility course. She loved her course on the roof at home, and if we were staying here, I needed to give her that outlet, even though our sniff-faris were so much longer and more interesting now.

I found a few traffic cones and an old rake and made a jump between the fields and the house. I found a few paint stirrer sticks, and I pounded them into the ground to make weave poles. I found some pallets, and I called Owen over to help.

Because Sean was burying a body.

"Hey, can you help me stack these? I want to put together an agility course for Grace and I need a raised platform with two ramps."

"Sure," he said, and we worked to stack the pallets together. "How are you feeling?"

I wiped some sweat off my head. "Glad that I have something to do," I admitted. "It helps."

"I've never seen a dog go through an agility course. How do you train them to do that?"

"Well, at first, we used a lot of treats . . ." I spent the next fifteen minutes explaining it to Owen.

When we were done setting it up, I whistled, and she ran over from playing in the sheets. I had arranged it the same way we'd had at home, so even though it was new equipment, she would know what to do.

She flew through the weave poles and sailed past the jump, then hesitated a little at the ramp. She shook her head and barked at it, and ran up one side, stood for a second on the platform, and down the other. She barked at it again for good measure and went over the jump one more time, then looked at me expectantly.

I laughed. "I guess she thinks she deserves a treat," I said. "Maybe I'll let her have one of the chicken eggs. She likes to crack them." It was a good idea, and one I followed through on.

"You seem . . . better," Owen hedged cautiously.

"I have to be. If I don't act better, I'm never going to *be* better. So it's 'fake it 'til you make it' time," I explained. I paused. "I wonder where the cultists ran off to."

Owen shook his head. "No telling," he said. "They went south-ish is all I know. They all ran together when . . . well, you know."

I nodded briskly. "Understood," I said. I went in to put away the previous week's laundry that had stayed on the line, and Grace followed me, panting happily. She loved crunching eggs, that was for sure.

We went up to the bedroom and started putting away clothes. Grace jumped on the bed as I made it, and it made me smile. She didn't know what I'd done, or if she did, she couldn't possibly care less. That was refreshing; she didn't treat me like I was broken by it.

I saw Owen upend the basin and refill it with rainwater to wash his own clothes. It was nice to know that even though he was a macho, militaristic, gun-toting guy, he still did his own laundry. I would've thought he would have outsourced that kind of thing to one of the ladies.

Granted, Laura would probably eat him for lunch, so maybe that wasn't a good idea.

Aspyn would do his laundry, though, I was sure of it. There was something too gentle about her, as if she were even more broken than I was. She seemed fine, though, so it wasn't something I could ask about. As if I spoke of the devil, she popped her head in the door.

"I'm making peanut butter and jam sandwiches," she said. "Do you want some? We have strawberry and blueberry."

"Man, you guys have canned a shit ton of stuff," I said. "I didn't even know there were berries growing."

"They're at the back of the field, they might be wild," she explained. "They're coming up through the fence, which is keeping the animals off of them. Whoever lived here before might have planted them, though, since there's so many of them."

I thought about the family that had lived here before us: the two farmers and one son. Laura often wore the son's clothes, she was so petite; the rest of us had to live in T-shirts and track pants. I didn't know when the last time I'd had underwear for more than a day was.

I shook my head, trying to clear my thoughts. "Yeah, I'll take some strawberry," I said finally. "If you don't mind."

She beamed. "Not at all!" Aspyn seemed to be one of those people who genuinely liked taking care of others. I wasn't that magnanimous.

Aspyn popped back down the stairs, and I could hear her skipping every other step. Now that she had people—real adults, she called us—to make decisions for her, she seemed at peace. Even with me, with what I did.

It was something I could learn from her, that was for sure.

I finished folding and putting away Sean's clothes— mostly jeans and the ever-present T-shirts—and I noticed he'd forgotten the belt he always wore. It was on the floor near his side of the bed. I decided to take it to him.

I trailed down the stairs with Grace behind me, and went out to where he was burying the body. I couldn't see him anymore; he was covered in dirt. Sean was sweating and swearing as he filled in the hole.

"Remind me not to volunteer by myself for shit like this," he managed, groaning. "That my belt? Thanks, I knew I'd forgotten something."

I looked around. There was another shovel—a flat one, not really made for holes, but it would do to bury a body. And I felt like I had to do something, to make amends for what I did.

"He didn't even have time to be surprised," I said softly as we dug. "I just . . . and then he . . ."

"I know," Sean said, heaving the dirt back into place. "But you didn't mean to, Kiera. We're going to get through this. Hopefully the cultists have gone for the last time, and we can just live out the rest of our days on the farm." He paused. "Have you ever thought about having kids?"

I blinked a little. Was this really the appropriate time to have this discussion? I wondered as I filled the hole. I mean, I guessed wherever we had to have it was appropriate enough.

"Sometimes," I admitted. "I'm not getting any younger. I'd like to have kids, I think. One or two."

Sean nodded, leaning on his shovel for a moment before starting to stamp down the dirt with his feet.

I joined him.

"I've been thinking about it ever since we met Brayden," he said finally. "I know we haven't spent much time with the kid, but the family they've created . . . I want that for us."

"Yeah," I said, leaning against him, exhausted. Grace was currently invested in catching a grasshopper, so she was entertained through this particular conversation. "So . . . do we think we should? I mean, we're in the middle of a zombie apocalypse and I could turn at any moment."

Sean grimaced. "I don't think you're going to turn at any moment, Kiera," he said. "I think you're as safe as everyone else is, and while there might be a high likelihood in the cities, maybe there's something out here that makes it less likely. We've seen a shit ton of zombie animals, but no zombie people that weren't brought here by the cultists. We don't have any zombie neighbors; the houses look like they just up and left one day."

I thought about it for a few moments. "You're not wrong," I said. "We *don't* have any zombie neighbors. At least, we didn't when we were looking for antibiotics for Owen. That's kind of weird, isn't it?"

Sean shrugged, and we started walking toward one of the big tubs that held rainwater to splash it over our bodies and faces. There was a little bar of soap on one of the windowsills, and we washed everything we could while still being clothed.

"I think they saw the proverbial writing on the wall and got the hell out of Dodge," he said. "But it's really weird that they didn't stay here. We're so well-provisioned and protected, what were they running from?"

I nodded. "It's weird," I said again. "Maybe there's something we don't know about this place."

He thought it over. "We never went down in the basement, or up in the attic," he offered, before using the bucket to pour water over his soapy hair.

"Maybe that should be the next thing we do. See if the rooms are hiding anything," I said.

"Let's change out of these disgusting clothes and we'll go check them out," Sean said.

I was the one who grimaced this time. We were stinky. "Yes, please," I said. It was a mystery, but it was a mystery we were going to solve. Why did they leave? They had animals, crops, farmland and relatively low numbers of zombie animals. There had to be a reason.

There had to be.

The Basement

~ Sean ~

We had one of the lanterns we used at night, full of oil, as we crept down the basement stairs. They were concrete, built into the house, and steep. I went first, so in case we fell, I'd be the one catching Kiera instead of the other way around. Granted, I only had one and a half arms to deal with it, but it was better than nothing.

"It smells in here," I said as we started our explorations.

"Smells like what?" Kiera asked.

"Like . . . rot." I peered into a barrel and saw it was full of moldy corn. "Well, that might be one reason for the smell."

"We'll have to open these little windows and air it out," Kiera said, walking over and unlatching one of the small glass panes.

"Sure," I said, and I opened the second window. I could see better with the windows open; they had a protective cover on them, for some reason. And that's when I saw the door.

"Kiera," I said quietly.

"Yeah?"

"There's a door." I walked over to it and turned the handle. It was locked. "I'll be right back," I said. "I'm going to go grab my crowbar."

I ran outside and found my crowbar just where I'd left it, next to the rainwater tub. I had left the lantern with Kiera, so I felt my way down the stairs, almost tripping myself on the last few steps. I examined the door and tried to figure out where to pry.

"Is this a good idea?" Kiera said nervously. "Maybe there's something we're not supposed to see."

I worked the edge of the crowbar between the door and the wall. "Not supposed to see according to who? The ghosts of Christmas past? No, there's no reason for us to suspect that there's anything hidden behind the door. Maybe it's a safe and they're secret billionaires." I snorted. "Fat lot of good that would do us now."

Alas, the door was wooden, and it soon opened beneath my crowbar. I grabbed the lantern from Kiera and shined it into the small room. What I saw made me retch.

It was a zombie: a zombie chained to the wall, crouching on the floor, with two broken legs. It was a male, younger than Kiera and I. He was still wearing one of his band T-shirts. I gagged. "Kiera, it's a zombie," I said through bouts of coughing. "I think it's the son."

. . . *killkillkill . . . eateateat . . . killkillkill . . .*

I reached into the mind of the zombie in that weird,

quiet place in my brain and all I got were jumbled images and emotions. Whoever this zombie had been, he sure as hell wasn't anymore. He reared back and spat at me. It landed by my shoe and sizzled on the concrete.

"Why the fuck . . ." Kiera joined me at the doorway. "His legs are broken," she said. "Does he know that?"

I shook my head. "I don't know. I didn't feel any pain from him, just . . . this overwhelming desire to kill."

She shuddered. "That's creepy as fuck. What are we supposed to do about this? We can't just leave him down here."

I struggled to come up with a somewhat intelligent answer. "I think we need to put him down," I said gently. "There's nothing left of his mind. All he wants to do is kill us. And he can't even do that, with two broken legs."

Kiera grimaced. "Do we have to?"

I nodded. "We can't just leave him here. It's inhumane."

"Doesn't he have to be human to have something be inhumane?" she replied.

"You know what I mean," I said. I started toward the stairs. "I'm going to go get Owen. He deserves to be put down safely and without pain."

"I'm coming with you," she said in a rush. "I don't want to be down here alone with him."

We went upstairs, looking for Owen. He was cleaning his gun at the kitchen table. I knew ammo was precious, but I couldn't find it in me to do it myself. "We found a zombie," I said.

"A zombie? Where the fuck did you find a zombie?" Owen raised a brow.

"In the basement. He's chained to the wall and has two broken legs. Based on the clothing, I think it's the son," I explained. "He doesn't deserve to be locked up like that. Can you help him?"

Owen snapped the cartridge back in his gun and looked at me. "Are you sure?"

I felt like throwing up. I had been a zombie, and nobody had put *me* down. There was a chance he could get better, right? But all he wanted to do was kill, and those chains didn't look terribly sturdy.

"Yeah," I said finally. "He doesn't deserve to be chained up and stuck with two broken legs. He's the acid-spitting type, so he's faster than us if we let him go. I think he'd be a threat to all of us here."

Owen looked at me for a few moments, then at Kiera. "You're okay with this?"

"No," she admitted. "But it's not fair to him to torture him any longer. There's no Cure for this that we know of, and there's no way to save him. His bones aren't going to heal while he's a zombie, and Sean read his mind and all he could read was the feeling of killing."

He nodded and slung his gun over his shoulder. "I'll be back in a few minutes, then."

"Sean?" Kiera said as we watched Owen disappear behind the basement door.

"Yeah?" I found myself holding her hand without knowing I'd moved.

"Can we, like . . . pray for him or something?" She struggled to finish her thought. "I know it's not our usual

MO, but it just feels . . . so wrong to leave him down there, and to put him down like an animal."

"Sure," I said, a little bewildered. We weren't particularly religious people. It wasn't a dealbreaker by any means, but it was a little weird for Kiera to ask to pray for someone.

"You want to say some words?" I said after a minute.

"Yeah," she said, and cleared her throat. "To God, the universe and the far reaches of our galaxy, I pray that the son dies cleanly and does not have to be a killing machine any more. I hope his torture ends today, and he comes to rest. I hope that whatever happened to his fathers, he did not hurt them, and finds peace."

I stared at her for a moment. It was one of the weirder prayers I'd ever heard, but I had to admit this was not our forte. "Amen?" I said questioningly.

"Amen, gesundheit, bless this mess," she said. "Whatever."

We heard the gunshot, and Kiera sat down quickly. "We still have to look in the attic," I reminded her. "If we found a zombie in the basement, who knows what we'll find in the attic?"

She sighed and rubbed her temples with her fingertips. "All right," she said finally. She followed me upstairs and waited while I grabbed the pull string for the attic steps. They were rickety, not sturdy at all, and I felt every pound in my body pressing against those little steps. Kiera came up after me.

"Kiera . . ." I said. "Don't come up the last few steps."

"Why?" She, of course, came up the last few steps. "Oh, fuck . . ."

There was blood. A lot of blood. There were two men with slit wrists, holding each other with mummified arms. They had clearly dried out up here in the hot attic, and they had just as clearly committed suicide.

"Yeah," I said heavily. "I guess I have to dig a few more holes."

Tears sprung to her eyes. "I don't know if I can keep living here," she admitted. "Not knowing this."

I put my arm around her shoulder. "I don't think they would mind us living here," I said softly. "They didn't kill all the animals, so maybe they expected someone to take over for them. I think they just couldn't handle what happened to their son."

The zombie son had spit acid on one of the mummified men. There was an open wound, gaping, on his shoulder beneath a torn shirt; the skin around it was black. "I guess now we know for sure what acid-spitting zombies do to humans," I said. "Up close and personal this time."

Kiera's eyes were a little teary. "They just couldn't get over what happened to their son." She choked a little. "There's no way this wasn't intentional."

I nodded. "I know," I said, trying to sound vaguely soothing. "But they're at peace now, right? Isn't that the prevailing theory on the afterlife?"

She sniffled. "Yeah," she agreed. "It's just . . . this is such a beautiful house. They looked to have a beautiful life. And now they're dead in the attic and their son is dead in the basement and nothing will ever look the same again."

I began to tug her down the stairs to the attic. "Come on," I said. "You can help me dig holes or help Aspyn and Laura cook, your choice."

Kiera managed a little laugh. "I'll definitely take the cooking over the digging," she said. "Every time."

I pushed her gently in the direction of the kitchen and started outside to dig some more graves. This was definitely not in my plans for our little homestead. Two farmers committed suicide in my attic and their son was a zombie—now a dead zombie—in my basement. What even the fuck was that?

Using the shovel to punish the dirt, I heaved a plot of grass off the ground. "Now we're haunted," I said, starting to pant from the exertion.

"We're fucking haunted, and now I have to drag two bodies out of our attic," I said.

"We're what now?" Wyatt, Anna and Brayden stood in front of my hole.

"Haunted?" Brayden said. "What does that mean, we're haunted?"

I rubbed my forehead with my hand, leaving behind a smear of dirt. Anna shushed Brayden and gave me an apologetic look. "I'm sorry, we didn't know you were . . . talking to yourself," she said lamely. "We'll go inside and help the girls cook."

"Now your wife thinks I'm batshit crazy," I told Wyatt. "I'm digging two more graves. Wait, no, three."

He picked up the flat shovel and started digging.

"Who are the graves for? And why did you hesitate on the third?"

"The two farmers who lived here killed themselves in the attic after they locked their zombie son in the basement with broken legs," I explained warily. "There's blood all over the attic. Kiera is probably traumatized now. We might have to move to the house next to you, if she can't handle what happened up there."

"You're welcome to," Wyatt offered. He thought as he dug, and I could see the wheels turning in his head. "So what happened to the rest of the community, do you think?" As he worked, I noticed a tattoo beneath the sleeve of his T-shirt, and I wondered what it meant.

I shrugged. "Maybe they saw the son become a zombie and got the hell out of here," I said. "Maybe they wanted to end it all before they turned on their neighbors. And maybe the neighbors had the good common sense to get the fuck out of here."

"I guess that's one way to look at it," he said, a little blankly. He continued to dig. "Anna should talk to Kiera."

"Huh? Why?" I leaned hard onto the shovel to get the dirt free.

"She was a nurse. She saw a lot of death, mostly the oncology ward. Maybe she can help." Wyatt shrugged. "It's worth a shot."

"I know she talked to Owen earlier today, but that was more of a 'you did a bad thing in self-defense' talk, not a 'your house is haunted by two suicides and a zombie' talk," I said. "Maybe having that kind of perspective will make a difference. She's not dealing with this news very well."

Wyatt nodded. "I understand," he said finally, panting as he dug holes with the wrong type of shovel. "I didn't expect her to do what she did. But I don't blame her for it. She was in the middle of a zombie apocalypse in miniature and he was coming at her with a torch. I saw it, I was right behind her. That man was going after Kiera, no doubt in my mind."

I watched Wyatt through the corner of my eye for a few minutes. "That's what she said," I said finally. "I just think she didn't expect the hatchet to go straight through his chest. She might have been trying to wound him."

"Zombies are certainly easier to break," Wyatt mused. "I wonder if it's a bone density thing. Something to do with the acid-spitting, maybe. Biological changes in the body affecting the way bones break."

"I'd never thought of that," I admitted. "But it makes sense. I had a lot of injuries as a zombie, solely because I couldn't repair any of it myself. Fine motor skills were not my friend at the time. And I didn't feel any of it."

"It always surprises me when you talk about being a zombie so casually," Wyatt said. "I feel like if I had been a zombie I would've started screaming the second the Cure hit me and wouldn't have stopped until I ran out of breath."

I shrugged. "I had a lot of time to come to terms with my zombie-ism, I guess. I was a lot more sentient and communicative than other zombies in my Hex group. I've never told anyone this except for Kiera, but it was like my brain split in two: Zombie Sean and Not-Zombie Sean."

Wyatt looked interested. The hole was about three feet

deep now; time to move on to the next grave. "What was that like?"

"Horrifying," I admitted. "I remember everything I did as a zombie. Every kill, every Infection. I remember how it felt to bite someone. I still have nightmares."

"I can understand the nightmares," he said. "If you remember everything, that's got to be pretty hard."

I nodded. "Kiera's got nightmares too. She probably wouldn't love me telling you this, but if it'll help Anna help her . . . She killed a lot of zombies with her group. Hell, even the dog killed zombies. But they turned back into people after the Cure, and it weighs on her. What if they could have been saved, you know?"

I hit a rock and had to lean down and heft it over to somewhere else. Wyatt was quiet for a long time. "I was exposed," he said finally.

"Exposed to what part?" I asked.

"The Cure," he explained. "So I could turn at any moment, too."

"You might want to talk to Kiera about that. She's really freaked out by it. How are you dealing with it so calmly, seeing as how you have a kid and a wife?"

He smiled thinly. "My wife and I have an agreement," he said simply. "If I turn, she's going to punch a steak knife in the back of my skull and sever my spinal cord. Simple, easy, and if I go staring at the sun, that doesn't seem like such a bad death."

I muttered under my breath. "Maybe we need an agreement." I didn't know what Kiera would think; would she be relieved that she couldn't hurt anyone anymore?

Would she be able to be Cured, and would I have the strength to put her down if she couldn't?

I couldn't say I was any better than the men in the attic. If there was even the smallest chance that I could get Kiera back, I'd take it. And if that meant chaining her up in the basement, that's what I would do.

Not even being a zombie made me change my mind on that one. If there was hope, any hope at all . . .

. . . *no hope at all. I spread her rib cage with my fingers and the bones broke and snapped. She was screaming. I had had enough of her screaming; I bit at her throat, hard, and ripped something out of it. She couldn't scream any more. But she could bleed, and bleed she did. She bled so prettily on the leggings and workout shirt she was wearing; the only color I could still see . . .*

I shook my head, trying to clear it. "What's up?" Wyatt said.

"Flashback," I said curtly. "Not a great one."

We dug in silence for a long time. "What bothers you most about the flashbacks?"

I started digging the third hole. "That there's nothing I can do to stop them," I said finally. "That I'm hurting people—hell, I can still hear them screaming—that I'm killing people, and it doesn't even matter to me. A life is worth nothing if it isn't a zombie life." I paused. "Except for Kiera. Somehow, she was always real to me, always something to come back to."

"Is that unusual for a zombie?" Wyatt asked.

"I think so," I said. "My Hexmates didn't have the type of longing I had to be near her. I didn't want to Infect her, I didn't want to kill her, I wanted to be *with* her. It was different, somehow. I wanted her to be a zombie like me so we could be together forever, but I had no urge to Infect her myself."

"That's . . . romantic?" Wyatt asked. "I guess?"

I shook my head. "No, it's really not," I said after a while. "Being a zombie is not a good life to lead. I shouldn't have ever wished she would be a zombie. Not even while I still had Not-Zombie Sean to keep me in check."

Wyatt looked interested. "What did Not-Zombie Sean do?"

"He—I, I guess—was like the angel on my shoulder. Trying to keep me from killing, from taking steps that I couldn't turn back from. He hated the killing. Infecting was a little easier for him, though. I don't really know why."

"You talk about him like he's a completely separate person."

"He really was," I explained. "It was like having two completely different people in my brain fighting for supremacy. Sometimes he won, sometimes Zombie Sean won. But in the end, I was Cured, and Zombie Sean disappeared."

Wyatt hesitated. "Do you miss it?"

I thought about it for a while as we dug the third hole. "Sometimes I miss the simplicity, you know?" I began. "It was so easy: Infect or kill. The Hex made it more complicated, I had to think of others' feelings and desires, and I think that's what kept me cognizant through it all. I was working like I was part of a team, even if the rest of them weren't."

He shook his head. "You're a strong man, Sean," he said at last.

I shook my head too. "No. Just one who had something to come back to."

~

Wyatt helped me take the bodies down from the attic, and we all stood around the graves as the evening sun set. "Should we say something?" Aspyn asked.

"Sure," I said. "What can we say?"

Aspyn cleared her throat. "Two dedicated fathers lie here for their final rest. They fought hard for their son and had to do the unimaginable. They treated their pain the only way they knew how, and now they are reunited with their son in the afterlife. Please let them be at peace and with each other."

We stamped down the dirt and I put the three crosses Laura had made into the ground to mark the graves. "I guess that's it," I said lamely.

Kiera had come out with Grace to see what had become of the two farmers. "I'm glad you made those crosses," she said to Laura. "Makes it seem like we respected their choice, you know?"

Laura nodded. "I don't know what religion they were, so I might've totally missed the mark, but it was all I could think of to do."

Kiera sighed. "I've been thinking, and I think we should stay in the house, Sean. They clearly cared about their son and we did the right thing by reuniting them. Hopefully now they won't haunt us."

I raised a brow. "You were particularly worried about being haunted?"

"There are fucking zombies and you're concerned that I believe in ghosts?" she countered.

Wyatt chuckled. "I don't think we're haunted," he said. "I think we laid them to rest and now they're together, wherever they are. And their son isn't a zombie anymore."

Kiera sighed, and we started back to the house. Owen, Laura and Aspyn followed us, and Wyatt went across the street to his family. Grace trailed along behind us, jumping at grasshoppers.

"Is it time to listen to the radio?" Owen asked.

Kiera nodded. "Yeah, I think so. Hopefully there's no news."

We turned on Owen's little radio and sat in the living room in silence. There wasn't much to say; we had buried some (presumably) good people that day, and it wore on us. Aspyn was sitting on the floor with Grace, rubbing her belly slowly.

. . . National Guard has been deployed to cities across the US, the radio began. *Cities have become zombie strongholds, and we are trying to eradicate them. We can bring this world back into order. We can end this. I believe that we will come out on the other side of this, victorious . . .*

"Who the hell is this?" I frowned.

Owen clicked on the receiver. "Hello, broadcaster. Where did you get your information?"

I'm outside of Manhattan, he said. *The entire city has gone up in flames. Zombies are everywhere. The*

National Guard is trying to figure out how to save the rest of us, but so far, burning down the city is the only way to get rid of the damned things for good.

"I mean, headshots do it too," Kiera muttered.

They don't have enough ammo to gun down every zombie there is, the voice explained. *Who are you, anyway?*

I said, "A small party of survivors outside of Point Peak, Connecticut. We're holed up on some farmland and we're doing pretty good." I didn't feel like he needed to know how we spent our afternoon. "My name is Sean, and my wife is Kiera. Owen, Laura and Aspyn are with us from Point Peak and the surrounding areas. We've also got a family across the street. We're fairly well-provisioned."

I'm Brett, he said. I could see Kiera paling. She had relied a lot on Brett during the war, and he had died, losing him just like I'd lost the rest of my Hex family. She didn't need this reminder that she had failed to save him. *It's just me here, but I'm close enough to the city to get the broadcasts from the National Guard, so I try to report what I hear every evening.*

"We appreciate the broadcast," Owen said. "Do you have any more information about what's going on in the cities?"

Just that it's a hellish mess, Brett said. *National Guard is everywhere and nowhere. There aren't enough to deal with every major city in the US, so they're scrambling. I wouldn't be surprised if they just start marching down every major highway.*

"Well, that's great," I said. "Guess that's one more thing we need to worry about."

Kiera sighed and put a foot on Grace's back while Aspyn petted her. "Is there any information on how many people are getting Infected with the new zombie disease?"

Just that there's about a fifty percent "success" rate for someone to turn into a zombie, Brett said. *It's not a zero amount, so that's bad, but it's hit-or-miss as to who's going to turn.*

She slumped into the couch. "Great," she said weakly. She closed her eyes and became lost in her thoughts, or so I assumed.

"Well, we're too far away to come get you," Owen said bluntly. "Are you okay?"

I'm fine, he said. *I've got supplies, I live right next to a major grocery store and I've been stealing—is it really stealing if nobody works there anymore?—canned goods and pastas and stuff. I have a gas stove so I can still cook. Speaking of which, did anyone hear if there's any news about utilities?*

Owen shook his head, then realized Brett couldn't see him. "No," he said. "I don't know why natural gas is still working, but I haven't heard a single word about electricity or water."

I'll keep listening to the National Guard broadcasts, he said. *Do you want to make a plan to meet on the radio once a week or so?*

"That's a good idea," I said. "Not that I particularly know what day it is anymore."

It's Wednesday, Brett supplied. *Let's plan to meet*

every seven days from now on. I'll get as much intel as I can get, and you can keep me updated on what the National Guard is doing in Connecticut.

"Sounds like a plan," Owen replied. "Over and out."

You can take the guy out of the military, but you can't take the military out of the guy, I guessed. I looked at Kiera; she was not all right. "Kiera, I don't think you're going to turn," I said gently.

"You don't know that," she said, sounding withdrawn and depressed. "He said fifty percent. That means I'm as likely to turn as I am to not turn."

"Well, we'll cross that bridge when we get to it," I said firmly. "For now, you should put it out of your mind. We have a lot to do here, especially if we want to make our dead farmers proud."

She sighed. "I guess," she said listlessly. We all got up and started on evening chores. Kiera was sweeping the house, Laura was cooking dinner, Aspyn was across the street playing with Brayden, and Owen was trying different channels on the radio. I got up and started going towards the barn.

"Wait," Owen said, frowning. "I think I've got something."

. . . all major cities. Please remain indoors. If you or your loved one has turned, please go to your nearest food pantry or stay put. The National Guard is scouring the cities looking for citizens that have turned . . .

Well, that was great. "What the hell was that?"

"Something I think we shouldn't tell the girls about," he said quietly. "We're a little off the beaten path, so we should be okay, but I don't want to jinx it by saying we're fine."

"Is anyone else worried they'll turn?" I asked.

"Aspyn is," he said. "She was exposed to the Cure. But Laura was out in the woods for the majority of the zombie war, so she didn't get exposed."

"Well, that's good news, at least. You were exposed too, right?" I wondered.

"Yeah. I'm not worried about turning. If I do, I'll do my very last headshot before it turns into A Thing." He sounded so eerily calm about blowing his brains out.

"So who's immune? Me, Laura and who?" I ran my fingers through my hair and sighed.

"Wyatt was out of town," he said after a minute. "He had to fight to get back into the city. He wasn't exposed. But Anna and Brayden were, and Aspyn was."

"Great," I muttered. So we were outnumbered. I wasn't particularly worried about Kiera turning; it was just a feeling that I had. I didn't know where it was coming from, but it seemed sure of itself, somehow. "Well, I guess we'll just have to take it as it comes."

"You seem pretty calm about this," Owen remarked.

"Once you've been a zombie, it's kind of hard to ruffle your feathers," I explained. "I already did all the Big Bad Things and survived it. I have a feeling Kiera will be fine, and that's all I really care about."

Owen snorted. "Well, as long as your *intuition* says she's fine, then we'll have to believe it."

"I don't know what it is. I just feel like she's going to be okay."

"Maybe because there's no alternative?"

"What do you mean?" I asked.

"If she isn't okay, what does that mean for you? Do you stay here? Do you set her free? Do you ask me to shoot her, like you did for the zombie in the basement?" Owen was looking at me.

"I . . . I don't know," I said slowly. "I don't know what I'd do if she turned. Take care of Grace, she'd want me to do that. I think I'd stay here, because if I was alone, I might take the cleaver and end it all. I can't think of a life without her here."

Owen nodded. "I'm pretty glad I've ridden the single bus for the majority of my adult life," he said wryly. "Being in relationships just complicates things. If it's every man for himself, things get a lot simpler, pretty damn quick."

"Yeah," I sighed. "It does get complicated. But it's worth it."

He shook his head and continued messing around with his radio. I took that as my cue to leave, and went to find Kiera. Grace was sitting on Aspyn's bed as Kiera swept the floor.

"Does she know Grace gets on her bed?" I asked.

She chuckled a little. "I think everyone knows that Grace gets on their beds," she said. "She leaves little doggy hair presents everywhere she goes."

"I don't think Aspyn would mind, but I can't see Laura and Owen being okay with that." I leaned back against the doorframe.

"Well, they haven't complained yet, since I've been

keeping all the rooms clean. If someone has a problem with it, they can talk to me about it," she said.

"All right," I replied. I watched her sweep for a little while, thinking about what Owen said. Relationships *did* complicate things. But it was worth it. Seeing her smile when Grace did something silly, lying in bed with her at night . . . it was worth it.

I wouldn't know what to do with myself without her.

The Long Road

~ Kiera ~

I t didn't take long to sweep the house, and then it was time for bed. I climbed into the bed I shared with Sean, and stared at the ceiling. Fifty percent. That was incredibly high. I had a fifty-fifty chance of turning into an acid-spitting zombie and trying to kill my family and friends.

That news, paired with the four graves outside, made me feel like it was the end of the world, for real this time.

Sean slid between the sheets and used his good arm to wrap it around my waist. "You okay?" he said softly.

"No," I admitted. "I am very much not okay. Please don't let me turn into a zombie. Please don't let me hurt anyone." I was talking too fast.

"I won't," Sean soothed me. "It's going to be okay. We'll deal with it, if it happens. But it's not going to happen, so you have nothing to worry about."

Fear still gnawed at me like a dog over a bone. Well,

I presumed like a dog over a bone; I'd never given Grace one to find out. "I'll try to think of it that way," I said finally. I turned onto my side and pressed my forehead against his. "Thank you for not letting me be a zombie. I'm sorry I couldn't do the same for you."

He blinked a little. "Do you still feel guilty about that?"

"Of course I do," I said. "I cut your damned arm off and you *still* turned. I couldn't save you and I couldn't put you down. I couldn't do anything but leave you."

"You had to leave me," he said gently. "I don't blame you for not killing me; we didn't know if there would be a Cure or not, and by the time you knew, I was out with my Hex links. Too late for you to do anything about it. And I got the Cure, so I'm okay now. I'll take care of you, Kiera. You don't have to worry about taking care of me."

I rubbed my temples with my fingertips. "I always want to take care of you," I admitted. "I consider it my job, and I failed you."

Sean shook his head. "No," he said firmly. "You didn't fail me. You couldn't kill me, and that's fine, you set me free someplace that I hopefully wouldn't have hurt people. You didn't know about the Hex links and what my mind would be like when I turned. You had no idea of any of it until after the Cure."

"That's true," I hedged. "I didn't know what the virus had done to you. I never expected to see you again." I felt tears well up in my eyes.

He held me tightly against his chest, with his bad arm under my head. "I never stopped wanting to be back with you," he admitted. "I thought of you the entire time. Well,

Not-Zombie Sean did, for sure. I'm still not entirely certain which one of us stayed when we got Cured."

"That's . . . pretty interesting, actually," I said thoughtfully. "What do you think happened?"

"I think Not-Zombie Sean and Zombie Sean integrated, in a way," he mused. "Blended together to become New Not-Zombie Sean. I still have all the memories, but none of the Infection."

I nodded, laying my head against his chest. "Was it scary?" I asked in a whisper.

"Being a zombie? No," he said. "I wasn't ever afraid. I just wanted to Infect and kill, and Zombie Sean was totally fine with that. Not-Zombie Sean kept trying to talk me out of it, but he didn't scare me."

"Okay," I exhaled slowly. "I guess that makes sense. Maybe if I was a zombie, I wouldn't know I was a zombie, like you did. The zombies whose minds you read didn't really have concrete thoughts, right?"

"Yeah," he said. "Just kill, kill, kill. It was kind of freaking me out at first, but now I'm used to it. As used to it as you can be, I guess."

"I just . . . what does it feel like to not be yourself anymore?" I asked. "I'm afraid of losing myself. I like myself. At least, as much as any millennial can like themselves."

"I didn't really care," he said. "Not-Zombie Sean took care of all the worrying. I got all his memories, and Zombie Sean's . . . I hate to say confidence, but the way he looked at the world so pragmatically. It definitely changed me as a person, but I wouldn't say I'm worse for the experience."

I sighed, relaxing a little. Maybe if I turned into a zombie, that was it: I wouldn't know I was a zombie, and I wouldn't remember if I hurt anyone. I knew the new zombies were fast, so Sean would have to act quickly if I started to turn. I knew he'd ask Owen to put me to rest; I didn't think Sean could do it on his own.

"Let's get some sleep," he said finally. "Things always look better in the morning."

I stayed curled into his chest, closing my eyes hard enough to see stars. It wouldn't be so terrifying in the morning, right?

I had no Not-Zombie Kiera to answer me. I was alone, for now. It would be less terrifying in the morning.

It had to be.

~

We woke up and took care of the animals, like usual. I fed the chickens the grain that was stored in the barn; we'd eventually have to start feeding them the things we were growing. It was a nice ritual, feeding the chickens. They clucked around and wove between my feet and I felt like a Disney princess.

Sean was right, it did look better in the morning. Or, at least, I didn't feel so anxious in the morning. He had a plan, and that was what I needed to know. I needed to make sure there was someone to take care of it so I couldn't hurt anyone, and Sean would do that.

I leaned against the fence and watched the cows and the bull. It was calving season, and little cows were springing up everywhere. It was almost time to learn how to butcher cows for meat. I anticipated that would *not* be a Kiera job.

We really did have an idyllic little life out here. It was satisfying, and safe. No zombies wandering up to our doors anymore, and the only things we had to worry about were zombie animals and if it rained enough for us to take mini-baths. It was a peaceful life.

I weeded the fields and watched Sean milk the cows. I could hear Brayden playing across the street, and the pigs behind his fence oinking loudly. I wondered if Brayden had any interest in Grace, who was eating some of the giant bag of dog food I'd brought. I'd have to go over and introduce him officially to her.

After I weeded, I walked up the long dirt drive and went to the pigpen with Grace trotting along beside me. Brayden was running around in the grass, with Anna and Wyatt watching. They raised their hands in greeting, and I did the same.

"Hey Brayden, have you met Grace yet?" I asked.

He immediately stopped running and turned to me. "Doggy!" he cried, and ran over to Grace. For her credit, she didn't flinch or move away from him throwing his arms around her; she tolerated it pretty well, actually. She even licked his dirty little face.

"Yep, that's a doggy," I said. "Her name is Grace."

"Gwace," he said. He stepped back from his hug and pet her gently on the head. "Gentle with Gwace," he said.

"You've certainly taught him how to interact with animals," I called over to Anna and Wyatt. I sat down on an overturned bucket. "She can do tricks," I said to Brayden.

"Twicks?"

"Yep. Watch this," I said. I signaled for her to lie down and roll over. She stayed upside-down for a minute, wagging her tail hard, and completed the move. Brayden laughed with delight.

"Hold your hand out," I instructed Brayden. He did, and Grace put her paw on the palm of his hand. "She can shake, too!"

"Good doggy," he said happily. "Shake shake shake!"

"Laura's making breakfast," I said to the others as Grace and Brayden played. He showed her various stones and she sniffed them, which made him giggle.

"What are you having?" Wyatt asked.

"Eggs and moose," I said. "Same as the last few days. We've got to use that moose meat before it goes bad."

"Where are you keeping it now, without a refrigerator?"

"The basement is cool," I explained. "We just . . . had to remove the zombie."

Wyatt sighed. "I still can't believe what happened over there. That their son turned, and that they . . ." He looked askance at his own son.

"That they did what they did," I supplied. "I can't believe it either. The pictures on the mantel are so happy. I wonder how he got exposed. Did he go to school and get exposed there? Work-study? How does a teenager get Infected like that?"

Anna shook her head. "Brayden, be gentle," she said.

"I don't know. He didn't appear to be in college, which is where you found each other again, right?"

I nodded. "Yeah, we reconnected at the college when the Cure was dropped."

"So he must have been in high school. There's two pickups out back. Maybe he drove one to school, and the high school got Infected?"

"Hmm. I didn't hear anything about the high school," I said. "Granted, the only news I ever really heard was the CDC warnings about what was going to happen."

"Well," Wyatt said, "let's all head over to your place for breakfast. I'm getting sick of bacon."

I snorted. "At least you learned quickly how to butcher pigs," I said. "We haven't had to butcher a cow yet, but after Owen and Sean butchered the moose, I think we're in good shape."

We walked across the street to the white house with green shutters. The wraparound porch made the house seem bigger than it was; I loved it. Brayden and Grace were in front, with the adults trailing along behind.

I opened the door for Brayden and Grace and we all filed in and went to the kitchen. "Laura, we've got company," I said. "You got enough meat and eggs to go around?"

She thought about it for a second. "Yeah, I think so," she said. "They've been laying pretty reliably and that was a fucking—excuse me, freaking—huge moose."

Luckily, Brayden didn't seem to be focusing on her words at the moment. It was going to be hard to clean up our language around a kid. I wondered what Sean thought about having children. We'd talked about it, but not *really* talked about it. Could we even bring someone into this world safely? Who the hell would deliver my baby if I had one?

I shook my head. "Let me grab a few extra chairs," I said, and I went into the dining room and got some. "Grace, come here. Stay, please."

Wyatt laughed a little. "You say please to your dog?"

"And thank you. She's pretty smart. As smart as your kid, according to the studies I've read on border collies," I said.

He nodded. "I think I've read the same, actually," he said. "About the average intelligence of a three-to-five-year-old, right?"

"Yeah," I said. "She's definitely on the older end of the spectrum with how quickly she picks up tricks and things she needs to do. She gets into her Doge suit so easy that I barely have to do anything but zip it up."

"What made you create the Doge suit?" Anna asked curiously. She was cutting up the meat that Laura was serving on a plate for Brayden. Eggs didn't get the same treatment; I guessed scrambled eggs were soft enough not to choke on. What the hell did I know about kids? We'd need a damn manual to figure out what to do with one.

"I found Grace," I began. "She was in an apartment where there was no one else. She goes everywhere with me. I don't know what I'd do without her by my side."

"Makes sense," Anna said, using a fork to feed her son. "It's a pretty cool setup." She shook her head. "I don't know what we would've done without you. Doge suit and all."

"It really is kind of cool," I agreed. "She sure knows how to use those spikes. And I think she understands that it helps her stay safe." I paused. It was the first time I'd really spoken to Anna; I kind of liked her. She was agreeable, but had her own opinion.

"Smart dog," Wyatt said.

Sean and Owen came back in, and Aspyn came downstairs from her bedroom. Our entire little "family" was around the big table in the kitchen, and I couldn't help but smile. This was what we were going to do for the rest of our lives. And Anna and Wyatt could help us figure out what to do with a kid. Maybe even start a little school for them. We could find more people to move into the houses and really have a good community going here.

"I think we're going to be okay," I said softly.

Wyatt looked up briefly from helping Brayden and smiled. "I think so too."

In Silence

~ Sean ~

We were eating dinner when I heard it. Something crashed through the front window. I stood up and walked cautiously into the living room, only to find a brick with the words "They're coming" written on a piece of paper wrapped around it.

The rest of the family piled into the living room. I tried to look out the window, but it was pitch black with no moon. There was, however, some light at the far end of the road.

And it was getting closer.

"Turn off the lanterns!" I whispered. "Get down."

Everyone hid in the living room. Brayden started to cry and Anna put a hand over his mouth. "Shh, baby. It's okay. Just play the quiet game with me, okay?"

Grace was currently in residence under Kiera's armpit, clinging to her like the world was about to end.

Well, maybe it was. What the hell did I know?

We heard them coming and saw the lights growing brighter. It was the cultists, and behind them, an army truck full of National Guard soldiers.

Daven and the fat one, Paul, or so Laura had named them, were leading the way. There was a loudspeaker somewhere.

Please exit your homes. We are checking for Infection. You do not need to be afraid. This is only a test.

I frowned. "I don't trust them," I said slowly.

"I don't either," Owen murmured. "Let's stay low."

They finally reached the front of the house, and I could see Daven and Paul leading the way up the front walk. "Shit," I said. "Run. Run to the back of the house and hide. Now!"

We all ran in the dark, things clattering to the floor in our wake. I grabbed Kiera and pulled her into the pantry, trying not to breathe too loudly.

"They're in here!" I heard them yell. They knocked: once, twice. And again, once, twice. After that, I heard a *bang* as they presumably kicked in the front door. There was light under the door to the pantry. I held my breath and held Kiera. Shit, where was Grace?

We'd forgotten about Grace! I could hear her growling and it sounded like she was close. I opened the door just a crack and called for her; she stalked over to the pantry and climbed in behind us. *Thank God,* I thought. *That could've been bad.*

I could hear them talking. They were sweeping the house, and I could hear every shout and every order through the thin doors of the pantry.

"I've got one!"

"Me too. Move everyone into the living room." The lights grew brighter. "Commence testing."

The pantry door opened fast. We were pulled out without ceremony. I fought against the guy holding me, and he dropped me on the living room floor. Everyone else was caught, except for Anna, Brayden and Wyatt. I had heard the back door open. They must be hiding in the fields.

Laura was pissed, and Aspyn was terrified. Kiera and I were pretty mad, too. "What the fuck do you want?" I spat.

One of the National Guard Guys held up a little kit. "Tests your blood," he explained. "To see who's been exposed to the Cure and who hasn't." He started pricking everyone's fingers and putting strips into the handheld machine. He didn't ask first.

"Stop it! We didn't do anything wrong!" Kiera exclaimed.

"Well, it sounds like you're hiding people that have been exposed to the Cure and could turn at any moment," the NGG said. He pulled Kiera, Aspyn and Owen off the floor. "You're coming with us."

I reached for Kiera. "No fucking way!" I shouted. "Get out of here, we're not hurting anyone!"

The NGG turned on me with a gun in his hand. "How sure are you about what you're doing right now?" he said quietly.

Kiera was sobbing, but she shook her head through her tears. "Kiera, stay safe," I said urgently. "I'll come find you."

The NGG were zip-tying their hands behind their backs. Kiera was still crying, and I could see the red marks beginning to rise on her wrists. The NGG started pouring out of the living room, filling the truck, and throwing Kiera, Aspyn and Owen inside.

I ran outside with Laura. "You can't do this!" she shouted. She started banging her fists against the truck.

"Do you want to get shot? Because that's how you get shot," one of the NGGs said.

Laura backed away, but I could tell she was still extremely pissed off.

My heart was dropping into my shoes.

. . . left me on the stairs. The girl was crying. Why was the girl crying? She had blood all over her shirt. She closed the door on me, and I was alone.

I could feel the zombies in the halls above and below me. I looked down at my arm, which was covered in bandages, and wondered what the hell had happened.

I went exploring. These new zombies might be important. I was already starting to change, even from how quickly the girl had pushed me out the door . . .

I came back to myself just as the NGGs started pulling away. The cultists stayed behind, dancing and crowing in the dark with their torches.

"Oh, hell no," I muttered. I ran for it; I charged Mark with all the power I could possibly muster. I reared back and punched him in the face, not once, not twice, but over and over again. "This is your fault!"

Mark staggered back, groaning. "You took our

women!" he shouted through a broken nose. "You deserve everything you got!"

"Fuck you," I hissed. I punched him one more time for good measure, knocking him down onto the ground, and stepped on his neck with my foot. "You're not going to make it out of here alive unless you tell us where they're going."

He tried to roll out from under me and realized I weighed at least as much as he did, and I had more muscle from working on the farm. He groaned again, a hoarse sound, and wondered what I broke in his throat. Good. He deserved it.

Cowering away from my blows, he whimpered. "They're . . . there's an outpost, north of here. They're going that way. Please, just let me go!"

As the lights crept back toward the city, I saw Wyatt and Anna come out of their house. They rushed over to us in the starlight, but I couldn't stop myself from beating the shit out of Mark.

Anna started to pull me away. "He's gone, Sean, he's gone," she said.

I was breathing heavily and my hand was bloody. I had cracked my knuckles on his teeth. He definitely looked worse for wear. The cultists circled us, angry. There were four of them and the miscellaneous women left.

I looked up. Kiera was gone. Kiera was *gone* and it was the fault of these monsters. I planted my feet and stared at them.

Laura and I charged at the cultists. I was kicking Paul with the long hair, rearing my foot back and making impact with his stomach as hard as I could. He was shrinking back on the ground, and Wyatt pulled me away. "We don't have to kill all of them," he said urgently.

"They took Kiera," I whispered.

"I know. But killing these people is not going to bring her back. We need to make a plan."

I felt like I was broken. I couldn't protect Kiera. She was taken away from me, and she had to be scared. It was comforting to know that Owen and Aspyn were with her, but she didn't have me or Grace.

Speaking of Grace, she slunk out of the house, coming up to sit against my side as I sat down heavily, next to the guy I'd kicked. "Get away!" I howled—and Grace howled with me.

The cultists didn't have at least a modicum of sense in them. "You'll die here," the one called Jason promised. "You don't have enough people now to keep things going. You'll die here, and then we can come back and wait for the Messiah."

He stared at me for a long moment as I stared back at him, equally pissed. Logically I knew that Kiera was still okay, for now; the worst they could do was knock her around a little, I'd hoped. They needed her alive for . . . whatever they were going to be doing. Fuck. My mind was spinning and I could hardly cling to my sense of reason.

The women were pulling the men back, leaving the one on the ground across from me; Daven, I think. I wondered what we'd do with him. Laura knelt down and assessed his injuries. "I don't think there's any internal bleeding," she reported. "But he's certainly going to regret this in the morning."

I hugged Grace to my chest and tears welled up in my eyes. Grace was all I had left of Kiera. She wasn't going to be there feeding the chickens or making me laugh or training Grace. She was *gone*. And I was devastated.

"Are we . . . are we going after them?" I whispered.

Laura was panting, and Wyatt was standing over me, trying to take deep breaths. "I'm going to have to talk to Anna," he said slowly. He nudged Daven with his foot lightly, who rolled over onto his stomach, so that he didn't choke on the blood coming out of his nose. "I don't want them to go with us, and they have to keep themselves safe from these fuckers."

Laura nodded. "I'm in," she said. "Owen and I have really gotten to be friends, and I like Kiera and Aspyn. I want to make sure they're okay. We have to go get them."

Laura kicked the cultist one more time for good measure, and he groaned on the ground. "I say we dump him in the river," she said calmly. "See if he can find his way back from that."

"Makes sense to me," I said, and we grabbed him by his hands and feet and started heaving him toward the river that ran behind our house.

He continued moaning, and I didn't feel the slightest bit of remorse. He had taken Kiera away from me. *Nothing* could take Kiera away from me. I would *never* stop going after her. I would kill every cultist and their women if I had to, to get her back. We unceremoniously dumped the guy in the river, and came back around to the front of the house.

"He'll either drown or not," Laura reported. "Not our problem anymore."

I knelt down next to Grace. "We're going to go get mama," I said. "She's going to be so happy to see you. Let's suit her up and get our weapons. Maybe one of us can bring Owen's gun, does anyone know how to shoot?"

Laura volunteered. "My dad taught me how," she explained. "He's still got a good amount of ammo, but I'll try to use it sparingly."

We armed ourselves and started packing provisions. Anna and Brayden would take care of the farm chores, while Wyatt, Laura and I would go after Kiera, Aspyn and Owen. I had faith that they would do fine without us.

I was still in shock. They just . . . pulled her into a truck and drove her away? How could they do that? What the hell were they doing, testing people and taking them away? How was that possible?

"Let's bring Owen's radio," I said as we packed. "Maybe Brett can shine some light on what the fuck is happening, because I do not know. I don't know," I said again. I still felt broken. "I promised to protect her . . ."

Laura snapped her Meat-Siah onto Wyatt's backpack and gestured towards the door. "Well, they haven't been gone too long. It's totally feasible that we'll come up on them before they get back to wherever they're going. We can ambush them."

"The three of us, a Meat-Siah, a cleaver-rod, and Owen's gun . . . sounds like a plan I can get behind." I was in no mood for mercy. What if they *made* Kiera turn? Then she'd be taken away from me for good.

I was not about to have that.

"Let's go," I said shortly. We all walked down to the dirt road, following the path that the wheel wells left. We had our lanterns and extra oil, so visibility wasn't a problem. Grace trotted along beside me, as if to ask, "Where's mama?"

"I don't know, baby," I whispered to her. "But we're gonna find her."

The End?

Discover more awesome books and authors at
www.nefhousepublishing.com